Aestas

The Yellow Balloon

By J.P. Prag

A

FUTURE

INTERLUDE

INTERLUDE 05
:: VENUSIAN GUIDEBOOK

Lilit floated into the mess hall looking for something to calm her frazzled nerves. Even though she knew by heart every single prepackaged meal, snack, and drink that came out of the dispensers, she still went looking through the bins hoping to find a surprise. Eventually, she settled on a pouch of the same weak decaffeinated green tea she had chosen dozens of times before and cracked the built-in heating element at the bottom to get it somewhat warmed up—though certainly not hot. Watching her flexible carton slowly begin to reheat, she wondered how long ago it had been originally brewed before it was vacuum sealed. Sadly, she had a pretty good idea that it had been at least several years, and it did not make her look forward to choking it down, especially considering her upbringing on almost entirely fresh food.

With her package of lukewarm tea in hand, Lilit headed towards the seating area to find a spot to settle into. While some people found the idea of having chairs and tables in an environment lacking strong gravity to be a ridiculous waste of space and resources, at times like these Lilit was glad for the familiarity they provided. Although she could not be grounded physically, she hoped that partaking in a simple ritual from her long-discarded previously normal life would gently help mollify her free-floating emotional distress.

At this hour of the night—according to the clock they had chosen to live by on the ship—the mess hall was usually completely empty. However, to her surprise, delight, and relief, she saw one table with two noteworthy men at it. They appeared to be intently discussing one topic or another as their arms flailed in every which direction. Of course, she instantly recognized the bickering companions, even from this distance. Who could possibly mistake them for anyone else?

Knowing them as she did, Lilit was quite sure that what they were deliberating was unrelated to their current mission, which was exactly the type of effervescent distraction she desperately needed, too. Feeling overjoyed about running into the duo at that particularly low moment for her, Lilit swam over to join them. En route, she started smiling to herself as she wondered how these two had become her best friends in the whole universe and her most loyal co-conspirators. It wasn't that long ago that she had the rather ordinary existence of a young woman living on Aestas and not as the interplanetary criminal she had transformed herself into—one who was definitely guilty of everything they accused her of. With a huff, she resigned herself to their higher purpose. Everyone aboard this vessel was in the exact same boat, so to speak.

Upon approaching their sitting place, Lilit did a somersault in the air and performed three rotations before making a near-perfect landing in the chair. Strapping herself to the seat so that she did not drift away, she pushed the interior straw up out of her terrible beverage, took a sip, winced at its abysmal flavor, and then finally inquired, "`Sup, boys?"

"Must you always take such risks?" chided Ahmad. "Why can you not just take a seat like a sane person and perhaps avoid bashing your head? Do you know how hard it is to corral blood in microgravity?"

"Give the lady a break," Durojaiye rebuked his tablemate. "It was not such a dangerous thing, and we all need to keep our spirits up on this long journey between worlds. A little fun is not a bad thing every now and then."

Lilit chuckled as Ahmad and Durojaiye squabbled with each other as they always did, even the first time she had met them. Oh, they pretended they were always at each other's throats, but it was obvious to her how much love they shared. And she was so happy and fulfilled to be a part of that love, as well. Just being in their presence had an instant calming effect on her, granting her permission to compartmentalize her trepidations and anxiety away and just enjoy being with them. For a little while, their company would allow her to forget about the troubling message she had received so that she could remember why it was worthwhile to be alive despite having to go through all this anguish.

Delving through her own mind, Lilit wondered how this state of being had come to be. Suddenly, that line of thought made her recognize a failing in her own relations with Ahmad and Durojaiye, something she couldn't believe she didn't already know after almost five years together. She decided that she would rectify that oversight right then and there.

"You know, I just realized this," Lilit seamlessly segued, interrupting the debate that they had picked back up after greeting her, "but I don't think you guys ever told me how, exactly, you crossed paths. I mean, I obviously know where it happened, but what were the circumstances, how did it actually happen? When we all met for the first time, you told me that you had only known one another for a couple of weeks."

"Ah, this is a tale I must tell," Ahmad declared, "because he would recall it wrong and make a bunch of things up. I remember and report the factual events perfectly, unlike certain people I know."

"Fine, fine," Durojaiye conceded, "you tell the story. But I am going to provide color commentary and correct you when you are wrong."

"I am never wrong!" Ahmad declared. "However, I will allow this, for the sake of peace."

Lilit's heart lit up at this exchange. This was the type of stuff she adored about them and why these two had become central to her life. "Alright," she said, "I'm listening. Go on already!"

"I will if you two will stop interrupting," Ahmad censured. Once he appeared satisfied that their mouths would remain zipped shut, he cleared his throat and commenced the account.

Interlude 03

"I was shaken from my stupor of staring out at the yellow dot growing minutely larger in the distance," Ahmad began, "when I heard the person floating to my right ask, 'I wonder what it would be like to take a walk outside?' Turning toward him, I peered at the man who had just spoken. Blinking to regain my focus, I blurted out, 'Excuse me, what?' not sure I had caught his words correctly.

"To my great surprise, I found I did not recognize the fellow at all. Under his bright, single-colored dashiki and matching pants combination, all I could tell was that he was dark-skinned, clean-shaven, and amazingly—despite several months of drifting in microgravity—still noticeably muscular."

"Oh, Ahmad," Durojaiye teased, "I did not know you were looking at me so intently. I am blushing now!"

"That is not what I meant!" Ahmad said in defense of his description.

Undeterred, Durojaiye kept it up. "Not that Ahmad ever had a muscle tone to speak of to lose, so he must have been jealous!"

"Ah, I cannot help that I have always been a rounder person, no matter what lifestyle I have led," Ahmad claimed. "It must be genetic! And I think you are looking at me wrong, as I am the right size for my height. I just look bigger because of it."

Lilit could not resist and said, "Well, the good news is that being back in microgravity has helped you gain a couple of centimeters!"

Missing the joke entirely, Ahmad agreed, "Yes, quite so. But let me tell you something: even for someone from the unnamed sand dunes on the outskirts of the United Arab Emirates, I am, sad to say, somewhat short."

"But Durojaiye is not that much taller than you," Lilit observed from her stature, which was almost a full head above both of them.

"I just wear it better with my glorious musculature," Durojaiye offered.

"Anyway," Ahmad said, attempting to take back the reins. "Putting all that together with his accent, I deduced that the man previously unknown to me must have been of Nigerian origin."

"You did no such thing!" Durojaiye accused. "You are adding facts to the past with things you learned at a later point."

"That is slander!" Ahmad cursed. "And I confirmed it when I heard your name. You said in your typical clipped, but perfectly pronounced English, 'Oh, pardon me, I did not realize I had spoken out loud. Ah, I do not believe we have met! Many apologies, my friend, please allow me to introduce myself.' And then you gave a proper introduction. At that moment I thought that yes, I was spot on. With a name like that, you were definitely Nigerian."

"You will notice, Lilit," Durojaiye interposed, "that Ahmad has admitted that I gave a proper introduction, but said nothing about himself. He was quite rude, but I am happy that he has confessed this himself so I did not have to bring it up."

Aghast, Ahmad jumped right in saying, "Per usual, you mispresent what was happening and leave out pertinent details! My lack of respectful greeting at that moment was because as you held out an open hand with an offer of a handshake in the Western style, horror overcame me."

"Right," Durojaiye agreed, "you hesitated for a moment, concerned about what type of microbes could be growing on this unfamiliar weirdo after we had all been confined so long to the ship."

"No, no, that was not it," Ahmad protested. After Durojaiye stared at him for a number of seconds without saying a word, he said, "Okay, maybe it was a little. However, I decided it would be ill-mannered of me to not accept your invitation and took your hand firmly in my own. But that is when my terror took hold and made me still my tongue. Much to my chagrin, you released your hold on the safety straps attached to the full-length windows in front of us."

"Here we go..." Durojaiye trailed off. Lilit realized that he had undoubtedly heard this contention dozens of times before, probably even more so since this journey had begun.

Appearing not to notice the comment at all, Ahmad ranted, "We had been given strict instructions to never let go of the clutch-devices lest we go flying out of control and break something or injure ourselves or someone else. As such, I gripped on to my own strap out of concern for both of our precious and irreplaceable lives, solidly holding your palm so that you would not sail away due to the momentum from our greeting."

"Now we're getting somewhere!" Lilit encouraged Ahmad in an attempt to hasten the story along.

"Yes, well," stuttered Ahmad, "I continued to hold on tight as I introduced myself with all the proper—I repeat, proper—politeness. I said, 'It is odd that although there are only a few thousand people on this transport, I do not believe I have ever seen you before.' To that, my dear friend here announced that it may be because he generally kept his own personal time."

Lilit thought about that odd phrasing for a moment. From her understanding, back on Earth, the clocks in different geographic regions were set according to the hours that were most reasonable for their vicinity. Of course, this had been greatly complicated by the advent of the colonization of other worlds. On Earth's moon Luna, for instance, it was daytime for about two weeks and then nighttime for around the same time. Meanwhile, on Mars, a sol was roughly thirty-nine and a half minutes longer than a typical Earth-day. That bit of extra time each rotation did not seem like much, but it quickly became evident that throwing off natural circadian rhythm even a small amount created many adverse and debilitating health effects for all Earth-originating life.

In the end, because people living on Luna, Mars, the dwarf planetoid Ceres in the Asteroid Belt, and other similar places had to live underground in order to avoid the deleterious impacts of solar radiation, they all ended up going back to a twenty-four-hour based clock anyway and picked a time zone comparable to one back on Earth. Usually this was the area that most people came from—or, more likely, the one that the monetary sponsors originated from despite the fact that the generally poorer laborers outnumbered them twenty-to-one. That was exactly what had happened with Aestas, too, in the distant past. Consequently, that was the same chronometer they were now keeping aboard this craft. Being a native-born citizen of the colony, Lilit had no idea what part of the Earth shared the hours she had grown up with and lived in her whole life—aside from that one regrettable experience she was still trying to put behind her.

Similarly, Lilit surmised, the ship Ahmad and Durojaiye had originally left from Earth on more than five years prior probably maintained an internal clock based upon its point of origin on the ground. The interplanetary transport that carried them was a dedicated ferry, going back and forth from Tsiolkovsky-Pearson Station at the end of the space elevator above Volcán Cayambe in Puerta Estrella, Ecuador—one of the few Earthly locations Lilit knew and could point to on a map—to a receiving platform in orbit around Venus. The Terran Government had made it abundantly clear they considered her own homeworld to be second rate, so no one would have a ship that matched up to Venus's time. At least, that was not the case until her and her team's most recent... acquisition.

After leaving Earth, Ahmad's and Durojaiye's final destination was, of course, her birthplace: Aestas, the first of the planned soaring sky-cities above Venus's hellish surface. Named after the Roman goddess that is the personification of Summer, Aestas was basically a dirigible filled with an Earth-like atmosphere that allowed it to stay aloft in Venus's much denser "air". To the disbelief of many Earthers, Mars had proven to be highly resistant to every terraforming effort HSA—the Human Space Agency—had thrown at it. Thus, an early twenty-first century proposal called "Project HAVOK" from HSA's ancient predecessor organization NASA was revived with the idea of putting floating habitats on Venus.

While the pressure on the surface of Venus was almost a hundred times that of Earth and the temperature could reach a blistering 738°K—hot enough to melt lead—that was not true higher up above the clouds. There, the pressure was more tolerable and it was far cooler. Although still too hot to handle, it was well within the range of even twenty-first century refrigeration technology to cool the interior of an object residing at that level in the stratosphere.

More importantly, Venus had an induced

magnetic field to protect it from the solar radiation that kept the denizens of places like Luna and Mars from seeing the sun for but a scant few hours a month. And most of all, the gravity was ninety percent that of Earth, a difference that was barely noticeable. Gravity and magnetic fields had been found to be the key factors in keeping Earth-based-beings alive, healthy, and functional. As such, it was a constant struggle in places that lacked them, which was basically everywhere else.

However, this was not the case with Aestas, a metropolis that now thrived with hundreds of thousands of people. The city actually propelled itself across the terminus line where the sun met the darkness, creating a twenty-four-hour-ish "normal" cycle. Lilit's people lived on its solid platforms, grew food and trees under a visually-larger sun, and had a perpetual summertime thanks to the city's movements and the general conditions of Venus. It was as close to freely living on the surface as any of the colonies got.

Compared to almost all other planets in the Sol System, Venus spun in the opposite direction—retrograde, albeit very slowly, with a sol on Venus lasting even longer than its full rotation around the sun—perhaps because some other large terrestrial object slammed into it in the distant past. And unlike Earth's and Mars's highly angled axial tilts and elliptical orbits, Venus stood nearly straight-up as it circumnavigated the sun in an almost perfect circle. All these factors made it so Aestas's environmental and navigation systems could more easily create and maintain a true paradise.

Really, Lilit thought, Ahmad's and Durojaiye's ferry should have used the same hours as Aestas. It would have made so much more sense to synchronize up with the local time at their destination over the course of their long three-and-a-half-month journey between worlds instead of having a sudden shift when they finally arrived. Still, although prior to meeting these two she had never left her planet, even she knew that it was odd—to say the least—to find someone who was living on their own personal clock, especially at that point in their voyage.

Interlude 02

"Lilit, are you even listening anymore?" Ahmad scolded.

"Ah, sorry!" the contrite Lilit jumped as she bumped up against her seatbelt. "I got a little lost in my own thoughts about clocks and history and class warfare..."

"It is alright," consoled Durojaiye, "we are all concerned by what we are doing here. It is useful for your mental well-being to let your mind wander and get a little distracted from time to time."

"I know," Lilit intimated, "It's just that... no, never mind. Ahmad, you were saying that Durojaiye was keeping his own time?"

"Well, I suppose I can repeat myself," Ahmad grumbled. "What I said was that it was a surprise to hear that and I asked him why."

Durojaiye reinserted himself into the conversation noting, "And I said, 'Yes, well, I suppose I am just holding on to the last vestige of my old motherland.' But please record for the official transcript that I did not yet offer the name of my country of derivation.

This, I know, irked Ahmad at the lack of confirmation for his prior assumptions based on stereotypes."

Ahmad gave Durojaiye a look that all but canonized his account of events. Through his clenched teeth he said, "As I recall, you declared that when we arrived you would have abundant time to make the full transition."

"Oh," Lilit chimed in, "this is where I can offer my professional expertise!"

"I do not believe that is your job anymore," Durojaiye proffered.

"Hush, you!" Lilit playfully admonished, although under the surface there was a twinge of guilt and longing for her forsaken prior life that she would never admit out loud, not with the way people needed her to be now.

Slipping into her old shoes, Lilit lectured, "Durojaiye, what you thought was true enough. After you guys disembarked at Aestas, you would have had several months of physical therapy ahead of you to gain back the calcium leached from your bones and to learn how to ambulate again. These sessions could take the typical new arrival anywhere from three to six months, sometimes even up to a year. During that time, you would not have been allowed freedom of movement and instead would have been confined to the inside of a complex that was not completely dissimilar from being trapped within the ship you just got off of.

"To tell you guys the truth, not everyone was successful at these adaptations, either. In some semi-rare instances, a particular individual would never be able to fully acclimate to being on Venus for any variety of reasons, much like some people couldn't cope with living on top of some really tall mountain on Earth in a place like... um... ah... what's it called..."

"Tibet," proposed Ahmad.

"Yeah, that's it, a Tibetan mountain!" Lilit declared. "While some have no discomfort, others can never make it work. In these situations, the people often have to give themselves over to a type of indentured servitude aboard interplanetary shuttles—just like this one—attempting to make up the debt for the cost of their passage and eventual return to Earth. In reality, few have ever escaped their involuntary labor, but it is a concern the governments of the Sol System have chosen to turn a blind eye towards."

Durojaiye clapped and said, "I am impressed with how well you can still recite these pertinent details, even if we are all well aware of these facts now... for obvious reasons. We were lucky to have found her, Ahmad, do you not agree?"

Ahmad looked like he wanted to come up with some witty quip in response, but instead simply nodded in agreement and said, "I do."

"Listen, I will take over the storytelling for a bit," Durojaiye pronounced. "Attempting to make conversation, Ahmad said to me, 'When we land, you can stop thinking about taking a walk in the vacuum of space. We will be very safe down there.' It was exceedingly kind of him to worry about me, though unnecessary."

"I did not know that then," Ahmad asserted, "though you oftentimes still give me reason to worry. But then you bemoaned, 'Yes, stuck inside that Yellow Balloon.'"

Lilit gasped and yelled, "Durojaiye, you didn't?! Oh, that's so disgusting!"

"To my eternal shame, it is true," Durojaiye acknowledged. "As I recall, Ahmad reflexively cringed much the same as you, and it showed on his face before he could stop it."

Lilit hated the term "Yellow Balloon". It was a derogatory phrase used by those on Earth and the other colonies who felt that Aestas was a complete waste of time and resources, things that could be—by their biased estimations—better spent elsewhere, notably projects that would cater to their own selfish needs and benefit them directly. Apparently, Ahmad had felt the same way about the pejorative axiom even before coming to Venus.

As if reading her thoughts—which was not an uncommon occurrence—Ahmad said, "Everywhere I had been on Earth, I met many people who felt this way about Venus, including my own parents. They were not supportive of my decision to immigrate to Venus, and made no qualms about letting me know. 'Yellow Balloon' came up quite frequently in their criticisms of my decision. Hearing it from someone on the same journey as me was quite disturbing."

"Yes," Durojaiye contritely agreed, "and seeing Ahmad's reaction, I realized my egregious error. I wailed 'I am so sorry; I have offended you. Please forgive me! It is just that sometimes I think about the fact that without those protective barriers, we would be sublimated almost instantaneously. Or if the city's elevation dropped just a little bit, the pressure would crush us all.' To be honest, I then began to list more ways we could die in the hostile vastness of Venus and outer space in general."

"During that rant," Ahmad cut Durojaiye off both in the present and the past, "my watch started beeping. Taking a look at it, I said, 'I beg your pardon, I have overstayed my time by the windows. My rad-count has already exceeded my daily allotment and I must return to my quarters.' Although most of the ship's exterior walls are filled with machinery, water, and insulation—anything to slow down and hopefully stop the constant bombardment of cosmic rays—it is well known the solution is hardly perfect."

Lilit was also aware that the meter-thick windows at the bow of the ship were the only things that allowed a view of anything other than the interior bulkheads. It was a reluctant concession the astronomers and physicists gave the shipbuilders and psychiatrists, with the compromise being that each passenger would wear a watch at all times that would measure their radiation exposure and absorption. The talk of it made her reflexively check her own, though she had not been near the edges of the ship in quite some time.

Ahmad continued, "It was then that I noticed that Durojaiye had nothing on his wrists but braided ornaments. 'Durojaiye, where is your watch?' I exclaimed in sheer panic and concern for the man I had just met. I then asked, 'How long have you been here? Please, come with me back to the quarters. Maybe we should take you to sickbay to have you checked out?'"

"As I told you then and every day since,"

Durojaiye interrupted, "you do not need to concern yourself with my safety. I informed you I would be fine and I was, as you can plainly see. HSA is over-protective of us and has guidelines that are far below what we can handle."

"Somehow, this man is impervious to the death he regularly seeks," Ahmad proclaimed. "He said to me, 'I have done this many times; it is no problem. But if you wish to go, you may do so. Do not stay on my account.' How many times have you done the same thing since we got on this vessel, huh?"

In response, Durojaiye sheepishly smiled wide, showing off an array of bright white teeth.

Unable to hide his annoyance, Ahmad said, "Having no intention of killing myself on his account, I implored Durojaiye one more time before wishing him peace and safety, leaving him alone. On the way back to my own quarters, I slowly pulled myself along the attached rails, wondering how a person could be both so fatalistic and reckless at the same time. I could not piece together the enigma that was Durojaiye; I could not make sense of this man. I am afraid understanding him is still a work in progress."

"Would not many people say the same about you, Ahmad?" Durojaiye challenged.

"This... is true," Ahmad conceded. "As a child, I

became infatuated with watching a bright yellow spot making loop-the-loops on the low horizon. When it was the morning star, I would wake up early every day to see it. Conversely, when it was the evening star, I would drop everything, even abandoning a fútbol game with my friends to track it with my small, second-hand telescope. As I got older, my parents decided that I needed a better education than could be provided in the little village near our homestead and sent me to a private boarding school in Abu Dhabi. Sadly, the city was filled with bright lights at all times and I was unable to see Venus or most other dimmer celestial bodies.

"Unfortunately for my parents, in the cosmopolitan capital I was exposed to something far more dangerous: ideas. There were people from all over the world who made Abu Dhabi their home, either permanently or temporarily. More importantly, there were occasionally persons from off-world who helped me learn that not only was it possible to go to that wandering star, but to actually live there. Nevertheless, it was recommended that should I desire to do so, I must bring something to the table that they wanted and needed.

"As such, I spent the next several years learning about water reclamation, soil production, genetic seed manipulation, and other skills that could make me indispensable to any of the colonies. Should I ever get to Aestas, I wanted to make sure they would have no reason to refuse me, but instead would embrace me as a long-lost brother finally returning home."

"Wow, that was quite a long side-trek through your entire autobiography during what was supposed to be the story of how we met," Durojaiye expressed in the driest tone possible.

"Shut up, Durojaiye!" Lilit said in defense of Ahmad. "Ahmad, that was a beautiful revelation, and as your primary native Venusian contact—and still technically your official Coordinator—I am delighted to embrace you." With those words, she unbelted from the table, swam over, and smothered Ahmad in a hug.

After holding on for over a minute, Ahmad attempted to push her off and said, "Ach, that is enough already!" Lilit giggled but held on for another few moments before letting go and reattaching herself to her seat.

Lilit turned to Durojaiye and prodded, "See there, you could learn from Ahmad's example; I've discovered a lot about him today! All you need to do is open up a bit more and, on occasion, let us into that convoluted brain of yours."

"You know I cannot do that," Durojaiye simply stated in return.

Sighing, Lilit yielded, "That I do." It was an argument they had had plenty of times before and she wasn't in the mood to hash it out again. She had wracked her brain enough times trying to figure out when Durojaiye was being completely straightforward and when he was dancing around the subject with carefully considered statements. It amazed her that he could be so honest in some areas, and so protective of his secrets in others. "Okay, Ahmad, since I know Durojaiye will not even tell us what he did at the window after you left, what were you up to?"

"That is not true," Durojaiye interjected. "I can tell you what I did at the window."

Lilit sarcastically retorted, "Wow, will the

miracles of this day ever cease? Yet, given your proclivities, I wonder if it will be interesting or revealing in any way."

"No, of course not," Durojaiye admitted. "But what does that have to do with answering the question? You understand that I will have no choice but to tell you, if you ask me politely."

"Do not fall for his trap," Ahmad warned. "You know how this will go for us if you do."

Exhaling, Lilit asked in halting, forced words, "Durojaiye, what did you do by the windows after Ahmad left you?"

"It is funny you should ask," Durojaiye said with a lit-up smile that showed off his brilliantly white teeth. "Once Ahmad was gone, I discovered that the others who were there before had left while we were talking. Apparently, our conversation annoyed them so much that they opted to return to their quarters rather than listen to us any longer."

Lilit laughed and declared, "Well, I'm sure with no one around, you felt it was quite pointless being there by yourself."

"You are spot on," Durojaiye divulged. "I stayed for a short while longer to see if anyone else would come by. When no other souls appeared, I returned to my quarters, only slightly more irradiated than the recommended dosage."

Scowling, Ahmad pondered, "I do not understand how you can be so nonchalant about such things."

"We have already traversed this ground many times in the past," Durojaiye chastised. "As such, it would be best to move on. I am curious about what happened with you after we parted ways."

After giving him a brief look of annoyance, Ahmad launched into his saga saying, "Well, anyway, after getting back to my quarters and strapping myself into the bed, I began to feel trepidation deep in the pit of my stomach, that fear of my old mistress named rejection rearing its ugly head. I had been stung by it more times than I cared to recount, and deep down I knew it was still a distinct possibility despite my hopes, dreams, and preparations. Aestas had already existed for several generations before my arrival, and by that point you natives had outnumbered us émigrés by a large margin. I know you have trouble seeing it, Lilit, but that makes you an insular community, and I have had unfortunate experiences as an outsider in such a place before."

"You're right," Lilit huffed, "I don't get what you're talking about at all."

"How to explain?" Ahmad rhetorically asked out loud. After a short pause in which he signaled for his friends not to interrupt his train of thought with their questions, comments, or suggestions, he continued by saying, "Ah, yes, I think this will make some sense, please bear with me.

"On Aestas, people are completely dependent upon each other for their collective survival. Disagreements must be resolved without resorting to violence—or at least nothing more than the occasional fisticuffs—otherwise it could literally kill everyone. This had created a very socialist, somewhat communist society, albeit more like a hippy commune than a totalitarian regime; but only by a slight margin.

"The closest comparison to something on Earth are the kibbutzim in Israel, at least the few that remain. Most of the kibbutzim had in the distant past morphed into a blended form of capitalism such that, at this point, they are more like a housing subdivision with a community farm. Still, a few clung to the old ways dating back to before the modern state was even founded.

"It was to one of these that I decided to move. I knew that I needed to prepare myself for what life on Venus would be like, and it seemed like the perfect place to gain some experience. Yet despite the Emiratis having had peaceful relations with the Israelis for more generations that I can recall, I was still treated with immense distrust. After only a few months, I left the kibbutz and returned to my parents' home with my tail between my legs. The experience set my plans back years as I questioned and doubted everything."

Lilit was not sure that made anything clearer for her as she had no frame of reference for the places and groups Ahmad had described, but she chose to honor his request and not interrupt.

Finishing his explanation, Ahmad said, "Slowly, though, the need to escape the gravity of my progenitor planet so that I could start anew once more became overwhelming. That yellow dot in the sky beckoned me with the beauty for which she was named. As the desire to be within her sheltering womb reasserted itself, I imagined that I would feel safe and finally, finally be at home. When I began to drift off, I wondered how we could have traveled some fifty million kilometers and Venus was still just a small speck in the far-off distance. My last thought before completely falling into a restless sleep was...

"'When will I see my love with my own eyes?'"

From Nameless to Righteous

CHAPTER 01

After clearing the decontamination chamber, Lilit stepped out directly into her workstation area. She didn't understand why she had to go through the process since at this juncture she was still separated from the new arrivals by an impermeable wall of plexiglass, but the powers that be on Aestas were always exceedingly cautious about the potential transfer of pathogens. Sighing, she gave in and accepted that in an enclosed environment like theirs it was a reasonably prudent precaution. Still, being separated from people during first introductions always made things difficult. Lilit felt that it was necessary to physically be in proximity with her new clients in order to understand and assist them.

Looking around her assigned rectangular compartment, Lilit continued standing just beyond the entrance as she brought up a virtual display to go through the mandatory checklist before beginning her day. The screen was only visible to her through the ocular implants she received as a child, even earlier than she could remember. Everyone born on

Venus had them, and a fair amount of the immigrants chose to undergo the same procedure if they had not already done so at their point of origin. If they came from one of the other colonies like on Earth's moon Luna, the planet Mars, the dwarf planetoid Ceres in the Asteroid Belt, or the handful of other places in the Solar System that humans had begun to settle, then they were more likely to already have a pair installed. Space was always at a premium, as was access to the resources to build and store tangible components like giant monitors. Thus, in the colonies it became almost mandatory to find ways to work around these limitations with technologically-based augmentations.

Those who came from Earth—which was the vast majority of all migrants—were a different story entirely. As far as Lilit was concerned, Earth was a magical land with unlimited amounts of everything readily at hand. In her head, she pictured humanity's progenitor homeworld as nothing but endless stretches of open land with people below the surface mining its rich resources. Although she was aware that this vision of hers was quite inaccurate, the image was reinforced with how Earthers behaved even after arriving on Venus.

Because people living on Earth could get away

with being wasteful and having lavish—if ultimately meaningless—possessions, they could also afford to be suspicious of the idea of sticking sophisticated computers inside their heads. As such, more often than not, they chose to avoid doing so. Of course, there were Earthers who still went through with the practice, but they were a minority of the population. Most opted to continue to own corporeal objects to do their work on, or, as a compromise, put on temporary overlay devices like glasses so as to interact in virtual spaces.

Over the few years that Lilit had been performing this job, she was still surprised by how many of her clients had no idea what she was doing as she typed and waved her hands in the air—just as she would appear to be pantomiming if someone were looking at her at that moment. In actuality, she was going through a tedious list on her personal screen that basically confirmed that there was nothing in her area at all aside from what she brought in with her and a few required pieces of equipment that were needed to communicate with those outside her little niche. She supposed that it was possible that whoever had been assigned this station before her had left an object behind or that an émigré had done something nefarious like burning a hole through the plexiglass, but neither situation nor anything remotely like them had ever happened to her before. All she could see at that moment were the blank wall and door she had come through behind her, the empty walls on either side of her that did not grant her visibility into the other workstations, and the desk and chair in front of her adjacent to the clear window that looked out to the client area.

Beyond that transparent partition, she could easily make out the queue of people waiting in wheelchairs. They were arriving from orbit in small batches on the "skimmers", a type of ship that could transform between a dirigible to float in the skies of Venus and a small rocket that could reach the receiving platform in orbit. Unlike on Earth, Mars, Luna, and the other terrestrial bodies, Venus did not have a space elevator because they could not anchor it to the ground. No human nor robot worker would be able to survive long enough under the crushing surface pressures to attach it, even if the line itself did not instantly snap from those same forces. Using an actual dedicated conveyance vessel like on Earth in the ancient-times before the advent of the space elevator was an inefficient but necessary methodology to move people and goods from space into the colony, and vice versa.

Although her sidewalls were opaque, once beyond the plexiglass the separation dividers were semi-transparent to allow light to pass. Through those partially-translucent barriers to her left and right, Lilit could somewhat make out the shadows of immigrants in their rolling carriages. Apparently, she had somehow fallen behind her colleagues who were already interviewing people from this cohort. She was sure this was going to come up in her next efficiency review meeting. When the time came for that, though, she would have no choice but to take the "constructive criticism" with a smile and promise to do better. After all, her supervisor was also her cousin who got her this job in the first place, so she was forced into forever being grateful.

Amazingly, despite these small detriments like her overbearing cousin and the pointless checklist she was still plodding her way through, Lilit did enjoy her occupation. Most of all, she was good at it. No, scratch that, Lilit decided, she was fantastic! Among all of the officers since she started, she had the lowest rejection rate at less than three percent. The average for her whole department was eight percent, so she really was the crème de la crème. Lilit hoped that management never got it into their heads to promote her; she wanted to remain right where she was on the front lines.

Completing her tiresome list, Lilit connected to the new arrivals database and ticketing system. With this done, she was finally allowed to take a seat at the desk, although she found the chair to be uncomfortably warm still. Whoever had last been there had vacated not too long ago. Lilit was a bit surprised they had not run into each other outside of the decontamination chamber. Putting the thought aside and placing her water bottle on the surface in front of her, she created a set of virtual monitors to separate out the relevant details from the personnel files she was about to use in the interview process. Every agent had their own favored style on how to access the data, and Lilit preferred to see as much of it at once in different locations so that she could turn to view them as needed. Not everyone was good at multitasking in this way, but it felt natural to her.

Pulling the next-up request from the ticket manager program, Lilit placed the pertinent information for her first immigrant of the day in front of her. Activating the microphones hidden around her to broadcast to the outside hallway speakers, Lilit announced, "Durojaiye Yakubu, please come to the window at booth number sixteen."

CHAPTER 02

A short, dark-skinned man in a colorful outfit rolled up to her window. He flashed a smile full of bright white teeth and said, "Hello, I am Durojaiye Yakubu, your humble servant, as someone close to me would say." His voice carried through the speakers hidden inside her chamber on the other side of the glass, just as Lilit's would now do for him.

With his introduction, Durojaiye attempted a small bow from his seat. Lilit smiled and giggled a little at the show of chivalry. In her experience, some people even tried to shake hands through the separation barrier, oftentimes mimicking the motion in the air. Lilit chose to do whatever they did, so she bowed from her own seat and proclaimed, "Nice to meet you, Durojaiye! I'm Lilit Sarkisian, and I've been assigned as your Coordinator with the goal of helping you make the transition to Aestas and Venus."

"What does that mean?" Durojaiye asked.

Lilit was taken aback a bit and inquired, "Didn't they explain this to you before you left Earth?" Everyone who came to settle on Aestas was usually exceedingly prepared. Frankly, it was a necessity in order to avoid being shipped back. Lilit began to feel a knot form in her stomach as she saw her failure rate about to arc skyward because of this one man.

In response, Durojaiye claimed, "My coming here was a rather last-minute decision, so I did not have long to prepare."

"Oh," was all that Lilit could manage in a confused tone. "Well, think of a Coordinator as equal parts immigration officer, social worker, physical and occupational therapist, psychologist, job recruiter, real estate agent, and smiling face of the neighborhood welcoming committee."

"In other words," Durojaiye summarized, "we are going to be seeing a lot of each other!"

"That's right," Lilit confirmed. "Here on Venus, we do not believe in passing people along through a bureaucracy of different agencies and individuals. Instead, we work one-on-one with new arrivals through the entirety of their onboarding process. If you ever need anything, I am your one contact and gateway to all things here on Aestas."

"This is most excellent," Durojaiye declared. "You sound exactly like what I am going to need so that I can complete my assignment."

Lilit crinkled her brow as she questioned aloud,

"Your assignment?" Not waiting for an answer, she turned to her invisible monitors to look through Durojaiye's work and life history. While she was reading, she said, "I think I'm a bit confused here. Do you have some type of job already waiting for you here? I'm not seeing anything. Actually, your record is rather... odd."

"How so?" Durojaiye probed.

"Well," Lilit began, "usually people come here with a set of skills and education that can contribute to the collective needs of the colony. But from what I can see here, basically, you have barely left your own home village. I'm sorry, I'm not familiar with the name of this place."

"It is in Nigeria," Durojaiye offered. When Lilit did not show any signs of recognition, he added, "In Africa. Do you know where that is?"

Lilit blushed a bright red. "I know this is going to sound awful," she confessed, "but not really. I mean, I think I could pick it out on a map, but I get confused with the big continents that have similar shapes. As a native Venusian, the political and geographic boundaries back on Earth have never really sunk in."

"You have never been?" Durojaiye queried.

"To Earth?" Lilit clarified. Not pausing for a response, Lilit admitted, "No, no. Much like you, I have rarely left my hometown, either. The furthest I've ever gone is to the docking platform in orbit as part of my training for this job."

"Ah, so we are very much alike!" Durojaiye proclaimed with delight as he clapped his hands together. "What about your family? When did they come here?"

Lilit suddenly realized that the interview had been spun around on her and she was no longer in control. Nevertheless, she went along with it anyway despite feeling that she was being manipulated. "My ancestors came here on the first settlement mission. I am as indigenous of a Venusian as anyone can be. Over twelve percent of the population here can trace their family tree back to the same two people, me among them."

"It must make it difficult to find a mate," Durojaiye sympathized.

"Well, that is part of the reason we have to keep importing new blood into the gene pool!" Lilit expounded with a broad smile on her face.

"I am sorry; I am already spoken for," Durojaiye plainly stated.

Turning bright red again, Lilit stammered, "I... I... I wasn't coming on to you! Our relationship is meant to be a professional one!"

Even while saying that, Lilit knew that it was a lie. Not that she was attracted to Durojaiye and wanted to start a sexual relationship with him, but she knew that it had happened often enough with other Coordinators. Management turned a blind eye to this blatant ethical violation because it did actually serve the government's agenda of diversifying their DNA. Lilit's own cousin who got her the Coordinator job was one such offender, and that was part of the reason she was no longer a field operative. Working intimately close with people for months and years on end tended to create unintended connections. It really was a pressure cooker situation for some, but not Lilit. She had a way of compartmentalizing everything in her life.

This unexpected embarrassment was just the thing Lilit needed to jolt her out of Durojaiye's hold and back onto her intended task. She turned back to her monitors to more deeply peruse Durojaiye's records and history, looking for clues as to his intentions. Unfortunately, nothing in particular stood out. He appeared to have had some civil service experience, but that was common enough. Actually, the lack of detail was far more concerning than the absence of useful skillsets or education. The Terran Government was nothing if not fastidious with their record keeping. The only explanation that Lilit could think of was that Durojaiye must have acted as some type of independent contractor or laborer. These fields and positions were often only loosely chronicled using official means, or were paid under-the-table and avoided government scrutiny altogether.

Sighing after finding nothing relevant, Lilit finally gave up and just inquired, "Let's get back on track, Durojaiye. You said you already had some type of work lined up?"

"No," Durojaiye disputed, "you assumed that based on the words I carefully chose. I said I had an assignment."

"Okay, an 'assignment' then," Lilit conceded. "What, pray tell, is this assignment of yours?"

Without a hint of irony, Durojaiye simply avowed, "I am a spy."

CHAPTER 03

Before Lilit could react in any way, she heard a voice from far away yelling, "He is kidding! Do not listen to him!"

Looking behind Durojaiye, Lilit saw another one of the immigrants attempting to roll down the aisle to her station. He was not making much progress as he did not seem to have regained a lot of strength in his arms yet to push the wheels along. Although, by the looks of him, Lilit doubted that he ever could have had much power within his flabby exterior. Whereas Durojaiye appeared to be in peak physical shape, the newcomer looked like a beachball. Lilit began to feel a pang of guilt at the thought and filed it away for future self-improvement. Even in a place like Aestas, prejudice had not been completely overcome. Sure, predetermined judgements based on the superficial components like skin tone had been largely put behind them, but plenty of other ones remained, especially socio-economic concerns.

Peering at the man coming down the lane, Lilit could not place what region on Earth he may have originated from. It did not help that people of various façades had moved all over the planet. The only thing she knew with certainty was that he was darker than her and lighter than Durojaiye. That didn't really narrow things down.

As the stranger rolled up to the window, Durojaiye smiled in delight. Something sparkled in his eye, but the newcomer did not seem to notice. Instead, he continued to stare straight at Lilit and pleaded, "Please forgive Durojaiye; he thinks that he is funny."

"Excuse me, sir," Lilit reprimanded, "but just who are you?"

"Oh, many apologies," the heretofore unidentified man said. "My name is Ahmad Al Zaheri and I just want you to know tha—"

"Hold your horses, Ahmad!" Lilit commanded as she raised her hand up to the glass. She created a second virtual monitor setup and sent a digital request for permission to pull up Ahmad's record. A manager would have to manually approve the ask as Coordinators were not supposed to pick and choose their own clients. In the dropdown to enter a reason for the override, Lilit selected "Spouse or Domestic Partner" and submitted it. A brief moment later, Lilit's cousin granted the authorization and Ahmad's information filled her secondary setup.

Ahmad tapped his hands nervously as Lilit looked over his details. Raising her head, Lilit reproached him, "Ahmad, nothing in your record here shows any type of legal connection to Durojaiye. How long have you known each other?"

Ahmad fumbled for a bit before asserting, "It has only been a few weeks now, but it feels like forever."

Lilit smiled at this and felt her own anger at being suddenly interrupted melt away. Relaxing her own countenance and making understanding gestures towards Ahmad appeared to finally allow him to calm down, too. "Oh, so you two met aboard the interplanetary shuttle? That's so sweet!"

"Yes, exactly," Ahmad proclaimed. "Although nothing about Durojaiye should be considered sweet. He needs me to look out for him, otherwise he is likely to wind up dead."

"Based on what I've seen so far, I can't disagree with your assessment," Lilit granted.

"Well, I do!" Durojaiye protested. "I have been more than capable of taking care of myself for the decades before we met, and will be very willing and able to do so during my time here and beyond. I keep telling you: you do not need to worry about me."

"Though you say this, I have no choice but to

continue to do so," Ahmad countermanded.

"You two are absolutely adorable!" Lilit gushed. "Alright, I get it, you don't have to tell me anything more. I see how quickly things have gotten serious!"

"Now I am confused," Ahmad perplexed. "I do not understand what you mean."

"She thinks we are a couple," Durojaiye explained to his companion.

"A couple of what?" the still lost Ahmad asked.

"A romantic couple," Durojaiye began. "Because I spurned Lilit's advances earlier, she now believes that you are my beloved who is keeping her from syphoning off my DNA to expand the gene pool."

Lilit tried to interject during the entire replay, but Ahmad beat her to it, "Me, in a romantic relationship, with him?!"

"What is wrong with me?" Durojaiye demanded.

"Where to begin?!" Ahmad exclaimed. "Who would want to bed you... aside from Coordinator Lilit here, I mean?"

Lilit wanted to scream but she could not get a word in edgewise between the duo. Instead, Durojaiye responded with, "My wife, Chigozie, back in my home village. And I can prove it with the children we have."

"What wife?" Ahmad asked. "What children? You

have never mentioned any such thing before. Do you not believe that this would be pertinent information one would readily share with a good friend?"

"You never asked," Durojaiye accused. "You have been too busy lecturing me on handrail safety and Venusian culture."

While they were bickering, Lilit took a deeper dive through Durojaiye's record before declaring, "He's telling the truth."

"Huh?" was all Ahmad could respond with.

Durojaiye turned back towards Lilit and declared, "It is okay, you can tell him what you are seeing on your screens."

Taking his permission to reveal personally protected information at face value, Lilit noted, "Ahmad, it's all right here in his profile. Durojaiye, is your family coming to Venus later? It's rather unusual for a married person with children to come here alone."

"No, they will not be joining me," Durojaiye confessed. "I will return to them when I complete my mission. Until that time comes, I will not be able to see or communicate with them. I will miss them terribly, but this is a temporary situation that is beyond my control. I know what must be done, so I will see it through until such a point that we can be reunited."

"You mean this alleged espionage mission of

yours?" Lilit scoffed. "You do realize that by telling us you are a secret agent, you are officially the worst one in all of history."

"You mean, this spy thing is real?" Ahmad asked aghast. "That this is not just one of your bad jokes? That you really are some type of infiltrator?"

"More like a mole," Durojaiye conceded. "Lilit, please be at ease; I am not here to do anything nefarious or cause any damage. Quite the contrary. I have been assigned here to act as a citizen of Aestas and do whatever is asked of me by you or whoever else is in charge. If you need me to pull weeds, that is what I will do. Should you want me to construct a new skimmer, I will do that exactly as the directions are laid out and never deviate. A key part of my assignment is to observe and report back about regular life here on Aestas. Earth Central Command is looking for intelligence on what it is like to be a Venusian, on getting into your minds and hearts. Therefore, I will be a Venusian so that they can learn and plan and scheme and prepare for how you might respond to a variety of stimuli."

"How could I possibly trust you to freely roam around my home after a damning admission like that?" Lilit insisted.

"How do you make the decision to trust anyone

who comes up to this window? How will you decide if you should trust Ahmad?" Durojaiye countered.

"Hey!" Ahmad shouted. "Unlike you, I have actually worked tirelessly and prepared to be here. I came to Venus of my own volition and want to be unconditionally accepted into my new home."

Lilit looked through Ahmad's records and verified this reality. He had degrees and proficiencies in just about every useful field for someone living on Aestas. Looking up at him and forgetting to formally receive permission to reveal details about his life, she said, "Ahmad, I'm quite confused. You are, for all practical purposes, overqualified. Why did it take you so long to finally get here?"

Not giving him the opportunity to answer, she then turned towards Durojaiye and said, "Your record indicates almost no useful skills whatsoever. You say you'll pull weeds or build a skimmer, but how do you intend to do any of these tasks? You don't have any prior experience doing either of them, or much of anything else worthwhile, it would seem."

Durojaiye was quiet as he appeared to have no answer. Suddenly, breaking the silence, Ahmad declared, "Then I shall teach him."

"Ahmad, what are you saying?" Lilit cried. "Do you realize that by intertwining yourself with this man you are tying yourself to his fate, whatever it may be? He is, I might add, a person who has already broken your trust after just a few weeks of knowing him."

Not deterred at all, Ahmad immediately entreated, "Coordinator Lilit, please, I am begging you to let Durojaiye stay and to make me responsible for his education so that he might be found suitable."

"Why would you offer this?" Lilit charged again. "What has he done to earn such loyalty and sacrifice from you? I should lock him up in a holding cell on the docking platform and send him back to Earth on the next shuttle!"

"No," Ahmad demanded, "that will not do. I believe that Venus is the land of new beginnings. It is why I have come, and it can be that for my dear friend here. Durojaiye, whatever your past is, whatever your reasons for being here are, they do not matter. I can help you see Aestas as a fresh start for you, too."

CHAPTER 04

Durojaiye wiped his eyes with his sleeves to stop the tears that were starting to form there, put on a sad smile, and noted for all, "See, you always think you have to look out for me, that I cannot do anything on my own."

Ahmad returned a similar expression and retorted, "And once again, I have been proven right."

"Very well," Durojaiye accepted. "Thank you, my friend. One more time, I am in your debt."

"And I, yours," Ahmad agreed.

With the deal between them apparently settled, Ahmad and Durojaiye looked away from each other and back towards Lilit. Each sat there doing nothing but patiently gaping at her with expectant visages. Completely torn, Lilit had no idea what she should do anymore. All the surety from her professional experience evaporated as she began to feel like a green rookie again. Nothing even remotely like this had ever happened to her during all her years on the job, nor had she heard about similar situations. Coordinators had a lot of autonomy, but with that came a

"

significant amount of power. She knew that she held the future of these two men in her hands. Should she elect to do so, she could turn them into indentured deckhands on the first shuttle back to Earth.

Utterly paralyzed by indecision, Lilit could not take it anymore and spun her chair around so that they would stop staring at her with their puppy-dog eyes. She pretended to busy herself by looking through their records yet another time on her virtual monitors, but she was not learning anything new. Ahmad was a top tier candidate, even though he apparently didn't realize it. The only mark against him was his age, but that was not enough reason to turn him away. Lilit realized that she already desperately wanted to make sure Ahmad would succeed, that she felt responsible for him.

However, she began to fear that if she sent Durojaiye away that Ahmad would follow. He had made some moral decision for inexplicable reasons and decided that he was obligated to ensure Durojaiye succeed here. Lilit could not imagine what had happened on that shuttle to engender this type of attachment, but it was definitely there and she was not going to be able to break him of it anytime soon.

As Lilit pondered more deeply about the situation, she began to realize that having Durojaiye around might actually be an overall beneficial thing. While on paper he certainly lacked any conventional talents, there was something intangible about him. Most importantly, as far as she was concerned, he appeared to inspire bravery and determination in Ahmad, something he clearly lacked alone. It was like the sum of the two was far more than just the parts. Together, they made a better and far more capable being than either could ever be individually.

Lilit also hated to admit it to herself, but she found Durojaiye interesting and charming, too. His frankness, honesty, and vulnerability were all on full display, characteristics Lilit found quite refreshing. Soft skills like these were often overlooked, but Lilit recognized that they were just as important as being able to culture bacteria. Whatever it was he was really doing on Aestas, it did not seem like he was going to be a danger to anyone but himself.

Suddenly, tears of her own began to flow and they made her virtual displays appear blurry. She was glad that Ahmad and Durojaiye couldn't see her as she pulled a handkerchief from her pocket to wipe away the evidence. Once finally composed, she twirled herself around and examined the duo for the last time, resolving herself to make a final determination. While she hoped that they had not noticed anything that had just transpired, she later learned that the red puffiness around her eyes had easily given her away.

"Durojaiye," Lilit prodded, "you've heard what Ahmad is willing to sacrifice for you. I'm going to ask you the same question, then. If I decided to reject Ahmad's application, what would you do?"

Not skipping a beat, Durojaiye declared, "Without Ahmad, I have no hope of prevailing on Aestas. Over our weeks together on the transport vessel between worlds, it became clear to me that my only path to the results I seek is through and with Ahmad. Deprived of him, I fear I will not be able to accomplish anything I have set out to do and be. As such, if Ahmad were to be asked to leave, it would be necessary for me to go with him and return to Earth as a total failure, despite the consequences I and my family would face."

"It would be that bad for you?" Ahmad concernedly inquired.

In response, Durojaiye just smiled and nodded. He held out his hand and, after a moment, Ahmad took it in his own.

"Coordinator Lilit," Ahmad announced as he and Durojaiye continued to hold tightly to each other, "it has been decided. You are either going to accept both of us, or neither of us."

"If that is how it is going to be..." Lilit attempted.

"It is," Ahmad affirmed.

Lilit thought for a moment more before she pronounced with as much formality as she could muster, "Okay then, it appears I have no choice. Ahmad Al Zaheri, Durojaiye Yakubu... against my better judgment, you have both passed provisional screening and have been granted the privilege to enter Aestas."

A palpable relief spread through the plexiglass as Lilit continued, "I will assign each of you your temporary quarters in the Quarantine District and will take you over there later today after I finish interviewing the other candidates. We have strict protocols related to pathogen transmission, so when you next see me, I will be in a full hazmat suit.

"Over the course of the next several months, I will be visiting you daily under the same conditions in order to make sure that anything you are carrying inside of you is completely wiped away and to monitor your internal exposure to the uniquely Venusian biosphere. Basically, in the end, your entire microbiome will be replaced with a new one. It is only after that point that you will be allowed to enter Aestas proper.

"Both during your quarantine and after you

arrive in the city, I will be working with you on your physical and emotional therapy. It is only when I deem you clear that you will be allowed freedom of movement and occupation. Before then, you will be extremely restricted in your activities, both in place and time. At any moment, I can revoke your privileges and return you back to whence you came. You also have the right to leave at any time should you so choose, but the government of Aestas will not pay for your exit under any circumstances.

"Do you understand everything I have told you and agree to these terms?"

"I do," both concurred in unison.

"Great," Lilit said, "please look down at the screen embedded in the desk in front of you. There you will see what I have described in greater detail. Read it over carefully and, one at a time, sign it in the open field at the bottom. This will be your official immigration contract."

Neither spent much time reading the contract and quickly scrolled to the bottom and signed with the stylus chained to the desk. Once done, Lilit verified their signatures on her end and heralded, "Congratulations gentlemen, though I may come to regret this, today you have taken your first step towards becoming official members of our society!"

CHAPTER 05

It was mid-morning and Lilit was waiting outside the decontamination chamber that connected to the Quarantine District. After nearly four months, Durojaiye and Ahmad had finally cleared the necessary hurdles to be released into her care inside Aestas proper. Truthfully, Durojaiye had been ready to go for a couple of weeks, but he insisted on postponing his departure until he and Ahmad could leave together. While Ahmad had tried to demur and send his friend out ahead, Durojaiye would not hear of it. Since Lilit was ultimately in charge of the decision on when to move them on to the next step, she elected to use her sizable authority to maintain the status quo until Ahmad was ready, as well.

As much as she hated to admit it to herself, Lilit had to concede that she was playing favorites. Her other clients were fine enough and some were downright delightful, but nothing got her ready to jump out of bed in the morning more than the chance to meet with Durojaiye and Ahmad. The banter between the three of them was so natural that she often forgot that she was actually at work and not just visiting their holding unit to have a good time. She had to program her onboard A.I. to literally yell at her when it was time to leave, otherwise she'd miss all her remaining appointments. Despite knowing it was wrong to be so negligent to the other immigrants who needed her just as much, they just did not stimulate her mind like these two did.

Durojaiye continued to be an enigma, but she was now wise to his verbal machinations. Sometimes she tried to probe deeper using her own psychological training, but it appeared that Durojaiye had been prepared for such tactics and had tools of his own at the ready to resist her. On the other side, Ahmad could not shut up and had yet to learn how to filter any of his thoughts. It was not that he was naïve—far from it, given his extensive knowledge—just that he had no concept or concern about what boundaries were supposed to be.

For instance, one day Ahmad just blurted out to Lilit, "Ah ha! You are Armenian!"

"I don't know what that is," Lilit responded.

"It is not a what, it is a where," Ahmad reprimanded. "It is a country in the Caucasus region."

"Okay," Lilit said, "then I don't know 'where' that is, or why I should care."

"This is sad," Ahmad declared. "Knowing where one originates from is very important. It helps us understand who we are and what our people have had to overcome. No one in your family ever said anything? Specifically, about the meaning of your surname?"

"Nope, never came up," Lilit exhaled, afraid of where Ahmad was going on this tangent.

"Well, it took quite a bit of combing through the Archives," Ahmad began, "but I believe I have figured it out. 'Sarkisian' is somewhat derivative, but when I trace it back to its foundational components, it basically means 'Child of the Servant'. Does this not sound like you exactly? You live in service to people like us and Aestas in general, a descendant of others who have done the same or similar."

Lilit tried to maintain her serious expression even though she wanted to burst out laughing and said, "I think you put way too much credence into stuff like this. Shouldn't you be doing more of the exercises I assigned you?"

Even though she tried to shame Ahmad into feeling like he needed to do more physical activity, she could not deny that he had already surpassed the required proficiency markers. More so, he continued to improve every week. Despite this, he somehow remained as rotund as ever. Lilit could not figure it out. By monitoring all of his caloric intake and tracking all of his joule-burning activities, she believed that he should have been shedding fat. Instead, he remained the same as always, like it was a protective layer over his strengthening muscles.

Not taken aback at all, Ahmad tried a different approach. "But you should familiarize yourself with the Armenian people. They have a rich and sorrowful history, one that is about surmounting the worst that we humans can do to each other. In the early twentieth century, they were the victims of a mass genocide at the hands of those who wanted to control them from afar. And even after they thought their enemies were defeated and their plight was over, they discovered that the rest of the world did not want to hear about their problems and were selfishly only concerned with their own affairs.

"For the next century and beyond, the other nations of the world pretended that the culling of the Armenian people did not happen so that they could maintain happier relations with their powerful former overlords. It was solely in the name of political expedience that the majority of other countries—including the largest and most formidable—chose to avoid doing the right thing of acknowledging the factual history and pain of the Armenians. By refusing to learn from the past, the entire Earth was doomed to repeat it over and over again. And they did just that, and continue to do so to this day."

"Thank you for depressing me," Lilit admonished. "Now I know that I come from a people who were trampled on, who no one cared about, and whose existence could be wiped out without anyone noticing."

"No, no, you misunderstand," Ahmad insisted. "This is a story about perseverance and beating the odds. I know about their plight because in the end they did win. It took a long time and incredibly hard work, but it was accomplished. The moral is that any smaller group can defeat a much larger rival if they can just continue to hold on to hope."

Later, with this conversation still stuck in her head, Lilit talked to Durojaiye about it during their one-on-one session. She wanted to get his perspective without Ahmad providing further commentary. To her surprise, Durojaiye was very much in Ahmad's camp saying, "I believe in this case that you should listen to Ahmad. He has great insight into this type of thing."

Skeptical, Lilit charged back, "You mean I should accept Ahmad's idea that my name and origins have a direct impact on my current life?"

"No, that is not what I meant," Durojaiye corrected. "What I took away was the importance of history informing the future, and about transcending the odds and triumphing over much larger rivals. There will always be times of great strife, but I believe that you, Lilit, are one of the rare few individuals who have the strength to stand up for what is right and make it a reality. If you never give up your hope and always push ahead, then you will undoubtedly succeed over those who want to hold you down."

Suddenly, Lilit was jolted from her thoughts by her onboard A.I. alerting her to an incoming voice call. The metadata that popped up in front of her eyes indicated that it was coming from one of the security guard stations inside the Quarantine District, with a name she did not recognize attached. Activating her inner-ear speaker and near-mouth microphone that she had chosen to have surgically implanted, she spoke aloud, "Hello, this is Lilit."

"Hello Ms. Sarkisian, this is Protector Aritza from the Immigration and Quarantine Center," the voice on the other side said.

"Yes, I am aware," Lilit teased.

"Oh, uh, of course, ma'am," Protector Aritza stammered. They must have been a relatively recent hire since they were being so formal with her. Lilit could not remember the last time she had been called "Miss" or "ma'am", but instantly recalled that she did not care for it very much, either. She was still young and unencumbered and full of life! No one should be treating her like a crusty veteran whose best days were behind her. Lilit decided that she would have to work on this newbie and teach them all about her sprightly vitality.

However, in the meantime, since Protector Aritza refused to continue, Lilit prompted, "What can I do for you?"

"Oh right," they finally commenced after apparently remembering that they had initiated the call. "I'm calling to let you know that your wards Ahmad Al Zaheri and Durojaiye Yakubu have cleared decontamination and are ready to leave for the outside world and be released into your care. Are you in the designated location to accept them?"

Lilit recognized that this was actually the official handover process, so she shifted her mind into business mode. "Yes, I am in the appointed position and ready to receive them."

"Please send confirmation codes," the inexperienced Protector requested. After Lilit had done so, there was a pause on the other end while they seemingly reviewed what had been sent over. At last, they declared, "Confirmation codes obtained. I will now open the doors and hand over control to you. As a reminder, if there are any issues at all, you are to contact the Protector Force immediately and alert us to the situation."

"Of course, of course," Lilit agreed. She had done this dozens of times before, but it never stopped irking her. They were talking about people and their lives here, but the Protector Force and the Aestas Government via the Managing Council always treated humans like they were mere objects that had to be logged and catalogued. She understood why it was necessary, but still didn't like it. Nonetheless, she felt that if she were in charge, she could find a better compromise that balanced the needs between security and compassion.

"Alright, the exit portal will release as soon as I hang up," Aritza announced. "Thank you, and good-bye now."

Without waiting for Lilit to also give her farewell, Protector Aritza disconnected. Putting their abrupt departure aside, Lilit saw the access gateway unlock and slide open. To her surprise, Ahmad and Durojaiye were not standing there waiting to come out, nor did they immediately walk through the now available egress. Approaching the aperture so that she could peer inside, she was surprised to hear Ahmad's and Durojaiye's voices engaged in one of their infamous squabbles. Lilit could not believe it; they had become so engrossed in their conversation that they did not even notice that they were free!

"Hey you guys," Lilit yelled into the chamber, "shut your mouths and get your butts out here!" That command certainly was not in the handbook, but she knew how to talk to them to get them going. Once again, she had to admit to herself that she was way too familiar with this pair, but also that she did not care to change that. While she realized that they were becoming friends, she did not feel it was compromising her ability to do her job of acclimating them to Venus. If anything, their shared closeness was perhaps beneficial, especially considering all the idiosyncrasies of this duo.

Following instructions, Ahmad and Durojaiye did as told and emerged from inside the chamber. As soon as they were outside, the door closed behind them and locked. Another person or group of people would be awaiting their turn to pass through to the wider colony soon enough.

Both Ahmad and Durojaiye put their hands above their eyes and squinted. Lilit went into her bag and fetched a couple of pairs of cheap sunglasses. Holding them out she said, "Here, put these on. This is the first time since you left Earth that you have been in direct sunlight, and you must be aware that you've never seen Sol quite like this!"

Ahmad put on his glasses, looked up, and said,

"Yes, I always knew it would look about one and a half times larger, and I ran all the simulations, but nothing prepares you for seeing it in person. Truly astounding."

Lilit glanced over at Durojaiye who, although he had taken his sunglasses, had yet to put them on. Instead, he was looking directly at her. "Something I can help you with, Durojaiye?" Lilit asked.

"No," Durojaiye began, "it is just that I have not seen you with my own eyes before now and I want to be able to do so. When we first met, we were separated by plexiglass and I could only see a part of your upper torso. Then, for the past four months, you have been in a hazmat suit. As such, this is the first opportunity I have had to truly see you, and under real sunlight, nonetheless."

Lilit put her hand on top of her head and spun around in a pirouette as her light skirt flared outward. "And what do you think?" she jokingly inquired.

"Perfect," was all Durojaiye said.

Lilit blushed, punched Durojaiye in the arm, and said, "What would your lonely wife back on Earth—who, I might add, is raising your kids all by herself—think if she heard you flirting with a young lady such as myself like that?"

"Oh, it was not a flirtation," Durojaiye contended. "It was a simple fact. Besides, she would understand the relevance to my assignment."

Putting her hands to her chest, Lilit said with false abhorrence, "Chigozie would be okay with the things you say to me in the name of doing your job? Why I never!"

Laughing, Durojaiye insisted that it was true, but Lilit still did not believe him. Suddenly, they both realized that Ahmad had not jumped in and admonished either of them. Turning to Ahmad, Lilit saw that he was still looking up, but with the biggest smile across his face as tears streamed down into his prominent beard. Placing a hand on his elbow, Lilit asked, "Are you okay, Ahmad?"

Ahmad suddenly appeared to realize that he had zoned out. He lowered his head so that he could look directly at Lilit as he spoke, wiped away his tears, and declared, "Yes, yes, I am fine. It is just... I am so happy. After so many years of doubt, I am finally here. I am finally Venusian."

"Not yet," Durojaiye corrected. "We still have to pass Lilit's final tests before we can become citizens. At this point, we are still just extended-stay guests who are hanging on by a thread and could be thrown out with a moment's notice."

Watching Ahmad deflate, Lilit shrieked, "Durojaiye! That was plain mean! Ahmad, don't listen to him. If I am going to kick anyone out, it will be him. You, on the other hand, are well on your way to becoming one of us."

Ahmad did not bounce back as she expected and instead requested, "Please do not deport Durojaiye. He has come a long way under my tutelage, and I believe he can prove to be useful to you and the rest of Aestas."

"Ahmad, I was only joking around, pulling your leg a little bit," Lilit quietly proclaimed. "Both you and Durojaiye are making fine progress towards being able to make your home here. It's my job to ensure that happens. Besides, despite my threats and bravado, it actually reflects poorly on me if you are unable to join us. So stop worrying, and start enjoying yourself!"

At the end of Lilit's speech, Ahmad visibly perked up, clapped his hands, and asserted, "Excellent, then all is well! Now then, what comes next?"

CHAPTER 07

"First up," Lilit declared, "is your inaugural official tour of Aestas! We'll start on Level 1 here, go for a lunch at my favorite restaurant, and then I'll bring you downstairs to see how the sausage gets made—so to speak—before taking you to your new temporary quarters in the Confinement District. Let me call a transport and we'll get going."

"If we could," Ahmad interrupted, "I would prefer to walk. We have only had a small track to do endless loops on for months, so I would be much appreciative if we could move around without any incumbrances."

Surprised, Lilit said, "Well, sure, I guess, if you are feeling up to it. I don't want to push you guys too hard, especially on your initial day out. What about you, Durojaiye?"

Laughing, Durojaiye stated, "I cannot let my rotund friend here show me up! If he feels he is able to handle it, then I have no choice but to do the same, except in a superior manner!"

Once Lilit was able to stop the two from trading barbs with each other, she proceeded to take them down some of the main boulevards on the top floor of the floating colony. As they were walking around, Lilit explained that it was designed to be mostly flat with the aim of maximizing the available farmland, as well as having recreational fields. She brought them over to an orchard of fruit-bearing trees, but emphasized that it was against the law to pick from them without a license. Protectors could be seen on patrol here-and-there, but Lilit told them the real enforcement came from the mechanized insects.

While there certainly were real bugs flittering about that had stowed away in the shipments of soil and fertilizer from Earth, Lilit highlighted that the artificial batch did the heavy lifting of pollination and surveillance. She warned that if the miniaturized robots caught anyone taking produce that they were not supposed to, they would latch onto the person in an unreachable spot and send out a signal to the Protectors to pick them up. "And as a reminder," Lilit lectured, "there are cameras everywhere—including on the mechanical flying creatures—and any illicit activity will be reported both back to the Protectors and to me."

"Can we not even go to the bathroom alone?" Durojaiye muttered.

"Well," Lilit admitted, "there really aren't

cameras in public restrooms or in your personal living spaces, but there are monitors of other kinds. For instance, we closely watch wastewater for signs of infections so that we can quarantine people before anything spreads. Thus, in some ways, you could say that no, you will never go to the bathroom alone ever again."

"I cannot decide if I am in awe or horrified," Durojaiye lamented.

All this conversation of bathroom etiquette made Lilit's bladder start to tingle, so she showed her companions where they could go to summon an elevator to take them down to the lower levels. While they called it "Level 1", it was actually at the peak of the colony with the numbers rising as the floors descended underground. Ahmad and Durojaiye both found this confusing, but Lilit insisted that they would get used to it. She further explained that this setup was necessary so that the largest possible area would be available at the uppermost point of Aestas in order to maximize their "outdoor" space. They could have built further upwards, but since their city was essentially a three-dimensional oval, that would only mean less available land.

Taking an elevator down three floors, they entered into the Commercial District. Going past various storefronts, Lilit expounded that the entire story was dedicated to commerce. Anything they wanted or needed, they could find for sale there somewhere. "That is," Lilit teased, "once you have access to your own money again. For now, you are wards of the state, and we are in complete control of your finances. Once I clear you from confinement into the general populous and make you a citizen, your accounts will be transferred back to you."

"Whatever is left of them, you mean," Durojaiye corrected.

Lilit cleared her throat, regained her composure, and attempted to clarify their understanding. "Yes, that is true. Of course, we have been charging you a maintenance fee for your food, housing, and immigration and coordination services."

"What happens if we run out of funding in our accounts before we are able to leave confinement?" Ahmad concernedly asked.

"Ahmad, if you are worried that we'll send you packing should that occur," Lilit began, "please put your mind at ease. You, more than anyone, should know that is not the Venusian way. Yes, an immigrant may end up in debt, but all services would continue as normal. Should such an event occur, I will work with you on a payment plan that will not leave you destitute. But if you don't mind if I reveal something about your finances in front of Durojaiye…"

Despite the fact that Lilit was still trying to make up for her earlier breach of protocol of revealing personal details without explicit consent, Ahmad did not wait for her to finish her formal request, immediately cut her off, and stated, "You need not ask. You can say anything about me in front of Durojaiye."

"And I feel the same," Durojaiye acquiesced.

Amazed by their openness with each other after such a short time together, Lilit noted, "Alright, then. The thing is, I've seen all of your accounts plenty of times and can tell you that you are both very well-funded. I cannot see a scenario where I would use even a fraction of your remaining savings. In all honesty, I've never had people of your economic standing under my care before. I'm not saying it doesn't happen, but it is rare for such cash-flush people to immigrate to Venus; not to mention for them to be together under one roof. It's quite a happenstance that you two were able to link up."

"Indeed," Durojaiye agreed.

Exhaling with relief, Ahmad professed, "I am very glad to hear this. Since I spent so many years preparing, I took a large percentage of my earnings and put them in a separate fund just for this day."

"Perhaps we should use our vast wealth to give Lilit a bonus or a tip?" Durojaiye offered.

"Can we do such a thing?" Ahmad exclaimed as he clapped his hands together. "Lilit, you have been most accommodating with us! And by us, I mean mostly Durojaiye, who is a real pain in the backside."

Giggling, Lilit put her hands up and asserted, "No, no; no such gesture is necessary or allowed. Besides, if I did it now, even with your permission, it would be embezzlement. Afterwards, it would look like a bribe being paid in arrears. I'm more than happy with my regular salary that you are essentially paying for right now anyway, and will continue to do so with your taxes in the future."

Ahmad did not look pleased by this and avowed, "Well, I will find a way to repay you somehow, then, no matter what. You can count on that!"

When Lilit attempted to demur, Durojaiye jumped in and said, "I agree, and believe there will be an opportunity to do so. Count on us, Lilit, for whatever your future needs may be."

Blushing once again, Lilit was happy to see that they had finally reached a set of public restroom stalls. "Ah, here we are, the bathrooms!" Lilit exclaimed by way of a distraction. "I'm going to jump into one now; you guys should go ahead, too. We still have a lot of exploring to do, thus no one gets to say they don't need to go. And if you finish before me, please do not wander off! Your implants are now coded to me, so if you get too far away from me outside the Confinement District, alarms will go off and the Protectors will swoop in and arrest you!"

"Yes, mother," Durojaiye mocked. "I look forward to having my waste be thoroughly reviewed for malicious content."

Sticking her tongue out, Lilit closed herself in the hermetically-sealed single-person stall. It had taken far too long to get here and she was practically dancing in her need to empty her bladder. Much relieved, she cleaned up and stepped back outside to find Ahmad and Durojaiye patiently waiting. "Everyone good?" she asked.

After receiving confirmation, they found a new elevator and headed up one level.

Upon swiftly arriving and exiting at Level 3, Lilit quickly showed Ahmad and Durojaiye the Industrial District. Like the Commercial District, it also took up an entire floor, but there was much less to see. Some areas had windows that the three could look in through, but Lilit could not explain what they were seeing inside. Despite this, both Ahmad and Durojaiye seemed excited by the sites, so Lilit did not want to dampen their spirits.

After that, they went up to Level 2 where the machinery was held that kept Aestas functioning. Most of the story was severely restricted to visitors except for the technicians who had been cleared. Lilit let the two know that the Quarantine District they had been in was actually on this floor, too, tucked away in a far-off corner near the arrivals gate at Level 1. Once they started talking about Level 1, both Ahmad and Durojaiye expressed a desire to get away from the life-critical equipment and back out into the open. Lilit was happy to comply as she, too, did not really enjoy being in such enclosed places.

At that, they returned to the surface with the sun now high overhead and angling towards setting. Of course, it was really Aestas moving around the terminus-line on Venus that made it appear like the sun was rising and falling each day, but the illusion worked on their hominid brains. For Lilit, who had never left the planet, it was just normal life and she had no comparison.

Once back in the sunlight, Lilit finally brought them to her chosen restaurant in the open area: Lusaber. She had intended to arrive there earlier in the day, but after deciding to walk the whole way as well as go on that side trip to the bathrooms in the Commercial District, she had to switch up her desired agenda. It appeared to work out in their favor, though, as there were far less people out-and-about as most had returned to work after the typical lunch hour. Thus, they were able to immediately get a table without a wait.

After they were seated, Lilit explained, "This is a bistro that specializes in the uniquely crafted Venusian cuisine style. The owners have a very old permit from the colony's founding that allows them to operate a kitchen here on Level 1. There are very few structures like this, but this place is an original. Basically, the ancestors of the current chefs helped to create and develop what is now the native fare."

"And what," Durojaiye asked, "in particular does that entail?"

Lilit expounded that part of it was the ambiance itself, eating al fresco out in their treasured wide-open space. Even when people bought meals down in the Commercial District or prepared food in their own apartments, they would tend to drag their fare up to the top level so that they could eat outside. "After all," Lilit contended, "we always enjoy a perpetual summertime here. There's never a worry about the weather. It's not even like some of the farms you told me about back on Earth, Ahmad. Here, everything is drip irrigation and underground feed lines; no need to worry about sprinklers suddenly going off! We have at all times been very careful with water management, which in turn helps maintain this ideal environment. Everything below is so closed off; consequently part of the Venusian culture is about taking advantage of what no other colony has: an outside surface area."

Turning towards the food itself, Lilit elucidated that at this eatery in particular, the plants and herbs were picked onsite right when they ordered. "The Venusian way," Lilit proudly declared, "is about the freshest and brightest tastes. I guarantee you've never had anything like this!"

Once their food arrived, Ahmad and Durojaiye admitted that they were forced to agree with Lilit's assessment, despite the fact that she lacked a frame-of-reference for what Earth provisions were like. While talking about this, Ahmad and Durojaiye seemed surprised to learn from each other that both had mostly eaten prepared and prepackaged foods their entire lives, though they each came from a very small village. "Over the centuries," Ahmad lectured, "most areas lost the ability to produce their own food as production became centralized and a lot became lab-grown or synthesized."

"I don't want to give a completely false impression," Lilit offered. "In the Industrial District, we do produce foodstuff in vats, too. It's just not as pronounced as it is on Earth because it is so resource intensive. Animal-derived and facsimile look-alike proteins are quite expensive and most native Venusians have never eaten them. It is something that you immigrants seem to consume more often, as well as the rich—but they do it more as a status symbol than a desire. Our culture is much more focused on whole foods with as little processing into other forms as possible. Of course, we still make breads, preserves, and the like, but what we can get at an eatery like this is the true Venusian style."

After finishing their meals—and Ahmad almost licking his plate clean—Lilit turned the conversation into what type of work they would want to do once she released them from the Confinement District. Patting his belly, Ahmad said, "I would do quite well right here in the gardens. If I could spend every day out here monitoring the plants and helping them become even more productive, I would be very happy."

"Hmmmmm..." Lilit considered. "Well, the thing is, those types of jobs don't open up very often. I'm not saying it's impossible, but is there anything else you'd consider?"

Ahmad stroked his beard as he thought for a moment before declaring, "I suppose, to be honest with you, that I am equally as experienced in systems maintenance and could fit in just as easily among the machinery below our feet as an engineer. I would prefer to be out in the open, but unlike you, I am similarly comfortable in open spaces as I am in enclosed ones for long periods of time. I have done it all during my travels, and am just happy to contribute to Aestas in whatever way I can!"

Seeing that she was not going to make much headway with Ahmad, Lilit turned to her other ward and asked, "And what about you, Durojaiye? Has

Ahmad's training helped you developed an area of interest to pursue?"

As Durojaiye put his finger up and was about to speak, Lilit cut him off and declared, "And not about your so-called mission from Earth Central Command! I've heard those words from you enough times about how it's your 'duty and obligation' and how you are working on it all the time and blah, blah, blah, blah, blah. Enough of that! Let's talk about the reality of life right here in front of you on Aestas."

"You say this," Durojaiye interceded, "but I do bring a certain skillset to the table as a spy."

"Oh, do tell," Lilit deadpanned.

Either not picking up on her tone or choosing not to, Durojaiye continued, "You see, my particular talents could translate well to equivalent fields like strategy, recruitment, marketing, or other such interests. Perhaps I could become a corporate recruiter."

When Lilit frowned at this suggestion, Durojaiye tried a different tack. "How about this: I could be a community organizer."

Lilit raised an eyebrow and probed, "Oh, is there a cause that you want to organize around?"

"Of my own?" Durojaiye scoffed. "Of course not; that would not be in line with my... well, you know what. But I could do something in support of others."

After paying the bill for lunch—which Lilit would, anyhow, later charge back to Ahmad's and Durojaiye's accounts—the trio again entered the elevators to descend into the lower depths of Aestas. This time, Lilit brought them to Level 5 and below, which were the locations of all the living and working quarters. The units towards the edges were the most desired as they offered a rare view of the outside world. Lilit explained that the apartments varied in size and were assigned based on many factors, including historical ownership, how large a family was, and if it was also used as a workplace.

"I would like to say," Lilit began, "that it is all completely doled out fairly, but that would be untrue. The rich and powerful like members of the elected Managing Council somehow seem to find themselves with the best and largest suites. Some of them even have interior staircases that span two floors. Then, there are people like me who inherited their place through sheer nepotism!"

Lilit had tried to deliver that last line as a

witticism, but neither Ahmad nor Durojaiye laughed. Dejected that it had landed so poorly, Lilit pushed forward. Finally, they came to an area that she explained would be Ahmad's and Durojaiye's home for the next several months: the Confinement District. The zone itself was interior, so there would be no windows to view the external cloudscape lazily drifting below Aestas.

"Great, more bulkheads to stare at," Durojaiye whined.

"I'm sorry," Lilit conceded, "but all new arrivals have to go through this."

"And the guards?" Durojaiye asked, pointing with his chin to the armed Protectors standing outside the entrance to the district.

"I agree, it seems like a bit overkill," Lilit began, "but they are very strict here about the movements of new arrivals. Once you go through that door, you cannot leave the Confinement District unless I sign you out or officially approve your authorization to become full citizens."

"So why not do that now so we can skip the middle man?" Durojaiye pleaded.

"As much as I would like to," Lilit admitted, "that is not something I can do. Believe me, if I was in charge, things would be run differently, but I'm as much a slave to the bureaucracy as you are. There are a number of milestones you will have to hit and that I will have to report on in order for your next phase to begin. We can discuss all that later. For now, let's head in and get you to your new temporary quarters. Your luggage was already sent ahead earlier."

Begrudgingly, Durojaiye agreed to continue, while Ahmad did not protest at all. Signing in with one of the Protectors, Lilit entered the new arrivals neighborhood and pulled up a virtual map in her direct line-of-sight. "This way," she prodded as she followed the lines on the screen that only she could see. Eventually, they came to a nondescript door that looked like all the others and Lilit waved at a plate so that it would slide open.

Inside was a studio space with two twin beds, a small kitchenette, and a separate bathroom in the back. "Wait," Durojaiye exclaimed, "you do not mean to say we will both be living here in this tiny space?! I thought we were finally going to get our own bedrooms, at the very least. There is no way that this room was ever meant for two unrelated people."

"Again, I'm sorry," Lilit granted, "but we're in the middle of a bit of a space... shortage... here on Aestas. Sadly, I'm afraid to tell you it won't get any better once you get out of here. Yes, the apartments are bigger, but you'll still have to share for the foreseeable future. The Managing Council is trying to work with the Terran Government and HSA on this, but well..." She let the thought trail off with a shrug—as if this was all the explanation that was needed.

"What is really going on, Lilit?" Ahmad concernedly prodded. Lilit wondered how he kept seeing through her when she tried to play it close to the vest. Perhaps it was when he dropped saying her formal title of "Coordinator" and started to be comfortable just calling her by her first name alone.

Lilit ruminated on how much she should tell them. If it were anyone else, she would have tried to deflect and told them not to worry about it, but with these two she felt the need to be honest. This time, she kicked herself for letting them get so close to her, and promised herself that after this she would revert back to a much more professional, arm's length relationship—as it should have been.

Taking a deep breath, Lilit began, "Listen, I don't want you to freak out."

"That is not a good way to stop us from freaking out," Durojaiye chimed in.

"Durojaiye, mouth shut!" Lilit reprimanded as she made the same gesture with her left hand. Once it appeared that he was going to comply, Lilit continued, "This is not the official government position, so please keep it to yourselves, but Aestas is over capacity. Between our natural birthrate and immigration, we simply have more people than we can handle. It's causing quite a strain here, but most notably with housing. We can handle most of the other logistics—at least for the time being—but we just lack the space for more human beings. Unfortunately, there is nowhere to build without sacrificing another critical part of the city."

"I did not hear about any of this back on Earth," Ahmad declared.

"Me either," Durojaiye concurred.

"It's not surprising," Lilit stated. "The Managing Council here is trying to keep it all hush-hush, but it's getting harder to hide when it's right in everyone's faces all day long. Besides, there were articles and studies from way back when that predicted this was going to happen, but we were always told not to concern ourselves; that things were well in-hand and would be taken care of. I have a friend who works for the government—specifically, the Managing Council itself—who has told me about some of the behind-closed-doors shenanigans going on. From what she's been able to glean, the Terran Government is actually well aware, but isn't doing anything about it."

"Why not?" Ahmad inquired.

"I can't figure it out, either," Lilit admitted. "But the bottom line is that we need a second Aestas, a new floating city. We were never meant to be the only one, but the Terran Government and HSA continue to drag their feet while we suffer. And, like I said, this isn't a new problem, either. Basic statistics showed this was coming to a head as far back as two generations ago. Yet, nothing has changed in all that time. If anything, it seems like the Managing Council has become complicit in our anguish."

"If the Managing Council is part of the problem instead of the solution," Durojaiye offered, "then perhaps they need to be replaced."

"Yeah, good luck with that," Lilit sighed in resignation. "Sorry, I don't mean to be a downer; I've just been dealing with this for... well, my entire life. I try not to mix my politics into my work, so please forget about it and forgive me for even bringing it up."

"No, no, it is fine," Durojaiye consoled. "We understand and appreciate what you have told us and all that you have done. Right, Ahmad?"

Caught off guard, Ahmad stuttered, "Yes, yes, of course. Lilit, think nothing of it. You have done no wrong here."

"Besides," Durojaiye said, taking back the reins,

"there are many lessons and tools from Earth's past that could be applied here to Venus, things that may assist in brining about these necessary changes. For instance, starting a petition or holding a protest or forming a nonviolent popular resistance group are all possibilities, among plenty more options that could be attempted. All it would take to get going is a little organization and reaching out to others to talk about their concerns. Lilit, do not fret: you are not so defeated yet, you have hardly begun!"

Lilit interjected, "That sounds very nice and all, bu—"

Before she could finish, Durojaiye interrupted by declaring, "We could even help!"

"We can?" Ahmad queried.

"Of course!" Durojaiye confirmed. "One thing we can easily do is find like-minded people who want to join and help with such a cause; others who see things as you do, Lilit. But I am afraid we will only be able to get started once we are finally free of this insufferable confinement."

From Righteous to Symbol

Chapter 10

An incessant ringing that was reverberating through the air finally woke Lilit from her deep sleep after repeating for what must have been at least the third time. Recognizing that the noise was coming from her doorbell, Lilit asked her onboard A.I. for the time. In response, a clock appeared in her personal virtual space and she saw that it was nearly one in the morning. Wondering who it could possibly be, she then had her A.I. shift her perspective to the exterior camera. From that vantage, she saw that it was Ahmad—looking quite out-of-sorts and rather agitated—standing there and about to press her doorbell button again. Throwing her thin blanket aside, Lilit almost walked straight to the entryway before realizing that she was wearing nothing but an old, holey, mostly sheer t-shirt and panties.

As she was trying to find a pair of shorts to slip into and a bathrobe to put on, the ringing commenced again. Groaning, she donned a pair from the dirty pile that smelled like the gym, added a second t-shirt that was at least opaque, and simply gave up on the robe. Now mostly clothed, she went to the main room and pushed the button that unlocked the front portal and allowed it to slide open. Before she could say anything, Ahmad barged inside and started yelling, "I cannot take it anymore!"

Quickly closing the door behind him so her neighbors wouldn't be disturbed by all the late-night cacophony, Lilit responded, "Nice to see you, too, Ahmad... especially at this hour."

Mortified, Ahmad seemed to finally realize what he had just done and launched into an apology. Lilit cut him off, knowing that he would not be in her home at this time of the night if it was not something serious. "Instead of apologizing," she said, "why don't you take a seat and a deep breath, and then tell me what's going on with you."

Ahmad sighed as he sat down on the couch. Lilit seated herself on the ottoman across from him and—as she put her hands over his attempting to stop them from trembling—again prompted, "What is it?"

"What... I mean... who else could it be?" Ahmad rhetorically asked. "It is Durojaiye. Or more correctly, it is the two of us, stuck in a small space together for over a year now, ever since we got to Venus. First it was the quarantine, then it was the Confinement District—by the way, I still do not see the difference. It is so redundant! Why not just a continual quarantine that extends into the concepts of confinement instead of th—"

"Ahmad, focus!" Lilit commanded. "Stay on track. What's going on with you and Durojaiye?"

"Oh right, right," Ahmad yielded. "I wish I could point to something specific, but we are just at each other's throats all the time."

"I fail to see how this is different than any other day of the week," Lilit asserted.

"No, this is totally unlike all those other times," Ahmad insisted. "What you are thinking about is our friendly banter, pushing each other's buttons, challenging each other's intellectual prowess, standings, and beliefs. Now, though, we have been arguing, really fighting. I think I just need some time away to cool off. Would you mind if I crashed on your couch tonight?"

Lilit knew she couldn't refuse as she was in a very unique position. She still had a one-bedroom apartment to herself, so she had more than enough room for someone to be in the public-facing space while she maintained the privacy of her own bedroom. Voicing these thoughts, Lilit expounded, "I suppose when you look at my place compared to your own lodging situation, it must seem like I'm living in the lap of luxury."

"You know I cannot lie to you," Ahmad declared. "It would be untruthful for me not to admit to being jealous that you not only have a home to yourself, but one this large. It is amazing how much my worldview has changed. Back on Earth, this would be considered quite small, even in the major cities. But here on Venus, my perspective quickly transformed as my expectations diminished."

Lilit pondered the mystery—to her—that was called Earth. Everything she had ever seen in the media and heard from her clients made her often wonder why people would ever leave a place with nearly unlimited room and resources to live inside a bubble that was small enough to walk most of in a single day. While she had no desire to ever leave and was quite used to everything, she had heard from many like Ahmad about the difficulties in making the transition and tempering their viewpoints.

"Ahmad," Lilit began as she returned from her thoughts, "can I ask you something?"

Ahmad laughed and said, "You never need permission to ask me anything. I am always happy to answer you, if I can."

Lilit smiled at this simple truth. Ahmad was always eager to share, whether she wanted him to or not. In comparison, with Durojaiye, it was not exactly like pulling teeth, but it was not easy. He was willing to tell her almost anything and everything, but she had to figure out how to pose the right questions to get the answers she sought. If she did not make a specific query, he would not offer it up on his own. Between her and Ahmad, they seemed to have grilled him sufficiently to get all the pertinent details about his life, but she still felt like she was missing something. She just was unable to put her finger on what that might be, and therefore couldn't elicit him into revealing it.

Returning her thoughts to the person in front of her, Lilit prodded, "Seeing what it is like here, going through what you are now because of it, do you have any regrets about coming to Venus?"

"Me?!" Ahmad exclaimed, almost jumping out of his skin. "If I have given you any impression that I am unhappy being on Aestas, then I must protest. This is my dream come true. I beg you not to make any demerits against my record!"

"Geez, Ahmad!" Lilit countered, "I would like to think that you know me a little better than that by now. You are aware that we're friends, right? And that I'll always protect you?"

"Of course, of course," Ahmad conceded. "I

suppose that old habits die hard for me, and it is difficult for me to have people like you and Durojaiye in my life, people I can count on and who are also looking out for my well-being. For so long, back on Earth, I was truly alone. And I mean that in all possible ways: mentally, spiritually, and physically."

"Well, allow me to put your mind at ease by letting you in on something," Lilit spoke in a hushed, conspiratorial tone. "It's not just you who is going through problems related to their living situation. Stuff like this is happening all over. You are hardly the first one of my clients to come to me in distress to discuss their accommodations, though you are definitely the first one to show up at my home—and in the middle of the night, no less!"

"Again, I am truly sorry about that," Ahmad attempted once more.

Lilit smiled and said, "You are forgiven, but only because you are special to me. Tell me: does it feel good having corrupted a public official into doing your bidding?"

Ahmad laughed at this and responded, "Yes, quite so. Though I do not know how it happened."

"Me either," Lilit admitted. "Yet here we are, and I wouldn't have it any other way."

Nodding in agreement, Ahmad rejoined, "You

said that your other clients are having similar difficulties? Have you been able to do anything for them?”

“Yes... and no, not really,” Lilit began. “However, I can’t get into specifics for confidentiality reasons. Suffice to say, everyone has roommates who they would prefer not to continue living with and shouldn’t have to put up with. All I’ve been able to do is act as a mediator and peacemaker between them. I wish I could do more, but it is out of my hands and way above my paygrade.”

“Hmmm... I understand,” Ahmad pouted.

Lilit frowned and disclosed, “Listen, even I’ve been under intense pressure from the powers that be to bring in a lodger and share my space.”

“Why do you not have boyfriend Brad move in, then?” Ahmad inquired.

Blushing—both at the question and because of Ahmad’s habit of always calling him “boyfriend Brad” like it was his title—Lilit admitted, “Actually, I broke up with him a week ago.”

Sucking in a deep gasp, Ahmad spit out, “What?! Why did you not tell me about this? Wait, does Durojaiye know yet?”

“No, no,” Lilit interceded, “Durojaiye doesn’t know either. I don’t know why I haven’t told you guys yet. I guess, it really didn't feel important. I mean, I suppose Brad just wasn't that important. I didn't really like him that much anyway, but he was hassling me to move in just as much as the government is! For real, were we going to become a 'serious' couple co-habitating together just because of this housing crunch?

"I get it, I really do, and I sympathize with him. He's in even worse straights than you guys, living with two other people in a one-bedroom like this one. But why should I give up my whole life for someone I only kind-of like just because I feel sorry for him?"

"Oh, no," Ahmad cried as he hung his head and looked down at his feet, "I am just as insensitive and needy as former-boyfriend Brad. Here I am, doing the exact same thing and imposing myself on you." At this, he stood up and said, "I will take my leave and deal with my own problems by myself."

Standing up to stop him, Lilit pushed Ahmad onto the couch once more and said, "Sit back down; I wasn't talking about you." As Ahmad tried to inter-ject, Lilit hushed him again and declared, "You will stay here for the night, but just for tonight. Besides, it's too late for you to be out wandering the halls until dawn. In the morning, with a good rest and a cooler head, we'll go to your place and talk with Durojaiye together to clear the air. Sound good?"

Ahmad stroked his beard in active contemplation before finally proclaiming, "I accept these terms as fair and equitable for all parties."

CHAPTER 11

The next day—after sleeping in a little late—Lilit and Ahmad went to his quarters. Inside they found a despondent Durojaiye, who admitted to being quite concerned about his roommate being missing all night. Lilit shifted her brain into professional mode and began to mediate the conversation between her two former wards, now full citizens of Aestas, and her dear friends.

"I must admit," Durojaiye was in the middle of saying, "that I, too, am very on edge with our living situation and how we have been forced to set up our shared space due to it. Even though, Ahmad, you are my favorite person..." Durojaiye paused as he thought about what he had just said before continuing, "besides you, too, Lilit, of course. I mean, not including Chigozie and our children, that is..."

"It's okay, Durojaiye," Lilit offered, "we get what you are trying to convey here. We're important to you. Please go on."

"Yes, exactly," Durojaiye agreed. "It is just that all of this is a lot to take, and is creating a significant amount of unnecessary stress. It does not help that Ahmad and I work together, too, so we are never apart. I am basically Ahmad's assistant, so either I am helping him or he is supervising me! We never have any time away from each other and cannot seem to escape one another's gravity well."

"But that is also what Level 1 is for," Lilit gently reminded them. "You do need to spend quality time apart for your own mental well-being. You could each take up a separate hobby and get away from each other for a while. At the same time, you may meet other like-minded people."

"Actually," Durojaiye interceded, "I have been talking to other people, especially other recent arrivals who I became acquainted with when we were all in the Confinement District. You could call it a support group, of sorts. We all thought it would be better when we got out of there, but somehow it has become difficult on another level.

"Ahmad, if I may, I would like to apologize. From speaking with other members of our cohort, I know it could be much worse. You are a good man, and do not deserve to be the recipient of my wrath. I was wrong, and out of line, to have treated you thus."

Ahmad hung his head and wiped away some tears before declaring, "No, I also need to apologize. I have done the same and even ghastlier to you. I feel terrible about the awful things I allowed myself to think about you. I should be more grateful for what we have."

"Then there is only one thing to do," Durojaiye announced.

"What is that?" Ahmad asked with trepidation. Lilit noticed that he was almost whimpering, most likely from his concern over what shenanigans Durojaiye must have in mind. Durojaiye was always pushing Ahmad into uncomfortable situations for him; it seemed to give him such glee. Chuckling to herself, Lilit had to admit that she got a little thrill watching Ahmad squirm, too.

With that thought, Durojaiye stood up, smiled, and opened his arms wide. Ahmad tried to balk, but Lilit would not hear of it and pushed him into Durojaiye's waiting hug. Once embraced, Durojaiye squeezed hard and Ahmad tried to free himself, but he was no match for Durojaiye's strength.

Clapping and laughing as Durojaiye finally let go, Lilit told them, "Durojaiye's friends are right; you guys are rather lucky. That is, you're lucky to have met me. I was able to pull some strings to keep this apartment solely for the two of you. Just to let you know, with another batch of immigrants eventually coming, there is a lot of pushback to open up your space to another person. I don't know how much longer I can fend them off."

"If only there was something we could do," Durojaiye lamented. "The members of the Managing Council are still living the high life and do not understand the plight of average citizens like us. They are off in their ivory towers with everything they could ever want while we are forced to squeeze water from stones."

Lilit sadly shook her head and said, "I was telling Ahmad about that last night, about how powerless I and the other Coordinators are to help you and the other immigrants out of the situation you find yourselves in without any fair warning."

"Are these things happening to all of us immigrants and being able to do something about it truly that important to you?" Durojaiye queried.

"Yes, of course!" Lilit exclaimed, "It's all extremely important! Your pain is piercing my heart. I can't stand watching people needlessly suffer, especially ones I am personally responsible for."

"So," Durojaiye probed deeper, "if Ahmad and I were just mere 'regular' clients of yours, or were under the watchful eye of one of your coworkers, you would still feel the same way about this?"

Lilit scrunched her eyebrows in a questioning gaze, trying to figure out where Durojaiye was going with his line of inquisition. In response, she said, "I think I've made my feelings abundantly clear over the past eight months, even though I should have kept my big mouth shut."

"To be fair," Ahmad interjected, "I believe we both have always been quite interested in your perspective and, thus, have pushed you to tell us things you would have rather kept to yourself."

Ruffled at having been so easily dislodged from her scruples—despite years of training to teach her how to avoid such traps—Lilit could only sigh in agreement. "I don't want you guys, or anyone else, to have to worry about these things that are out of our control. We just need to be able to live the best life we can with the resources we have been granted and the hand we've been dealt."

"I am curious," Durojaiye wondered aloud, "why you believe that the housing crisis is out of our control and that nothing can be done about it?"

"Hey, I didn't say 'nothing could be done about it,'" Lilit fought back.

"Oh?" Durojaiye intoned. "Then there is some hope you can offer us?"

Growling, frustrated that she'd gotten caught in

his web again, Lilit expounded, "There are a lot of good ideas out there that could ease the immediate pressures, and the long-term ones, too. I've read a lot about it, talked to others, and even come up with a few of my own."

"What is stopping them from being implemented?" Durojaiye asked.

"It's the same as always, the same old story told a thousand times: politics!" Lilit proclaimed. "I don't know what's the matter with Chief Councilor Xander and the Managing Council, but they really just don't seem to be on top of this. Maybe something else is going on, I don't know. To be honest, I'm not really up to speed on their current priorities. I may work for the government, but I'm hardly following the latest headlines. I know some people can't get enough of all the gossip from up on high, but I'm not like that. I just try to live my life in peace and harmony."

"Maybe they just do not know?" Ahmad offered.

"What do you mean?" Lilit asked. "How could they not know?"

"Hmmm, how to explain..." Ahmad began. "Ah, I have got it! You know about a country called the United States of America?"

"That's a big one I've at least heard of," Lilit allowed. "But please don't quiz me on any of their history or beliefs or customs or anything like that!"

"No, no," Ahmad assuaged, "it is nothing like that. Let me explain: the United States has a bicameral legislature, with one house supposedly focused on the will of the people, and the other on the needs of the individual States within the country as a whole. Nevertheless, as originally envisioned, neither of the chambers were representative of the people due to how the system was set up at that time. For instance, in the early twenty-first century, well over half of the legislators across both chambers were in the 'very, very wealthy' category. At the same time, over half of the population would have fit into the 'poor' classification, even by their own definitions."

"Sounds the same then as ever!" Lilit declared.

"True," Ahmad agreed, "but an equitable solution was not out of reach for them. You see, I am not insinuating that the rich people were 'bad' and poor people were 'good'; I am highlighting that there was a systematic disconnect in information. The very wealthy representatives were not trying to be mean to the downtrodden, they just lacked a frame of reference as to what was happening in their lives. There were very few poor people in their legislature, so their voices were often squelched."

"So, you're saying...?" Lilit wondered.

Ahmad smiled sadly as he stated, "That, unfortunately, the Managing Council simply lacks the insight that we all take for granted. We believe our plight is common knowledge, but maybe it is not?"

"How did they resolve things in America?" Durojaiye inquired.

"It took a long time," Ahmad admitted, "but they eventually amended their Constitution to allow a wider breadth of various viewpoints. It did not happen overnight and did not resolve all their issues, but it certainly eased a lot of difficulties and tensions just by having other voices at the table."

"An important lesson then," Durojaiye approved with finality.

"And, in many ways, we have Aestas today because of it," Ahmad claimed.

"What do you mean?" Lilit queried.

"Before they changed their legislature," Ahmad began, "they first updated their methodology of electing a chief executive—a President. During the first vote after that modification, an independent, a person completely separated from the major Political Parties of the day, was elected."

"How did that go over?" Lilit questioned.

Ahmad shook his head and said, "That is a story for another day. Right now, the most relevant part for us is that their leader planted the seeds for the Space Elevator. However, it was not until a more robust legislature—one that was not exclusively working towards disrupting the President's agenda—could be elected that any progress was made. Thus, without those changes in their Constitution, there would be no Space Elevator, which eventually paved the way to undertake the colonization efforts here."

"Wow," Lilit acknowledged, "I never really heard it connected that way before. You have a unique way of seeing history, Ahmad."

"More so, it does provide a blueprint, of sorts," Durojaiye insisted. "If it is as Ahmad claims, that the Managing Council is not taking any action simply because they lack the expertise and experience, then they must be informed. Nevertheless, a message like this could not come from people like us. Immigrants are the lowest rung on the ladder here and are not taken seriously. Only a native with a level of professional authority could possibly get through to them."

"I see," Lilit pronounced. "Listen, you know what? You've convinced me to give it a go! Although I've been thinking about it for a while now, this very minute I've decided that I will attend the next public meeting of the Managing Council and let them know what is really transpiring down here!"

"This is wonderful," Durojaiye said, "but how do you propose to get on the agenda? There must be a long list of petitioners."

Giving a wicked smile, Lilit declared, "Well, thanks to my friend that I told you about before who works for the Managing Council, I'll be able to get on the docket to speak. And when I do, I'll bring up all of your concerns, and we'll see what they have to say about it. And you know me; I won't hold back any punches!"

"This I do know," Durojaiye agreed.

"It's only a few weeks away," Lilit beseeched, "so please hold on a little bit longer."

Sitting at a small table outside at Lusaber, Lilit was still fuming from the Managing Council meeting the night before. Ahmad was across from her sipping his cappuccino, patiently listening as she perseverated over the same points she had just gone over.

"It's bad enough that they just brushed me off," Lilit began again, "but I couldn't believe how pompous they were about all of it, especially Chief Councilor Xander!" In a mocking voice attempting to impersonate Xander, Lilit quoted, "'We are aware of the situation and are doing everything we can.'"

"I am aware, too," Ahmad asserted. "I watched the feed live from home."

Appearing not to hear him, Lilit continued, "I pushed back on them, demanding concrete examples of what was being done, and they just shut me down again and again and again. They thought they could stop me by cutting off my mic, but I just yelled louder. And then they had the Protectors drag me away. Me: a native citizen; a descendant of the founders; and an important, productive, and loyal public servant who has the highest success rate in all Coordinator history!"

"I believe I may have recognized one of those Protectors," Ahmad attempted to deflect. "What was their name? Oh yes, it was Aritza, wasn't it? We became mildly acquainted in the Quarantine District, though I doubt they remember me. I do not believe I have seen them since I left there. They must have gotten a promotion or a transfer or something. Good for them, I say!"

Completely ignoring his non sequitur, Lilit demanded, "Are you even listening to what I'm saying? They forcefully removed me from the chamber and barred the door! How can the Managing Council do that? This is still a democracy! Don't they actually work for us?!"

"Sadly, Lilit," Ahmad attempted to intercede, "Aestas is not a true representative democracy. The Terran Government pre-screens who can even run for the Managing Council, so our options are unfortunately quite limited."

"Whose side are you on?" Lilit sneered.

"I am on the side of Venus, of course," Ahmad stated, "and I am on your side, always."

Realizing she was out of line, Lilit profusely apologized. Ahmad was quick to grant forgiveness, highlighting that he had done much the same to her only a few weeks prior. Speaking again, he said, "We all are on edge, still, about the housing situation. When Durojaiye and I were discussing it the other day, he made an interesting point saying, 'If the Terran Government is controlling all of our choices, are we really making any?'"

"Speaking of Durojaiye," Lilit pondered aloud, "where is he? He would probably have some good insights on this bureaucratic nonsense and how to impact the various involved governments, especially the Terran one."

"I do not know," Ahmad admitted. "He said he was going to meet someone after work and I have not seen him since."

"I wonder what he could be up to?" Lilit rhetorically wondered. "We did say we would gather here at this time, right?"

"That is how I recall it," Ahmad agreed. "It is highly unlike Durojaiye to miss an appointment. He is rather fastidious, in that sense."

Lilit frowned and said, "You don't think anything could have happened to him, do you?"

Ahmad laughed and declared, "I highly doubt there is a situation that Durojaiye could not worm his way out of. Besides, what could possibly happen to him on Aestas of all places?"

"Still..." Lilit trailed off as she picked at her fingernails, looking for something to distract her from her unwanted concerns.

After a moment of silence, Ahmad queried, "And what will you do when he arrives? Are you going to go over the details of the council meeting that we all watched... for a fourth time?"

"Hey!" Lilit yelped. "Are you making fun of me?"

In response, Ahmad just gave a sly smile.

"Arg, fine, fine," Lilit acquiesced. "I get it; I'm beating a dead horse. But when I start to think about it again, I realize I should ha—"

"If you are about to start this story anew," Ahmad interrupted, "then perhaps it would be best if I took my leave."

"No, no!" Lilit interceded as she jumped up and bade Ahmad to stay seated. "I'll stop, I promise."

"Very well," Ahmad agreed as he took another sip, only to discover his cup was empty. As he signaled the waiter for another one, Ahmad decreed, "Wait, I think I see him approaching in the distance from behind you."

At these words, Lilit turned around and saw Durojaiye advancing with two women in tow. Once they arrived, Durojaiye presented his new friends. "They actually wanted to meet you, Lilit," he announced.

"Me?" Lilit queried. "I don't understand."

"We all watched the council meeting," one of the women explained, "and were truly inspired by what we saw. When we learned that Durojaiye knew you, we asked him to make introductions. We're here to join the movement."

Lilt scrunched her eyebrows, still completely confused at what was happening. "What movement? What are you talking about?"

"Lilit," Durojaiye calmly explained, "the movement you started with your performance at the Managing Council meeting last night. Do you not understand? You, Lilit Sarkisian, are now the face of the people's struggle."

CHAPTER 13

Lilit was pacing back and forth inside the tent that had been set up earlier in the day. It was located behind the platform that they had erected on one of the public fields on Level 1 so that they would have a de facto "backstage" area away from prying eyes. She was still surprised that the permit to hold this gathering had been granted at all, given the animosity she and her companions were experiencing from the entrenched administration. Durojaiye had contended that someone in the licensing office must have been sympathetic to their message and had been intercepting their requests to make sure they were granted.

Glancing over at Ahmad, Lilit saw that he was sitting on some pillows in a corner and quietly reading on his tablet. Nevertheless, this sight only vexed Lilit further. "Why don't you get ocular implants?" she scolded. "Tablets are a waste of resources and space! If you really wanted to be Venusian, you'd embrace all of our ways!"

Ahmad looked up and gave a tired smile before

turning his attention back downward. It was obvious that he was not taking her seriously and knew she was just lashing out at him because she had no other outlet for her ire and agitation. Irritated by his lack of reaction, Lilit just let out a loud groan. She hoped it sounded quite annoying.

The tent flap opened and Durojaiye walked inside while also carrying his own personal tablet. Lilit's eyes bulged out of her head at the spectacle of it as she wound up her arguments so that she could properly reprimand him, too. Before she got the chance, Durojaiye simply stated, "Deep breaths. Come on now, with me: breath in... hold... hold... hold... let it out."

Much to her own chagrin, Lilit did as instructed. She hated to admit it, but it did help bring her heart rate down and reduce her anxiety. After a couple more minutes of guided meditation under Durojaiye's direction, she said, "Okay, okay, I'm calm again. Ahmad, sorry for berating you earlier; I went too far in my criticism."

Ahmad again looked up and smiled, but this time full-toothed. "Of course," he said, "I accept your apology with no reservations. You are forgiven, my friend."

Sighing because she hadn't even succeeded at

upsetting him enough in order to earn his forgiveness, Lilit turned to Durojaiye and asked, "How many are out there?"

"Our drones estimate that there are over two thousand people in the audience," Durojaiye perfunctorily answered.

"Two thousand?!" Lilit shrieked. "I can't go out there. Why would that many people want to hear me speak? I'm gonna pass out..."

Durojaiye put his tablet down on a nearby table and came over to try to embrace Lilit, but when he did so she started beating her fists against his chest. "How did you ever convince me to do this?" she screamed through the tears. Finally, worn out, she cried on his shoulder. Being taller than him, the position soon felt awkward and painful, so she lifted her head and sniffled unreservedly.

Ahmad appeared beside her, put a hand on her shoulder, handed her a clean handkerchief, and said, "Lilit, do not fret; I have no doubt that you have this, as they say, in the bag."

For some reason, hearing it from Ahmad instead of Durojaiye made it actually feel true. "Thank you," she said through the damp cloth. "It's okay, I'm better now. Durojaiye, please get Deb back in here; I need her to fix my makeup. And then go buy me a few more minutes to get myself in order."

Picking up his tablet and opening the tent flap, Durojaiye declared, "Consider it already done. See you out there!"

Once he was gone, Ahmad asked, "Are you really alright? You do not have to do this if you do not want to. It is not too late to call all of this off. No one would think less of you."

"No, I'm fine now," Lilit insisted. "And I have to do this. People are counting on me, looking towards me to help them figure out what to do. Ahmad, tell me: how is it that in just a little over two months we've gone from a handful of people to thousands who will not just willingly, but with great desire, show up for a stupid little speech?"

"It is more than the thousands who are out there today," Ahmad declared by way of a response. "For every person who came, how many are sitting at home feeling exactly the same? Two, three, four... ten? Lilit, the truth is, you have started something that is both personal and much bigger than any one person. It speaks to all caring and empathetic people, deep in their hearts."

"You make it sound like I've only made gains, but—to be honest—I've lost many things along the way, too," Lilit grumbled.

"What is it you have lost?" Ahmad queried, showing genuine concern.

"My anonymity, for one," Lilit noted. "And that is costing me in other ways, too."

"What do you mean?" Ahmad persisted in his probing, obviously using the psychological tools that Lilit had taught him.

Despite seeing through his ploy, Lilit continued, "Things are rough at work. I have clients who are requesting a transfer because I've become a magnet for hate. They are worried about themselves—and I don't disagree with their assessment, either. I'm a danger to them, both physically and politically! They are afraid that if they're connected to me, they'll end up deported back to Earth."

"Well, you are still my Coordinator, and I and most others have no intention of hanging you out to dry," Ahmad avowed.

"That's nice, however, I suppose you only have to worry about that while I still have a job. Oh, I've finally gotten the undivided attention of the Managing Council I sought, you better believe that. But since I work for the government, you should also know that there has been unbelievable pressure coming from way up on high to fire me."

"Yet, if they did that," Ahmad contended, "it

would look quite suspicious. They would not want that level of scrutiny."

"Damn right," Lilit agreed, "but they have other ways. My contract runs right up to when the next batch of immigrants arrives on the shuttle in a few months. They might not renew it at all. Or they could let me renew but never assign me any cases, so I won't have any work. Soon, you and all the rest of your cohort won't need me, and then I'll have nothing and they'll have no reason to continue paying me."

"Do not worry, I can always use another assistant," Ahmad offered. "Durojaiye is not as productive as I would have hoped."

Lilit broke into a hysterical laugh, snorted, and then gave Ahmad a quick hug. "Thanks," she snickered, "I really needed that. Alright, where's Deb already? Time to beautify my face so I can meet my adoring public!"

CHAPTER 14

Looking out over the cheering sea of heads, Lilit took one final deep, mind-clearing breath before connecting her surgically-implanted microphone to the previously assembled speakers that her team had set up. "Citizens of Aestas," she began, "how's it going?"

There was a rousing cacophony as people yelled out their problems in what had become the signature start to these rallies. It was a holdover from their earlier meetings when it was just a dozen or so of them sitting in a circle discussing their concerns and what could possibly be done about them. As their ranks swelled, they held what Lilit considered then to be large gatherings of hundreds of people. Since there was not enough time to let everyone speak, Durojaiye suggested they just have everyone yell their answer out loud at once. "It will be cathartic for them," he insisted. And boy, Lilit thought, he was certainly spot on with that assessment.

Ahmad, though, had really made a breakthrough that was much more useful to their movement. Sensitive recording devices were generously sprinkled throughout the area, surrounding the venue, and on drones flying above the crowd. Even though they could not possibly understand and parse through all the words, a trained A.I. could do so. Putting it to work, the A.I. took all the vocalizations and categorized them. As such, they had a regular poll of what people were thinking and what they were dealing with. Lilit tried to share their early data with the Managing Council, but per usual they brushed her off. Chief Councilor Xander in particular decreed, "Not a very scientific measurement, is it?" No one got under Lilit's skin as much as that blowhard.

Now, though, with a gathering of a couple thousand people, they would really be putting Ahmad's innovative technological solution to the test. Lilit had never considered being in front of a crowd like this before, but here she was. She would be lying to herself if she did not admit that there was something intoxicating about it. At the beginning, Lilit was quite comfortable as she worked one-on-one and in small groups with new people all the time. She enjoyed meeting and learning about unique individuals, but was pushed far outside her comfort zone as the number of those who wanted to speak with her and hear what she had to say grew.

Looking back, it was quite perplexing how their

little grassroots support group had so rapidly evolved into what she was seeing before her eyes. As attendees told others and she made subsequent appearances before the Managing Council, new faces kept appearing. During each step along the way, Durojaiye encouraged her to embrace what was happening while Ahmad provided the logistical and emotional support. She knew that she would be truly lost without them. At the same time, Lilit doubted that she would have put herself in this position in the first place if their lives had not become so intertwined in the first place. Apparently, this was the price of their friendships.

Putting all of that aside, Lilit shifted her compartmentalizable brain into speech-giving mode and launched into her prepared remarks that were being projected in front of her on her personal monitor.

"Thank you for letting me into your lives and hearts and telling me what is important to you. Unlike the Managing Council—" She was forced to pause as a large round of boos rang out. Signaling the crowd to let her finish, she stated again, "Unlike the Managing Council, I... am... listening!"

The crowd roared their approval, and Lilit smiled, waved, and blew kisses. Finally, she put on her most serious face and stated, "The truth is, they don't listen because they don't have to. As long as the Terran Government gets to decide who is even eligible to run for a political position, we will never have representatives who care about us. In order for us to address the very real issues we face here on Aestas—especially concerning our population explosion and the lack of housing for everyone—we must first and foremost have free and fair elections.

"You have all seen me on the media and social feeds as I have attempted to plead with the Managing Council, to open up their eyes and ears to the suffering of the Venusian people. Unfortunately, they consistently choose to be blind and deaf because there are no consequences for them. If there were an election tomorrow, they would win because the Terran Government will not let anyone challenge their regime. But we are not Earthers, we are Venusians, and we need our own independent leadership in our homeland!"

The crowd started chanting Lilit's name and she was forced to try to quiet them down again and dissuade them from their apparent desire. Breaking from her script she claimed, "I don't mean me! I'm just a regular citizen like all of you, trying to get by in life. I have a job and bills to pay. But because I was born here and have been nowhere else, Aestas is my entire universe. That is why I know it can and must change!"

This decree did not discourage the crowd from being in full-throated support of Lilit. Looking off-stage, she saw Ahmad and Durojaiye urging her to continue. A text appeared from Durojaiye that said, "Just roll with it. Go with your gut!"

Nodding towards her friends, Lilit closed all of her screens down and really looked at the people out there for the first time. She saw the visages of down-trodden souls looking to her for salvation, for a direction and a plan. Spotting her mother, Lilit knew what to do. "My entire extended family is here today. Let's give them a round of applause!"

The spectators did as she requested as many gawked around trying to figure out just who were Lilit's relations. "Yes, there's my mom and dad," Lilit began, "and my grandparents on both sides, my un-cles, aunts, and cousins. Hi everybody, it's so good to see you! I love you all very much, and am so happy you could be here to support me!

"But do you know what I don't have out there? I have no sisters, no brothers, no siblings of any kind. My parents made a very difficult decision to have only one child, me, because they were well aware of the population crisis that was looming. That means that I also have no nieces, no nephews, no next generation at all. I may descend from the first settlers here on Aestas, but I could be among the last of this bloodline if I do not have a child of my own. My entire clan could actually be wiped out and made extinct.

"And listen, I don't blame my parents and their siblings for making these pragmatic resolutions. It was and still is the logical, reasonable, and responsible thing to do. Our city simply cannot support the population we already have because of the negligence of the Managing Council, the Terran Government, and HSA. Those organizations have left us out here to twist in the wind of uncertainty, anguish, and desperation.

"Because of that, I cannot even make a determination for myself if I even want to have a child. I feel the pressure of existence here and know that, as things currently stand, it would not be right to bring a burden like that into this world. An uncaring Aestas Managing Council and Terran Government have ripped that choice from my womb. So long as they control our destinies, they can ignore our pleas for equality, freedom, safety, security, and being able to live fully as real human beings!"

Lilit slipped into her apartment in what she thought was a stealthy and undetectable manner and engaged the manual locking mechanism that Ahmad had installed. "I am greatly concerned," he professed at the time, "that someone might override the built-in locks and do something terrible to you. You have made a lot of enemies, both among officials and the populous."

Of course, she had dealt with various smear campaigns from hardline government supporters and been doxed long ago as a result. One of them had spraypainted "traitor slut" on her front door. For some "inexplicable" reason, every maintenance request she'd put in over the past month to have it removed was going unfulfilled. Strangely, whenever she or anyone else tried to clean it up themselves, Protectors showed up from out of nowhere and shut down their efforts. The Protectors would then calmly explain that only licensed professionals could work on official Aestas internal machinery.

Some of the Protectors had taken to apologizing

to Lilit directly when they were forced to show up. One of them that Lilit knew from work named Aritza said they would not have interfered if they were not ordered to do so. "You should talk to some of our historian friends, especially those from Earth, about soldiers who just blindly followed orders," Lilit recommended.

Blushing, Aritza said that they might just take her up on the offer. "Is there anyone in particular I should look up?" Aritza asked.

After recalling that the two had some shared past from the Quarantine District, Lilit gave them Ahmad's contact information in the hope that he would be able to talk some sense into them. Maybe if Aritza came around, Lilit thought, then other Protectors may also be willing to see they were on the wrong side of history. Suddenly, Lilit shuddered as she realized that she was thinking of people as assets the way Durojaiye saw the world. What she wanted was a better life for all of them, even the Protectors and jerks like Chief Councilor Xander.

Since her speech a few months prior in front of a comparatively paltry couple of thousand people, the protests had grown exponentially. Every day, the activists were out there engaging in passive resistance: refusing to do their jobs, blocking major thoroughfares, picking fruit en masse so there would be too many alarms to respond to at once, marching in front of councilors' apartments, and generally grinding everything down to a halt on Aestas.

When she had last asked Durojaiye for a crowd estimate, he said there were close to a couple of hundred thousand people. "However," he admitted, "it is getting difficult to count because the Movement is spread out everywhere around the colony and we do not have enough surveillance drones to know what is going on in all locations at once."

"The Movement" he called it in capital letters, and it was just that. Lilit wished not for the first time that they had taken a moment to think of a real name, but they were basically stuck with it now. When this all started, she hadn't imagined creating anything at all; she just wanted to get the Managing Council to listen to them and develop a plan. Somewhere, somehow, over time, they had become a Political Party unto themselves, and that in turn had inspired the counter-protestors.

She couldn't imagine why anyone on Aestas would be against what they were asking for. When she expressed that to Durojaiye and Ahmad, they both just laughed at her in a knowing way. Apparently, they had been through plenty of upheavals themselves back on Earth, and this was nothing new to them. "There is a book you should check out in the local Archives called **ALWAYS DIVIDED, NEVER UNITED**," Ahmad suggested. "It will answer a lot of your questions."

Lilit did not have time to read, though, as she was kept plenty busy organizing the Movement. As it was, she had not been home in days and was now sweaty, dirty, and feeling just plain gross. All she wanted to do was shower and change into clean clothes before heading back out there. Stripping out of her soiled clothing, Lilit peered at her unmade but inviting bed. Now she just desired to sleep at home more than anything else. She wondered if anyone would miss her for just one day?

Turning off all her messaging systems and even the doorbell, Lilit collapsed into bed naked before ever making it to the shower and promptly fell fast asleep.

Sometime later, she was awoken by a loud banging noise. Groggily, she realized that it was someone knocking at her door. Reluctantly, she connected her vision to the exterior camera and saw that it was Durojaiye pounding his fists on the door while Ahmad was pacing around behind him. She connected to the exterior speaker and said, "Go away!"

"Oh thank goodness!" Ahmad exclaimed. "Are you alright, are you hurt?"

"I'm fine," Lilit whined, "I said go away. I'll talk to you guys later."

"I am afraid we cannot do that," Durojaiye declared. "Check your messages."

Cursing under her breath, Lilit turned on her messaging system and saw there were thousands of unread ones. "Anything in particular I should be looking for?" she asked.

"It would be best if you would let us in so we can talk face to face," Durojaiye responded instead.

Looking down at her own birthday suit, Lilit said, "Ahhhhhh, I'm not really decent right now. Can you please give me, like twenty minutes?"

"I am afraid not," Durojaiye rejected, but with a note of concern in his voice.

Swearing out loud this time, Lilit told them to hold on a second as she found some semblance of clean-ish clothing to put on. With her private parts now covered, she unlocked the door and let them in.

Ahmad held her at arm's length and looked her up and down for signs of trauma. "When you did not answer and we could not find you, I feared the worst," he confessed. "I have never been so happy to have been so wrong."

"Good to see you, too, Ahmad," Lilit sarcastically responded. "It's been a whole, what, six hours?"

"For some, that is an eternity," Durojaiye offered.

"You are not helping," Lilit bit back. She was really not in the mood and now regretted not taking a shower before she passed out. She stank and she knew it. "Now tell me why you're here."

Without wasting a moment to even take a breath of air, Durojaiye summarized, "You have been summoned by the Managing Council for a closed-door emergency session. They are already waiting on you. They were going to send Protectors to drag you in if we had not intervened. Even then, we only have a few more minutes before they lose patience and break down the door."

"Are you saying there are Protectors out there who want to arrest me?!" Lilit shot back.

"Not arrest, per se," Ahmad declared, "just 'escort' you..."

"... in a forceful manner," Durojaiye finished.

Frowning and flailing her hands, Lilit beseeched, "How can I meet them now in my mismatched pajamas, with my disheveled hair, and my unmistakable aroma from days out among the protestors?"

"I am sorry," Durojaiye consoled, "but there is no time and no choice. We have to leave now."

CHAPTER 16

"Nice of you to finally join us, Ms. Sarkisian," Chief Councilor Xander said from the center seat at the raised semi-circle desk. To each side were the other Councilors, though over the past six months Lilit had come to realize that they were basically yes-men to Xander. "Although, I have to say, I do not approve of your choice of attire for these hallowed halls. This is a professional place of the people's business, and you should show it the proper respect with your dress and... hygiene."

Fuming, Lilit responded with, "Yeah, well, this is the best I could do with such short notice. Why don't we skip the pleasantries and get down to what I'm doing here."

"Very well," Xander agreed. "This so-called 'Movement' of yours—"

"It is not my Movement," Lilit interrupted. "The Movement belongs to the citizens of Aestas. I am just, as my dear friend Ahmad here would say, one of its humble servants."

Xander actually smiled at this and chuckled.

When Lilit did not react and continued to stare through him with an unwavering determined expression, Xander stated, "Oh, you're serious! You honestly think you are just some 'nameless member' of the Movement?" Turning to the other fellows of the council he asked, "Does she not realize what she is?"

"And what is that, exactly?" Lilit demanded.

Scoffing, Xander declared, "You, my dear, are the very symbol of the Movement!"

There was murmuring among the other councilors as they considered Xander's words and what should be done about them. Yelling above the din, Lilit inquired, "Okay, if that is the case, what are you going to do about it? Am I here to be arrested? I'd recommend against that, if I were you. As my other companion here, Durojaiye, would remind you: that would just make a martyr out of me."

"Oh, ho, ho," Xander chuckled. "The mouth on this one; and the things that come out of those pretty little lips."

Over the past several months, Lilit had grown quite familiar with Xander's proclivity for using sexist remarks to provoke an outburst from her, so she chose not to give him the pleasure of seeing her discomfort. Making a small cough after failing to elicit a retort from Lilit, Xander clarified with much less bravado, "No, no, Ms. Sarkisian, we have no interest in placing you under arrest. Quite the contrary, we are here to work with you to find a way to put a stop to these protests."

"Wait, what?" Lilit asked in disbelief.

Xander continued his pronouncement as if she had not spoken. "Everything the Movement has been doing as of late has been putting our colony in real jeopardy. I am talking about the 'death-of-us-all due to colony collapse' kind of danger. Before, you and the Movement were a mere nuisance; now you are an active threat to our survival."

"That sounds like you want to label us a terrorist organization and end the Movement by force," Lilit summarized.

"You've got it all wrong," Xander claimed. "Compulsion under gunpoint is the wrong approach and will only hasten the destruction of our home. As hard as it is for you to believe, I do care about the people of Aestas above all else. Everything I do is in their service, even if you cannot see all the chess pieces moving on the board."

"Oh, please enlighten this plebian, great and wise Chief Councilor Xander," Lilit chided.

Frowning himself, Xander attempted another approach. "Ms. Sarkisian, one thing you do not realize is how alike we truly are."

"In what way?" Lilit asked with legitimate curiosity as to where this could be going.

"Despite what it may look like," Xander laid out, "we, too, are just puppets of our far-off masters: the Terran Government."

"Xander!" one the other Councilors shouted. "What are you doing? You can't tell her this."

"We have to!" Xander screamed back. "In order to bring this to an end and save everyone's lives, she must know the truth. You know as well as I do how Earth Central Command will respond if we do not get things under control now."

Whatever Xander was describing was apparently enough to get the other Councilor to shut his mouth. "What are you talking about?" Lilit probed. "What's going to happen?"

Xander sighed before starting anew. "Ms. Sarkisian—Lilit, if I could." Lilit nodded in agreement. "Lilit, we have been in contact with the Terran Government about all of your concerns. Members of this council have been fighting the real battle behind the scenes for generations. There are people sitting right before your eyes who were doing so even before you were born. Despite your grandiose speeches, we are not dumb, blind, or deaf. We know very well exactly what is happening on Venus and have been pleading with the Terran Government and HSA to build a second floating city to end this intolerable overpopulation issue."

"Why haven't you said anything before now?" Lilit wanted to know.

"Because," Xander acknowledged, "if the general population knew that there was no hope for change, there would be pandemonium. We on the Managing Council spend all our time trying to keep things calm here while we wrestle with the Terran Government. If you want to know who is really acting dumb, blind, and deaf, it is them! Let me be as blatant as possible: I am in complete agreement with everything you and the Movement want. But if I gave in to you, Earth Central Command would show up one day and put us all down, as the Earthers say, like a rabid dog. Is that clear enough for you, or do I have spell it out?

"How about this: we have no defense against their weaponry and might.

"Even now, they are unhappy with us because of you. Yes, things have been difficult here on Aestas for a long time, and they will continue to be so for a good while to come. We are doing the best we can with the options we have available, and you are the one who is royally fucking up the system!"

Clearing his throat in an apparent attempt to regain his composure, Xander said, "My apologies, that was over the line. Lilit, honestly, I like you, I even admire you. You get to say all the things I am thinking without having to pay any of the consequences. But at the end of the day, your first priority is to this utopian version of Aestas and Venus that you envision, and my first priority is to the hundreds of thousands of lives under the dome. No matter what is to come, that is all that I am concerned about: the preservation of human life."

"What is the point of being alive," Lilit solicited, "if we are not happy and free?"

Xander rubbed his temples and said, "And there is the one difference between us, Lilit. You think these ideals of yours are worth dying for; I believe life is the most precious thing of all. Perhaps if you were in my seat, you would see things differently."

"I highly doubt it," Lilit chirped.

"We'll see, we'll see..." Xander retorted. "Anyway, that is what's happening in the real world. So, here's what I'm going to do: Lilit, I want to offer you a spot on the Managing Council, here right by my side." As he said this, he gestured to an empty seat beside him. "You will be able to directly influence and impact the Managing Council and will specifically be tasked with coordinating with the Terran Government and HSA. This will give you the power to do everything you have purported to want. All that we ask in return is an end to the protests."

Lilit was silent for a long time, looking at both Ahmad and Durojaiye who remained stoic. Finally, she turned to Xander and the rest of the council, looked up, and declared, "I refuse."

"What?" Xander asked, aghast.

Lilit stood up, slammed her hands on the desk in front of her, and roared, "I will not sell out the Movement. I will not sell out my friends and family. And most of all, I will not sell out my own soul. All you have offered me is a gilded cage. It's a trap, and I want nothing to do with it. Just because you're afraid, it doesn't mean I have to be."

Lilit's words lit the room afire as the voices of the other members of the Managing Council overtook all others with their objections and turned into a full rabble. Ahmad patted Lilit on her forearm in encouragement but otherwise he and Durojaiye did not attempt to make themselves heard over the cacophony of upset Councilors. Xander attempted to bang a gavel and bring order back into the chamber, but it made no difference. Finally, Durojaiye walked over to a large ceremonial metal bell and started violently kicking it to get its hammer to strike, causing a loud echoing ring to bounce off the walls of the enclosed space. Everyone stopped yelling as they covered their ears. Once the bell was quiet enough, Durojaiye spoke up.

"Everyone, everyone, please hold on. Perhaps there is a compromise that we can reach that all sides will find beneficial."

"Durojaiye, what in the holy hell do you think you're doing?" Lilit questioned.

"I fail to see where we go from here," Xander retorted.

"Perhaps compromise is the wrong word," Durojaiye offered, "as that entails everyone giving something up. What I mean to say, then, is collaboration, where everyone gains something through the creation of something new."

All eyes in the council chambers looked at Xander. He paused for a moment before leaning back in his chair and saying, "I'm listening."

"Please bear with me for a moment," Durojaiye requested. "I ask for your undivided attention without interruption. Does everyone agree?"

"Yes, yes," Xander said as he dismissed Durojaiye's concerns with a wave of his hand.

"And you, Lilit, Ahmad?" Durojaiye asked as he turned towards his friends.

Lilit and Ahmad looked at each other and nodded. "We trust you, Durojaiye," Lilit announced. "Go ahead, tell us what you're thinking."

"Excellent, I thank you all," Durojaiye beamed. "Allow me to summarize what we have learned here today. The Managing Council of Aestas would like to implement the policies of the Movement, but they are powerless in the face of the Terran Government. For decades now and despite their best efforts, they have been unable to persuade those with actual authority to provide relief. They fear both an implosion of society caused by this becoming general knowledge, as well as potential retribution from Earth Central Command should they lose their grip on the citizenry.

"Meanwhile, the Movement does not believe the Managing Council has done enough to mitigate the issues the people are living through. They find the Managing Council's approach to be wholly inept and ineffective. The Movement imagines that if they were to fully replace the Managing Council that they could do what has never been accomplished before. Is that all correct?"

Everyone in the room grumbled their concurrence, so Durojaiye continued. "Very well, we are all on the same page as to what the facts are. Now, the answer is quite simple. Since we in the Movement hold that we are superior to the Managing Council, let us prove it. Send Lilit to Earth to negotiate directly with Terran Government."

"What?!" Lilit screeched.

"Lilit, please do not speak until I am finished," Durojaiye requested. Once Lilit nodded after a moment of consideration—though the blaze of incredulousness never left her eyes—Durojaiye picked up where he left off. "Now, with the literal embodiment and head of the Movement off planet for at least nineteen months, the protests should die down and the Managing Council will have the peace and security it desires. At the same time, the Movement will have what it wants because Lilit will be able to bring our case directly to those who can actually make a decision. By doing this, she will be able to prove how inept the Managing Council has been if she is, in fact, able to achieve what they have been unable to. And should she fail, she will come back with the realization that you were right all along and will bring that message back to the Movement."

With his proposal apparently concluded, Durojaiye sat back down and folded his hands on the table in front of him. Everyone was silent as Lilit could see that no one wanted to be the first to speak. Xander leaned forward towards the desk and pursed his hands into a triangular pyramid shape, deep in thought. He then looked to the councilors on each side of him as some unspoken signal was apparently sent between them.

"Lilit," Xander spoke softly, "would you and your entourage mind stepping out into the hallway for a few minutes? We would like to discuss this proposal among ourselves first."

Lilit stood up, nodded, and said, "Yes, of course. Us, too. If you'll excuse us." At that, Lilit started walking to the door with Ahmad and Durojaiye in tow.

Once the door was thoroughly shut behind them, Lilit slapped Durojaiye across his face. "How could you?" she demanded. "What gave you the right to offer me up like that without even discussing it with me first?"

"I am sorry, it was a spur of the moment thing," Durojaiye claimed as he was rubbing his face. "Everything was happening so fast and spiraling out of control. I felt I just had to do something, anything, to get it back on track. I did not want to risk what would happen to you if Xander lost his patience."

Feeling the anger draining out of her, Lilit stroked Durojaiye's cheek and said, "I'm sorry, I shouldn't have hit you, that was very wrong. I don't want to make excuses for my behavior; violence is never the answer. If you no longer want to speak to me again, I'd understand."

"Lilit, I will never abandon you," Durojaiye avowed. "I will follow you to the very end."

"And I will too," Ahmad swore as be placed a hand on each of his friends' shoulders. "We will come with you to Earth and help end this, once and for all."

Lilit was quiet, and then tears started streaming down her face. "No," she whispered. "No, you can't come with me."

Shocked, Ahmad gasped, "What do you mean? Of course we will go! You cannot do this alone, no one could, it is unthinkable!"

"It's impossible," Lilit pronounced. "You two must remain behind to keep the Movement together. I need you to be my eyes, ears, voice, and muscles while I am gone. I'm afraid you are right, Durojaiye— that if I am not here, it really will fall apart from lack of cohesion. You must make sure that doesn't happen. The Movement absolutely must endure, it must stay organized, it must be powerful. Together, we've built an army here."

"Yes, and you are their Commander, and ours," Durojaiye noted.

"Then as your Commander," Lilit directed, "I am ordering you to stay behind and maintain the troops. I'll take some of the other 'lieutenants' with me... plus one more..."

CHAPTER 18

Out in the hallway, Lilit, Ahmad, and Durojaiye continued discussing the proposal, including how it might be implemented, what Lilit would do on Earth, who from the Movement should also travel with her, and other logistics. Seemingly, the Managing Council must have been debating something similar behind the doors that had been closed to them. As no sound escaped from there—even when Ahmad pressed his ear up the entryway—they could only guess. While all of this was going on, Lilit slowly began to convince herself that this was the right thing to do.

Eventually, one of the Councilors who had been sitting nearer to the edge of the raised desk opened the door and asked Lilit, Ahmad, and Durojaiye to come back inside. All of the cockiness the Councilors had demonstrated during the earlier session had dissipated and Lilit's group was now being treated courteously—with respect, dignity, and kindness. The proceedings took on a much more business-like and professional atmosphere. Once everyone was seated, Xander spoke for his faction again.

"We have discussed your proposal and taken an official vote. It has been decided: if you agree to these terms, then we will as well."

Lilit attempted to speak, but Xander raised his hand to indicate he was not through. "Lilit, before you say anything, I want you to know something. I would love nothing more than for you to succeed at this mission and bring some desperately needed relief to the citizens of Aestas. Should you somehow succeed, we have all agreed that we will resign from the Managing Council because your triumph would mean we were failures and fools all along."

"Well, Chief Councilor Xander," Lilit began, "While I strongly believe that you are all failures and fools without me having to make this long journey, I am prepared to accept Durojaiye's proposal, as well. However, before doing so, I have one final amendment to make."

Xander sighed, "Sure, what's yet another concession, especially after receiving such a magnanimous expression of eloquence from you? What do you have in mind? Would you like our first born?"

For the first time in hours Lilit smiled and said, "No, that won't be necessary. All I require is you, Chief Councilor Xander. I want nothing more than you. You will be coming with me."

"What?" Xander bellowed, "I will do no such thing! My place is here, running the Managing Council and overseeing the daily functions that keep Aestas afloat and functional."

"No," Lilit calmly corrected, "your place is where you can, as you say, protect the people of Aestas most effectively. For that, you must come with me to Earth. The only way to truly quell the protests is if we present a united front with a shared purpose. More so, if the Terran Government sees two deeply split political ideologies joining together for a common cause, then they will have no choice but to open their ears. Divided we fall, united we stand, yadda yadda, and all that jazz. The point is, in order for the plan to work both at home and abroad, we must come together as one singular voice."

Xander attempted to intercede again, but the Councilor who had held the door open for them before spoke up first, "Hold on Xander. I think we should hear her out some more. Is it just the Chief Councilor who would join your retinue?"

"Not at all," Lilit acknowledged. "I have already decided to have several members of the Movement join me, technical experts in various fields that can help craft the messaging and bring data and proof. I would expect the Chief Councilor would also bring along similar attachés, and perhaps advisors in areas where we lack familiarity, such as on the functions of the Terran Government and Earth politics in general. These are blind spots for us."

The Councilor looked at several of his compatriots and they all started nodding. "Yes," he agreed, "this all sounds very reasonable and logical. I believe we should accept this amendment."

Bug-eyed, Xander shot daggers at the wayward councilor before breaking out into a laugh. Wiping his eyes, he said, "Well played, Lilit, well played. You are a far better politician than I gave you credit for. Very well, it appears that I have no choice, as well. I am sure the others here will insist on me following your lead."

"Seems completely sensible to me," Lilit gloated.

"And while we're away," Xander added, "the other Council members will vie for my seat and take that power on themselves. Congratulations, Lilit, you have effectively removed me from being the head of the Managing Council. That is quite a feather in your cap to bring back to the Movement. I'm sure they'll be very impressed by your political acumen."

"That wasn't my intention!" Lilit protested.

"But that is exactly what has happened," Xander highlighted. "Did you imagine that everything would remain stationary—completely frozen in time—while we are removed from the public eye for nearly two years? That everyone back here would just be idly sitting on their hands while we are off on this grand adventure that you and your companions have cooked up? Life will go on, as always, except now it will do so without us."

Feeling like defeat was being snatched from the jaws of victory, Lilit remonstrated, "You think I wanted any of this? Do you really believe I desire to endure years struck with just you and your sycophants? Let me summarize how things have gone down been between us over the past six months:

"You've been an intolerable asshole to me and the Movement when you could have just shut up and listened for five minutes. If you had done that, none of this would be happening. The fact that we reached this point is because you have been so entrenched in belittling me and your concerned constituents instead of creating a solution, like you were elected to do in the first place."

"It is naïve to pretend like you have any idea what I was elected to do," Xander sneered. "All you see is what is in front of your face, not what is happening in the grand scope of the cosmos and humanity in general. A new era is about to dawn on all mankind."

"And you've missed the rot growing on the trunks of the trees because all you can see is the entire forest from above," Lilit retorted.

At these words Xander rose from his seat and bowed at his waist. "I suppose that is true enough, but all of these arguments do not matter at all. Lilit, I unconditionally agree to all of your terms. Now, we have less than a month to get ready before the next transport arrives, so there is no time to waste. Therefore, this meeting is hereby adjourned."

From Symbol to Leader

Chapter 19

As expected, the shuttle arrived from Earth on schedule and the passengers began disembarking over the next several weeks. Lilit felt a pang of regret and loss, realizing that—for the first time in years—she would not be there as a Coordinator to greet and assist the new arrivals. She honestly felt a little lost as she had nothing to do but prepare for the trip. Chief Councilor Xander's office had sent over some material to review and advice for what it would be like on Earth. Of course, Ahmad and Durojaiye could provide much of the same guidance, but they didn't have the insight into the political echelon that Xander and his attachés possessed. Still, she realized that there were certain logistical things she could only do when she got there.

The ordinary daytime temperature on Aestas was supposed to be around 300°K, but it was usually much warmer. Lilit realized that things had actually gotten worse over her lifetime as the population ballooned and they could not dissipate the heat as fast as they used to. However, due to Aestas's climate being a never-ending summer, she didn't own any cold-weather clothing. It was practically impossible to buy any on the colony, and most of it was just costume pieces for the theatrical performances that were staged in the parks on Level 1.

Lilit cringed when she realized the faux pas she had just committed when thinking about the temperature. While on Venus and pretty much every other colony they used the Kelvin scale, on Earth Celsius was still the dominant measure. At least the math was simple subtraction, but the numbers made no sense to her when she heard them out loud. The shuttle itself was kept at a temperature she had never experienced, almost 10°K below what she was used to. No, she corrected herself, she needed to force herself to use Celsius. She would have to make thousands of these seemingly trivial adjustments in order to be taken seriously on humanity's progenitor planet. Trying again, she said to no one in particular to enforce the lesson, "It will be about 18°C on there." Frowning at the sentence, Lilit noted that she didn't own a jacket. Why would she?

Ahmad and Durojaiye were surprisingly sympathetic, especially Durojaiye. Both were born in locales on Earth that were very warm and much closer to what life was like on Venus. Durojaiye, though, said that he had barely left his home village, so he did not really have the practical know-how and advice that Ahmad may have. True to form, Ahmad described many of his pilgrimages to much colder climes—including the one where Lilit would be spending the majority of her time—as well as the first time he saw snow.

"I've seen snow in person before," Lilit claimed.

"Do you mean the children's 'Snowfest'?" Ahmad asked incredulously.

"Of course," Lilit admitted, "what else?"

"Lilit," Ahmad said disapprovingly, "that is not snow. That is a machine that makes blocks of ice, shaves them, and flings it into the air."

"Isn't that what snow is?" Lilit innocently asked.

"No, no, no, not at all," Ahmad admonished. "Putting aside that most of it melts in the air and what little hits the ground is gone in half-an-hour, snow is not pulverized ice."

"I don't get it," Lilit pouted.

Ahmad stroked his beard before continuing. "Snowflakes form when individual tiny droplets of water crystalize in the air into unique shapes and flow down. You cannot just take ice and turn it into this, they are two very different things."

"That was no help," Lilit declared. "I still have no

idea what you're getting at."

Sighing, Ahmad asserted, "Oh, you will. When you experience it yourself, you will understand."

Thinking about this conversation, Lilit began to panic. She didn't know how she was going to manage without Ahmad and Durojaiye, but she could never admit that to them. If she broke down or showed any outward doubt, they would disregard her orders and join her on the voyage to Earth. She knew that could not be allowed to happen. More than anything, she needed them to remain on Aestas so as to protect the Movement and her investment into it. She had to remain resolute, for everyone's sake.

Meanwhile, with the last newcomers and cargo having at least been unloaded onto the platform in orbit, the turnover had begun on the shuttle. Already, both hers and Xander's teams had gone up to prepare for them. There was still a massive amount of distrust between their groups and Durojaiye had insisted on her taking a security detail. He had handpicked who would be a part of that group, as well as some others who were apparently part of his "intelligence" core. It looked like his experience as a spy was actually paying off for the Movement. Although it made Lilit feel icky, she could see the benefit of his wisdom. Putting aside her misgivings, she boxed them away as she had to do for so much of her life.

Lilit's parents had begged her multiple times not to go. Whereas the rest of the family was at least trying to appear outwardly supportive, her mother and father could not hold back their true feelings. "You are already our legacy," Lilit's mom had said, "you do not need to be anything more." Her father also expressed his own concerns. "You cannot trust Xander," he had lectured on more than one occasion. "He is always plotting something, ten steps ahead." Though Lilit tried to assure him that she had Xander well in-hand, she did not believe it herself and her father saw right through her bluster.

Finally, the day came for Lilit and the remaining passengers to board the skimmer and head up beyond the atmosphere. Lilit had managed to convince everyone else—even her parents—to say their goodbyes to her at the party the night before and not show up to see her off, but Ahmad and Durojaiye disobeyed her wishes and were waiting with her. Knowing that having others there might make her lose her nerve, Lilit wished that they had not come. Still, she found comfort and strength from her two closest companions. Suddenly, she started crying.

"What is it?" Ahmad asked as he gently rubbed her back.

Through the tears, Lilit exclaimed, "I'm just going to miss you guys so much!"

Durojaiye turned and forced them all into a group hug, more of a huddle like they were conspiring about a secret plan. In many ways, they were. "We will miss you just as equally," he said in his soothing and even voice. With their heads so close, Lilit could see that they were trying their best to hold back their own tears.

"Do you realize," Lilit asked, "that I will be gone for the same amount of time we've known each other? By the time I return, we will have spent half of our friendships separated by worlds."

"Your arithmetic is sound," Ahmad said, and they all had a good laugh at the ridiculousness of such an assertation. "But we will stay in touch, of course, as much as possible."

"Let's have regular live chats for as long as we can as the ship pulls away," Lilit suggested. "Every day, we'll talk over video until that is no longer possible. Then we'll use audio, and finally text messages, whatever it takes, however long the gap is."

"By the time you reach Earth," Ahmad expounded, "it will be about four and half minutes, each way, and will increase to nearly fourteen minutes before we are on the opposite side of the sun from each other. Then we will have to bounce our signals off several satellites to get around Sol since our radio-waves cannot penetrate it, which will only exacerbate the situa—"

"Thanks Ahmad," Lilit interjected, "that makes me feel so much better."

Dejected, Ahmad persisted, "But then, from that point onward, you will only get closer and closer until the delay is just a couple of minutes and you will be able to come home."

Breaking the huddle, Lilit wiped away any signs of distress and simply confessed, "I need you guys. And I don't mean to just hold down the fort while I'm gone. I need you, Ahmad. I need you, Durojaiye. Take care of each other while I'm gone. You both must promise me that you won't dare to let anything happen to either of you! The Movement is one thing, but you guys are far more important to me. You are my family, and I don't know what I'd do without you in my life. Do you understand me?"

"I do," Ahmad insisted. "And I need you, too, Lilit. I thought I was coming to Aestas just for what the colony and the planet could selfishly offer to me, but I have come to realize that what I was really missing in my life was you and Durojaiye. Whatever is to come, no matter how long it takes, I, as always, am your humble servant."

"You're no servant," Lilit contended. "You are a free Venusian, and I assure you that I will stop at nothing to make sure that becomes a true reality for you and everyone else."

"Thank you," was all Ahmad could muster.

Durojaiye had not spoken in a while and used the silence to chime in. "I need you, too, Lilit, in more ways than you could ever know. Of course, Ahmad, it goes without saying that the same applies to you. Lilit, please let your mind be at ease; we will be here waiting for you, anxiously awaiting the moment of your return."

Wrapped in nothing but an itchy, low thread-count blanket, Lilit spun herself around so that she could more easily peer "downward" from her position freely floating within the personal cabin. From this angle, she could get a better look at the slumbering Xander, who was strapped in to what passed for a bed aboard these transport shuttles. He was snoring loudly as being in microgravity had plugged up all their septums. Or was it "septa", Lilit wondered? Either way, it made it hard to taste and she had grown quite fond of spicy foods during the few months they had been flying through the void between worlds. It was one of the few things that could break through her dulled senses.

Perhaps that lack of taste had spread to her other faculties, too, and explained why she was sleeping with Xander. She then began to list through the other possibilities, counting on her fingers: boredom, avoidance, fear. Could it be something else, she asked herself? Whatever it was, she decided then-and-there that this was the last time. She pulled open her personal display and wrote in her journal: *If I need to get my rocks off with another person, there are plenty of other, far better options aboard. Plus, there will be more Venusians at the embassy in Puerta Estrella. More than that, Earth is filled with billions of people. Surely anyone, anyone but Xander would be a significant upgrade.*

She contemplated for a bit, tapping her lower lip in reflection. Then she started writing again: *Actually, that isn't completely true. Even though I'm sure that many of the members of the Movement—who are definitely superior to Xander in every way—would jump at the chance to bed me, that wouldn't be ethical. There's a real power differential between us now, and I am basically their boss. Also, if I started showing favoritism to one person, the others could become jealous and that would cause a breakdown in cohesion. I must keep the Movement united, no matter the personal costs to me. There is no alternative but to be absolutely uncompromisable for them.*

I doubt Xander has such concerns about his team since they are mostly looking out for themselves, anyway. He may be comfortable abusing his position, but I could never do that. That said, though, the Movement has become all encompassing, taking over my entire professional and personal life. Where am I supposed to meet someone if they are not already in or affiliated with the Movement in some way?

No, in reality, Xander was a safe choice. I hold no power over him nor he over me. We don't particularly like each other, so there is no worry about attachments. Both of us would actually lose the respect of our subordinates if they knew what we were doing, so we're stuck in a prisoner's dilemma where we'll both fail by going rogue and turning against each other. I just hope I haven't messed things up too much, because Xander's support is something I still need to make sure my plan succeeds.

Saving her entry and exiting out of the program, Lilit once again wished that she was gay. She had tried being with women a couple of times when she was younger, but it never felt right. This strangely made her think of and long for Ahmad and Durojaiye back on Aestas. It wasn't a sexual thing between them, far from it, but somehow it was emotionally more rewarding than any other relationship she had been in. She pondered if it would be so bad if she tried to take things to the next level with either of them—despite both being older than her, and Ahmad being significantly so.

Contemplating an intimate relationship with Durojaiye was actually a nonstarter. He was loyal to his wife Chigozie back on Earth and had made that crystal clear. Plenty of other women, men, and everything in between in the Movement had made propositions to Durojaiye, but he had rejected them all outright. He was only interested in learning if they had useful skills and could be assigned a role within the organization. Lilit had to admit that the Movement would not be what it was without Durojaiye, and that included his money. He and Ahmad had basically donated their life savings to the cause. She had tried to refuse to accept the funding, but they were both insistent, having come to the decision together long before discussing it with her.

If Durojaiye was out, then Ahmad—by process of elimination—would be the only available selection. However, Lilit knew firsthand that Ahmad would not be interested in any sexual relationship with her or anyone else. During their counseling sessions from when her former wards were still in quarantine and confinement, Ahmad admitted to sampling many different types of people and circumstances. "That said," Ahmad had confessed at the time, "none really interested me or gave me that 'tingling' feeling I have heard so much about, so I never pursued them further, even if they desired more from me. Besides, in fairness to them, I am sure my 'cold fish' response generally did not endear me to anyone who was looking for that sort of thing."

Accessing her observational files from those sessions, she read what Lilit from the past—who had lived a far different life than her own current one—had thought about Ahmad: *The subject appears to be more interested in inanimate objects like the planet Venus or the city of Aestas itself rather than other human beings. Still, it is more hero worship than objectophilia. Final official prognosis: no abnormal sexual deviation or dysmorphia that would be a danger to society.*

Lilit was glad she had taken advantage of the "generosity" of the Managing Council to pay for everything associated with this trip, including all the add-ons, no questions asked. Having access to her own personal Archives was proving both invaluable and comforting during the many low points of this voyage, of which this was certainly one of them. Although she and most other native Venusians had computerized implants, the vast majority of people did not understand how they functioned. The devices inside their heads were basically just a BIOS that ran a lightweight operating system interface. There was no local library; everything was saved to private collections in the Cloud.

It wasn't like every augmented person on the colony had recording and retrieval devices installed next to their organs! Instead, as Lilit knew, their implants were little more than dumb terminals. This arrangement also made them easily replaceable if something went wrong without having to worry about losing their individual Archives and setups. The only way these implanted devices performed any activity was if they had a network connection that granted two-way communication to the user's personal programs and files, which were preserved elsewhere.

Nevertheless, storage space was not infinite and still required a physical medium to exist somewhere tangible in order to maintain their data. On the shuttles between planets, that digital stowage came at a much steeper price. Like any cargo, the passengers paid by the weight and/or size of what they wanted to carry aboard. Lilit had a lifetime of data that she wished to take with her on this trip. If she was making this voyage on her own, she never could have afforded to bring her entire catalogue with her. However, thanks to the Managing Council agreeing to foot the bill, she was not forced to choose between what to take and what to leave behind. She only felt mildly guilty about wasting the taxpayers' funds to give her the ability to pull up her childhood drawings.

When they got to Earth, she would transfer everything to the servers in the Venusian Embassy, and then do the process in reverse upon her return. Unfortunately, Earth, in general, was not as open and accommodating as Aestas was about gaining instant access to personal data through accessible ports. More than likely, she would lose her connection as soon as she exited the embassy grounds. Before she left Venus, Ahmad had made her aware of portable devices that she could move at least some of her records onto that might be available for sale or to rent. With one of these machines, Lilit would be able to have handy access to a pruned selection from her libraries during excursions to other locations. After scolding Ahmad and Durojaiye so many times about carrying tablets around, she would soon look exactly like them toting about her own apparatus.

After finally closing out of the remaining files she had been perusing, Lilit realized that she had had enough. Shivering either from the cold or her poor decision making, Lilit found her undergarments and slipped them on before sliding into the thermal lined jumpsuit that she had found in the ship's holds. While she had gotten more used to the lower temperatures, she still did not like it. Perhaps that was why she had been willing to share a bed with Xander in the first place; she just needed something to help keep her warm at night.

Suddenly, the idea of letting Xander be inside of her made her nauseous. Rifling through the drawers looking for something to write with, she found a thick magic marker floating around. Lilit surmised that it must have been left by one of the former Earther occupants of the cabin because such items simply did not exist on Venus. Besides, she noticed that it lacked the connectors that generally kept items from flying freely about the ship, meaning it must not have been a standard piece of equipment.

Pushing the blanket she had recently been wrapped in against the wall and using it like a piece of notepaper, she forced her unpracticed hand to write one letter at a time in all caps:

N-E-V-E-R A-G-A-I-N

Lilit then tied the ends of the sheet to whatever handholds she could find in Xander's room so that he would be sure to see her message when he woke up. Task completed, she quietly snuck out of the room, hoping no one saw her leaving.

CHAPTER 21

"Welcome to the Venusian Embassy!" the bubbly young redhead with the nametag that read *Fiona Malone, Cultural Liaison* declared. "Is there anything I can get you before taking you to your room?"

"No, thank you," Lilit squeaked. "At least, not yet. There are a number of things I'll need once I'm settled in. Will you be the one helping me with that during my stay here?"

"My primary job is more of an emissary to the public," Fiona noted. "Someone else will be along later to assist you with all of those details."

"Of course, someone else," Lilit lamented. This was what it has been like ever since she, Xander, and the rest of their teammates had arrived on Earth months ago. In all her years as a Coordinator on Aestas, she hadn't considered what the process would be like in reverse. Even with people who were only visiting Aestas and not making it a permanent home, Lilit was their one-and-only point of contact for all things Venusian. On Earth, it was always someone else's job. By this point, she didn't really remember the names of half the people she had dealt with along the way.

Certainly, the process of getting from orbit to the ground was far simpler than on Venus, so she had to give the Terran Government credit for that. Shortly after docking at Tsiolkovsky-Pearson Station, they were placed in wheelchairs and swiftly brought over to the space elevator entrance. From there, the not unsubstantial time spent descending to the surface aboard the lift basically consisted of sitting around waiting to reach the bottom. During the controlled fall, Lilit was surprised that no one was available to prepare or work with them. Her first interaction with an Earther was not even when they reached the receiving station. Instead, they were rolled into yet another holding area, where they queued up to meet planetary entry officials.

Based upon her professional experience, the timeframe spent awaiting their turns was unnecessarily long. She could see from where she was sitting that most of the booths were unstaffed, thus they were delayed merely because the Terran Government had chosen not to put enough agents on duty. Since her time planet-side, she had come to realize that they probably had not hired enough personnel in the first place. It seemed to be fairly typical of Earth's approach to life in general.

When it was finally her turn, Lilit came to realize just how different from Venus things were about to become. The person she talked to was nothing but an immigration officer—no more, no less. Being that she was on a diplomatic mission, she was given some leeway, though she later heard from fellow members of the Movement about the unnecessarily invasive interrogations they were forced to endure. Some had been born or lived on Earth for a time and said they had forgotten just how rude people from their former home were compared to the process and lifestyle on Venus. One person was almost turned away before Lilit asked Xander to intercede. As much as she hated to admit it, Xander continued to prove to be accommodating despite their relationship becoming even chillier since she broke things off with him.

After receiving approval and passing through immigration—with Lilit ensuring everyone in the party was accounted for—they were consigned to yet another waiting area before being brought by people in hazmat suits to the Quarantine Zone. Instead of any type of interaction, the faceless workers just grabbed their wheelchairs and took them into their rooms. While Earth did not share Aestas's overcrowding and lodging issues, that did not mean that they provided massively large spaces for them. Her room was basically a three-meter by three-meter box.

Alone at last, Lilit began to feel disconcerted with her lack of access to her personal records. She was too far from the shuttle to pick up a signal from it anymore and was told everything was being transferred to the Venusian Embassy. However, she had no way of verifying if that was true. For her, it was like losing an appendage. She had never been cut off from her files and applications before. Attempting to even pull up a virtual monitor generated nothing but an error message in her line-of-sight. There was a typical Earther-style tangible screen on the wall that she eventually figured out how to turn on, though it took her a while. It was controlled by some type of physical remote, like the ones that she remembered seeing in old movies and shows from Earth. Once on, it played a linear broadcast on a "station". She felt like a complete idiot as it took her several hours to discover that there were actually many stations, and that she could select between them.

Over the ensuing weeks, various physical, occupational, and psychological therapists came for visits, though she rarely saw the same person twice in a row. Even when they did appear—which was frustratingly infrequent as on many occasions they failed to show up for appointments at all and seemed to refuse to communicate any change in plans—they only stayed for fifteen minutes at a clip. Lilit could not comprehend how this method was considered efficient or beneficial to their clients and patients in any way, but was told by everyone who had spent any time on Earth before that this was how things were in every field, but most especially in medicine.

Luckily, Lilit was well-trained in all of their techniques and started her own rehabilitation program to help herself and everyone else in quarantine—whether from the Movement, the government, or the civilian core in general. This actually won her quite a few more adherents. In private, several members from Xander's entourage told her that whether they had sympathized with the Movement or not beforehand, that she could now count them among the faithful. Lilit did not really trust anyone who was only willing to flip sides in secret, but thanked them for their support, nonetheless.

Due to Lilit's diligent handiwork, their entire cohort was able to clear the quarantine and confinement period in relatively short order. That did not mean that they were all progressing at the same rate, though. As soon as he was able, Xander left the isolated area, leaving behind several members of his retinue. Lilit, of course, could have done the same, but opted to stay behind until the last members of the Movement and the Managing Council support staff were ready to go. That was why she was so late arriving at the embassy.

However, Lilit's internment was not quite at an end. She and the rest of her entourage from the Movement had only been granted release to the Venusian Embassy and its grounds. They would not even be allowed out into the rest of Puerta Estrella and would instead only be granted leave once they had secured an appointment with the "Terran Government Subcommittee on Terrestrial Colonies". Lilit laughed at that name since Aestas was far from "terrestrial", but there apparently was no group more logical to talk to, according to Xander.

Once in her new room, Fiona transferred the access codes to Lilit so that the door would now only unlock for her and embassy security. "Is there anything else I can do for you?" Fiona asked without any sincerity in her voice.

Feeling snippy after being handed off yet again, especially under the auspices of a fellow Venusian, Lilit began, "Oh, yes, Fiona, please, something only another woman could understand."

Finally giving her a look of real concern, Fiona

declared, "Of course, Ms. Sarkisian, whatever you need that I can provide. What is it?"

Smiling, Lilit requested in a singsong voice, "It's just, well, it's a bit embarrassing, but... could you lower the gravity a bit? Everyone always told me that Earth and Venus are like twin sisters, but there's a real difference. I weighed around fifty kilos back home, but just being here has added, like, five on top of that. I feel so fat. You know what I'm saying?"

Not amused in the least, Fiona flatly declared, "Well, I'm sure you'll find some way to manage. If you'll excuse me."

After she left, Lilit felt a little bad about teasing Fiona so, and realized that she probably made a strategic error by alienating a member of the embassy staff. She decided to write Ahmad and Durojaiye and see if they felt her amusement was worth the risk. At a minimum, she thought that they would find it funny!

For months she had been using a tablet to write to them, but suddenly she realized she should finally have access to her systems. She attempted to boot up and was ecstatic to find everything was how she last remembered it. She supposed she would have to do a more thorough inventory and analysis to make sure nothing had been messed with, but for now she was happy enough to have her missing limb restored.

Following writing home and finally getting a member of the staff who could actually assist her with procuring all of her other necessities and wants, Lilit was now fully connected to the embassy's internal databases. After spending the better part of the past year getting nowhere, these simple acts felt like major leaps and bounds of forward progress. She was now anxious to get going and make her case in front of the representatives of the Terran Government.

Pulling up a map, she found where Xander's suite was and started heading that way. Knocking on the door, she heard Xander on the inside saying, "Come in." Finding the door unlocked, she did just that.

Stepping inside, Lilit was not surprised to discover that Xander had secured much larger accommodations than her. Whereas Lilit basically had a dorm-room with a bed, a desk to the side, and a separate bathroom; Xander had an open-floorplan front office and living space with an isolated sleeping and lavatory area hidden beyond a closed door. Although she could not see into it—and had no desire to ever go into Xander's bedroom again—she imagined that it was twice the size of her own.

Looking up from behind his desk, Xander exclaimed, "Oh, Lilit... I wasn't expecting... never mind. Glad to see you finally cleared confinement. Please, take a seat." At this, he gestured to the chairs in front of him.

Lilit did as offered, but landed with a thud. Although she had jokingly taunted Fiona, the effects of the additional gravity were palatable and she was still unsure of her own body in certain situations. While it was only a ten percent difference, it was noticeable, especially in how fast objects—such as herself—fell to the ground. Everything was just a little bit quicker than she was used to.

Noticing her discomfort at the loud smack her bottom made, Xander mollified, "Don't worry about it, Lilit, we're all still doing it, too. There's nothing to be embarrassed about. Even my own body doesn't react the way I expect it to."

Angered that Xander was able to see through her and express sympathy about it, Lilit bit back, "Just keep your thoughts on your own body and off of mine, Xander."

Putting his hands up in the air, Xander attempted, "That's not what I... what I meant was...

geez, there is no winning with you, Lilit, is there? Fine, since this doesn't appear to be a social visit, I assume you are here on business?"

"Yes, exactly," Lilit affirmed, compartmentalizing her brain into mission-mode. "Now that I'm out, I want to know when we'll be meeting with the Subcommittee on Terrestrial Colonies."

Sighing, Xander lectured, "As I have told you for months, even before we left orbit, they have agreed in principle to hear you out, but have not set a date."

Irritated, Lilit immediately barked back, "Oh, come on, Xander! What could possibly make it take so long to schedule one little summit? They've had ten months at this point and they still can't pick a single goddamn day to see us?"

"It's all part of the game," Xander admonished. "And you are playing right into their hands. They want you to be all flustered and upset so that you come to them like the raving, irrational, madwoman that you are. Then they can easily dismiss everything you have to say with video proof that you are nothing but a lunatic. Is that what you want?"

Seething, Lilit said through clenched teeth, "Of. Course. Not."

"That isn't going to do it either," Xander chided. "Lilit, I am trying to help you. Stop using our personal history as a wall between us and listen to me."

"We have no 'personal history'!" Lilit warned back. "You understand me?"

"Fine, fine, whatever," Xander conceded. "But my point is the same. It was your idea for us to work together as a team, so stop pushing me away and start using me as the tool you think I am."

All her frustration ultimately drained away as Lilit started laughing uncontrollably. Xander joined in, and they kept going until the tension bled out through their tear ducts. Finally regaining her composure, Lilit pronounced, "Fuck you, Xander, that was funny and you know it!"

In response, Xander just shrugged his shoulders before saying, "But it's true, isn't it?"

"It is," Lilit whispered. "I suppose, then, that I grant that you are right, at least in this one thing. But don't go making a habit out of it, okay?"

"You can count on me," Xander avowed. "Or, rather, you can count on my unreliableness for everything else going forward."

Frowning, Lilit pronounced, "You got one good joke in; don't push your luck with me."

Xander made a motion that he was zipping his mouth shut, locking it, and handing Lilit the key. Accepting his gift, Lilit responded, "Fine, I get it, we have no control over when they'll spring the meeting on us and they are going to do everything possible to ensure that getting on their calendar will be as painful as possible. If I let it get to me, then we'll never secure what we want. I must suppress my feelings of rage and put aside generations of mistreatment, otherwise it will just continue as it always has: with the Terran Government ignoring our pleas and us paying the price for their negligence. All we can do is prepare and practice so that when the time comes, we are ready."

Breaking his bonds without being handed back the key, Xander verbalized, "Exactly! And now that you truly understand our situation, Lilit, what can I really do for you?"

Lilit thought for just a moment before decreeing, "Schedule a conference room that can hold all of our team members. Starting tomorrow, it's all hands-on-deck. We must be ready."

CHAPTER 23

For over two months, Lilit, Xander, and everyone else who had made the journey to Earth with them drilled, plotted, and planned for the conference that still wasn't scheduled. Going for ten, twelve, fourteen hours a day, every day of the week, was wearing on all of them and they were showing signs of fraying at the seams. Xander recommended that they take an extended break from each other and start up fresh again afterwards.

"A vacation?" Lilit asked incredulously. "How can we possibly rest with what we're here to do? And besides, where would we go? We're all still confined to the embassy grounds."

Xander conceded, "That is a problem. Give me a couple of days to see what I can work out."

True to his word, two days later Xander walked into their conference room and presented everyone with ten-day passes to go anywhere on Earth that they desired. "Unfortunately, we do not have funding to pay for your trip, so you will have to use your own personal savings if you want to travel beyond this immediate vicinity."

Given the excitement in the room, Lilit had no choice but to agree to the holiday, but was able to delay its commencement by a week. Later that evening, she pulled the members from the Movement into her quarters and told them that she was giving each person a bonus payable immediately so that they could take advantage of this opportunity. In the back of her mind, though, she knew that she was going to need Ahmad to wire more money to backfill her extraneous spending. She hoped fundraising was still going well at home, but had read an earlier report from him that it was getting much more difficult to keep their donors' enthusiasm upbeat without her around.

Banking was always an interesting endeavor when dealing with the delays inherent with interplanetary travel and communications. Within the boundaries of a heavenly body, financial transactions were almost instantaneous—or close enough that no human being could really differentiate. However, no merchant was willing to wait half an hour to send a signal to another world, get the approval, and receive the response back. Further, using a beam across space for just one small matter would be a massive waste of limited resources. Data were queued up and sent out in large bursts on a regular schedule that was highly controlled. Commercial concerns were just one small tile of the overall mosaic.

Lilit knew that at some point in the past, the nascent Terran Government united the entirety of Earth under a singular currency. Ahmad had once explained to her that the economic union was what had initially brought the nations together; that their overarching system was originally created to act solely as a pecuniary body. It was only over time that the administration was able to slowly get the independent countries to cede part of their authority to the global alliance. What started out as a way to make trade easier as humanity expanded to the stars eventually morphed into a multi-planet overseer.

Simultaneously with the transition to a single legal tender, the Terran Government also digitalized all coinage. Every person and organization owned a virtual wallet that contained their funds, which was managed by an intentionally complicated and distributed structure that no one person or institution could possibly own or control. With humanity populating Venus, Mars, Ceres, and other far-flung places, it became clear that one wallet per person was simply impractical. As such, laws were passed that required everyone to have a "local" wallet. Therefore, funding was sent amongst wallets as needed during the regular broadcasts between the planets.

Aside from money, there were other troubling signs from back on Venus, especially concerning the animosity the revamped Managing Council was showing towards those representing the Movement. It appeared that Xander had actually tempered some of their more callous reproaches while he was in charge, but with him out of the picture, the rest of the Council was free to act capriciously and with unrestrained malice. When she asked Xander if he could do something about it, he shrugged his shoulders and said, "I can try, but no promises. My influence has been greatly diminished, as you know."

What was left unsaid was that Lilit was the cause of his fall from grace. Somehow, she had unwittingly brought about his rapid political demise. From what Lilit had been able to glean, he was becoming less involved with concerns at home and was focusing his energies almost exclusively on activities at the embassy. And it was not just their own project; he seemed to have ingratiated himself with the staff in contrast to the way Lilit had disaffected herself—especially, apparently, with Fiona Malone. Fiona's comings and goings from Xander's quarters at all hours had not gone unnoticed in their small, enclosed, and mistrustful community.

Lilit supposed that she was glad, in a way, that the response to her own lurid behavior was not necessarily automatically transferred onto the other members of the Movement, at least in the eyes of the rest of the Venusians and Earthers who shared their space. Nevertheless, this actually gave her something new to worry about. One of Durojaiye's so-called "intelligence operatives" came to her quarters one evening to express concern and speculation that some of their associates possibly had been seduced by the comparatively wide-open expanse of Earth. "They could decide to stay behind, seeking refuge here," he warned, "instead of returning back to Aestas to continue our virtuous struggle."

Lilit did not want to force anyone to do anything against their will. What purpose would it serve, she wondered, if she dragged them kicking and screaming back to Venus if they no longer wished to be there? But she agreed with the operative that the symbolism would be problematic. Still, she saw no solution that did not involve sacrificing her morality. Wishing to continue to further distinguish herself and the Movement's approach from Xander and the Managing Council, she decided that she would not play realpolitik with people's lives, no matter what anyone said, nor the cost that would have to be paid.

Pushing all that aside, Lilit tried to focus on the idea of partaking in a retreat herself. She attempted to think of where she would want to go, but realized that in all this time she still had no better idea where anything on Earth even was than before she left Venus. Then, she recalled, there were a few places she could easily recall the names of, even if she could not point to them on a globe. All it would take would be a search to find out what type of transport would be necessary to get her to where she wanted to be. She tasked her onboard A.I. with coming up with an itinerary and it quickly came back with the results. Looking at the findings and smiling, she announced aloud, "And thus it shall be done!"

The only trick, she presumed, would be finding a way to ditch her security detail and the intelligence operatives—who were oftentimes the same person. She didn't want anyone following her. This was something she desired to do alone.

Chapter 24

Standing outside the door, Lilit heard yelling in a language she did not recognize coming from inside the building. It seemed like the raised voice must have been directed towards the children because she could also hear them screaming and crashing into things. Her onboard translation program identified the cadence as being Hausa, but it was too muffled to make out the words for a full translation. The occasional one would be picked up and float before her eyes, although disconnected from any context. Whatever was going on behind that portal, Lilit decided it would be best if she waited patiently for it to finish before she attempted to knock.

She had already raised and lowered her fist several times in indecision. Why was this one action so difficult for her, she wondered? Over the past year and a half, she had literally stood up to a belligerent and powerful government and then flew to another world; yet this one deed was making her more nervous than all of that. Perhaps it was because she felt like she was violating some unsaid trust, breaking some upspoken agreement that all parties inherently understood without having to officially decree the terms.

Instead of moving forward, Lilit shifted her heavy backpack on her shoulders. Almost half of the weight came from the portable interface device that she had purchased back in Puerta Estrella. It did not have the capacity for all of her programs and files, so she did have to pick and choose what she would bring with her. Additionally, she had to dedicate a lot of space to Earth-based applications so that she could get around more easily. Having never travelled any-where aside from the journey between Venus and Earth, she did not know how to pack both her digital and physical wares.

Finally, things indoors seemed to quiet down, so Lilit channeled all her anxious energy into rapping her knuckles on the door. The person inside loudly muttered something that her translator picked up as, "What now?!" The butterflies in her stomach started flying and she thought about running away. Before she could take a step, though, the door swung open and a dark-skinned woman in a dress that covered her shoulders and arms and extended beyond her knees answered. When she first appeared she looked particularly annoyed, but after taking a quick look at

Lilit her demeanor changed to suspicion.

"Yes, is there something you want?" the woman perfunctorily asked as she seamlessly slipped into a perfectly clipped English.

"I... that is... what I mean..." Lilit stammered as she tried to find the right words. The other woman continued standing there impatiently awaiting whatever was coming before Lilit took a deep breath and spit out, "Are you Chigozie Yakubu?"

"I am," Chigozie slowly confirmed with a questioning tone. "And you are...?"

"Pardon me," Lilit began. "My name is Lilit Sarkisian. Your husband, Durojaiye, and I, we're friends, I mean, we're compatriots, freedom-fighters, back on Venus, on Aestas."

Chigozie stood up straighter, held out her hand palm first, and declared, "I know my husband's name." She then peeked her head out and looked left and right, apparently checking to see if anyone else was there who might notice Lilit standing in front of her home. Still, Lilit noted, Chigozie did not invite her inside, nor leave the safety of her own abode so that they might converse together outside more naturally.

"Ah, I didn't mean to imply otherwise," Lilit backtracked. "I don't know why I'm so nervous, I'm not usually like this. It's just, I've never been anywhere out in the open like this before or travelled so far or seen so many people in one place. It's all very over-whelming for me, so I apologize. Would you mind if I came inside? It would be better if we could sit down and converse together out of the sun."

"I would mind greatly," Chigozie declared. "It would be best for everyone if you remained exactly where you currently stand."

"Oh," Lilit said with disappointment. "I see. Have I done something to offend you? There are many Earth and regional specific customs that I'm not fa-miliar with, so if I have made some error, please let me know and forgive me."

"From my viewpoint, there is nothing in your be-havior that could be classified as wrong," Chigozie insisted, but offered no further explanation as the two women stared at each other in a silent impasse.

Not able to take the lack of response any longer, Lilit attempted, "Perhaps it would be helpful if I told you about myself? After all, you are at a disadvantage here. Durojaiye talks about you and the kids so much that I feel like I know you very well, but you might not be able to say the same about me. I'm not sure what he's told you about me... I mean, us... the Move-ment... and, and what's happening on Venus?"

"I have not spoken to or received a message from

my husband since he walked out this very doorway on his way to begin his mission," Chigozie claimed. "And we will not be able to speak again until he completes his assignment."

"So, he was really serious about that," Lilit rhetorically concluded.

"You did not believe him?" Chigozie gaped. "Is my husband not worthy of your trust?"

"No, no! That's not it at all," Lilit pled. "I suppose I just never properly internalized what it would mean to be so completely cut off from one's friends and family like that. Right now, it takes so long to get messages back-and-forth to Venus that I feel completely alone and isolated."

"And yet," Chigozie interceded, "you do get to hear from them, see videos from them, and send messages back in return, including with my husband?"

Anger and annoyance began to swell in Lilit's chest. Although she had no plan for how things were supposed to go with Chigozie, this interaction was certainly not what she expected. She decided to change tack before she said something she regretted. "Our situations are quite different. I can't hypothesize as to the conditions and reasonings of the deal that brought Durojaiye to Venus and the limitations that it has placed upon him. Whatever his perspective and internal rationalizations are, they are his to communicate or not. I cannot and will not speak for him, nor will I defend his actions. That is not my place, and therefore I will not presuppose anything."

When Chigozie did not even bother to provide any feedback, Lilit took in a lungful of air and tried, "As far as I'm concerned, Durojaiye is a fine man. He has been a loyal friend and a crucial driver of the changes that are needed on Aestas. I know there is very limited information available here on Earth, but we are in dire straits. Our population has reached a boiling point where our city can no longer support everyone. We must have a second city, otherwise we are all doomed. This is the cause I have taken up, and your husband has been instrumental in making that happen. I can safely say that without him, I would not be here today to negotiate with the Terran Government so as to hopefully provide necessary relief for our aggrieved people."

During all the time Lilit was delivering her soliloquy, Chigozie was looking her up and down like a prime piece of lab-grown meat. Not reacting to any of Lilit's words, Chigozie instead declared, "Oh, it is quite clear why he chose you."

Blushing, Lilit attempted to demur, "Oh, geez, no, no, that's not it all. Please, you've got to listen to me;

you're totally off-base here. I'm sorry, I think I've somehow made an even worse impression on you, but Chigozie, I'm telling you for the last time: you've got the wrong idea here!"

"No. I. Do. Not." Chigozie avowed.

"No, no," Lilit attempted to intervene again, "our relationship is strictly platonic, I assure you. Please don't be upset with him, or with me for just dropping in like this. I know I should have called first, but it was kind of a last-minute opportunity and I just wanted to see where Durojaiye came from and the people he loves with all his heart. If I haven't made it clear, he's a very important person to me, personally, and to our cause, the Movement. But that doesn't in any way mean that I'm saying he's not very important to you, and the kids, too!"

"And I am sure you are just as important to him and his cause," Chigozie accused without a hint of emotion.

"I keep telling you that you're reading into something that doesn't exist," Lilit pressed. "What can I say or do to get you to see things how they really are?"

Chigozie's eyes closed for a moment before she exhaled and said, "Forget about it, it is not important. What did you say your name was again?"

"It's Lilit, Lilit Sarkisian."

"Lilit," Chigozie rolled the word on her tongue, trying it out. "Lilit, I am sorry, but you cannot be here. I am afraid that I am going to have to ask you to leave and never come back."

"Wait, what?!" Lilit attempted, but she was too late. Chigozie had already shut the door in her face and barred it tight.

CHAPTER 25

The last of the members from Aestas Managing Council Support Team and the Movement exited the hotel lounge and headed to bed, leaving Lilit and Xander alone. "Oh great," an exhausted Lilit decreed, "there's no one left here to stop me from slapping your stupid face."

Taking it in stride with a laugh and a disarming grin, Xander said, "I'll forgive you for taking your frustrations out on me, but only this time!"

"Xaaaaaandeeeer," Lilit whined, "what am I doing wrong? Come on, you're the politician, this is your field. Why am I hitting a brick wall?"

After finally being granted an audience with the Terran Government Subcommittee on Terrestrial Colonies with less than a week's notice, Lilit, Xander, and their company had travelled to the designated meeting place halfway around the Earth and had been in all-day sessions for the past four revolutions around the planet's axis. Lilit quickly realized that most of the members of the committee were outwardly hostile towards her, questioning and doubting even the objectively most obvious facts that she presented. At one point, Lilit even requested an instant census from the colony and got the results back less than an hour later, and still the committee members doubted the accuracy of the population figures. Only a few of them—most notably Isra Emerson—showed anything remotely close to empathy and understanding, but even Isra seemed distracted for some reason.

Since Xander had not responded to her complaint, Lilit slammed her hands on the table and shouted, "Xander, are you even paying attention?"

"Lower your voice," Xander whispered, "we're in public here."

Looking around and pointing in every direction, Lilit noted, "We're completely by ourselves. Oh, are you worried about listening devices? Why would they care what we're talking about in private when they don't give a damn about what we say to their faces?"

"I just think a little propriety goes a long way," Xander pronounced.

Scowling, Lilit shot back, "And what have all these years of politeness gotten us, huh? Aestas is dying because of you and your twinkle-toes approach. Our shuttle home leaves in two months, and it's looking more and more likely that we'll have nothing to show for it!"

"I know, I know," Xander acquiesced, "and I'm concerned, too. Listen, I've dealt with these people and others higher up in the Terran Government for a long time, but I've never seen this type of vitriol before. Something has changed, Lilit, something big. We're missing some critical data here."

"What is it?" Lilit queried.

"It might be..." Xander trailed off. "No, never mind, it's gotta be more than what I'm thinking about. The main thing is that even though they have not wanted to provide us anything we've asked for in the past, they've always been willing to throw us some type of bone."

Accusingly, Lilit scorned, "You mean, you asked for a second Aestas and they increased our allotment of fertilizer at a reasonable price?"

"Something like that..." Xander agreed.

"And now you're afraid we won't even get a minor concession to show the people back home how effective you are, huh?" Lilit sneered. "Were you ever here to help me, or were you just playing a long game to get the booby prize?"

"I am only here," Xander stated in slow, measured words, "to ensure the safety of the citizens of Aestas; nothing more, nothing less. Your job, might I remind you, is to convince the Terrans that the way to do that is by allocating massive resources towards building a new colony on Venus."

Lilit despised admitting when Xander was in the right, and groaned as she lowered her head into her hands atop the table. Still face-down, Lilit grumbled, "Okay, okay, but what can I do?"

"These are government officials," Xander calmly explained. "If you want something from them, you have to give them something in return, something they actually want."

Lilit lifted her head up at that and hissed, "You mean a bribe?!"

"You misunderstand, nothing so crass," Xander said as he held his hands outward. "I'm talking about quid-pro-quo. What benefit do the members of the committee themselves, the Terran Government in general, and even the whole of the Earth get for do- ing what we want? We can't just talk about our needs and desires; we have to redouble our efforts on pre- senting the situation in a way that highlights how it can benefit them. Come on, Lilit, we drilled this very scenario over-and-over again."

"I know, I know," Lilit moaned. "It's just, in the heat of the moment, I can see that I'm not executing very well. Hell, they've rejected the examples and of- fers we prepared in advance, so I've got nothing in the tank. We need to regroup with the team and come up with something new to offer."

"Not tonight," Xander commanded. "I'm drained, and so are you. Everyone else already had the right idea. Come on, let's go."

At this, Xander rose and held out his hand to Lilit. She looked at it with curiosity until he finally put it down by his side. "You go ahead," Lilit offered, "I'm going to stay here and work a little longer." She had already pulled up her virtual whiteboard and was writing in the air.

Sighing, Xander departed without saying another word, leaving Lilit to contemplate their future alone.

Back in her room, Lilit still couldn't sleep and started reviewing reports from the Movement's activities back on Aestas. Really, she just filtered it to messages from Ahmad and Durojaiye, and especially the videos. She missed seeing them in person, so she had resorted to watching their images and voices to fill the gap. Sometimes, she even talked back to them, hoping to somehow magically get a response. At one point during the never-ending waiting she had been enduring, she attempted to program her onboard A.I. to respond like them. While it had no issue mimicking their voices, capturing their true essences and the sparks of their personalities was just a bridge too far for a computer. She knew plenty of people who lived with the "ghosts" of departed loved ones using this technological solution, but she could never get past the digital facsimiles' unnatural dispositions and lack of authenticity.

On a whim, she filtered the messages further to find ones that included the two of them together. For some reason, they generally dispatched individual posts and only occasionally sent a group communication. Usually, it was bad news, but once-in-a-while they seemed to realize that they should send pick-me-ups by having her resolve one of their endless squabbles over the most trivial matters. It was certainly a waste of money to pay for a transmission like that, but Lilit was glad they did. Finding an unopened file from a few weeks ago, Lilit hoped that this would be one of those to bring her a smile during these otherwise intolerable proceedings.

After opening the message, the two appeared in her line of sight and she immediately recognized that something was amiss. Ahmad stood there sheepishly while Durojaiye hid in the background expressionless. Ahmad spoke first saying, "Hello Lilit, how are you doing?" It was a classic stall as he was working up his nerve. "I hope you are holding your chin up high. We are all very proud and in awe of what you have been able to do thus far. We did not want to disturb you with this but..." Ahmad shrugged his shoulders as he tried to find his words.

Durojaiye chimed in then, encouraging his friend, "Perhaps it would be best if you just tell her what is happening without delay. Lilit is strong and understanding; she can handle anything we might throw at her. You should not underestimate her resiliency."

Apparently forgetting that he was recording a message, Ahmad turned around to lambast Durojaiye, "Of course I know of Lilit's prowess! It is you who have failed her, and you who should be admitting your shortcomings. As always, I have great faith in Lilit, while you are the one who doubts and expects me to soften these messages with my soothing countenance."

Durojaiye cleared his throat and pointed ahead. Ahmad jumped, turned around, and revealed his bright red face. Embarrassed, he said, "Oh, please forgive me, I have forgotten you were here." Lilit was laughing at this, a much-needed relief. Chuckling to herself, she wondered why they had not edited this out of the video or recorded a new one. Then she realized what must have happened: Durojaiye told Ahmad he was going to do just that, but instead sent the raw file just to mess with him and give Lilit a brief reprieve with their tomfoolery.

Continuing, Ahmad stood up straighter and put on a serious face. He must have thought that things would begin again here, so he jumped into it by declaring, "Unfortunately, this is not a social message. The Aestas Managing Council has taken your apartment by eminent domain and assigned it to new inhabitants. Durojaiye, other members of the

Movement, and I tried to stop them and did successfully delay them for months. Yet, in the end, we could not do anything to impede their decision. Even though Xander claims to support you, we are quite sure he had a hand in this in some way. Sadly, you are going to have to let that go for all of our sakes.

"Although it reeks of retribution for everything you have done through the Movement, it is still quite understandable given the situation up here. We need every bit of space and leaving your home fallow was no longer possible, it would appear. However, there is something good to take away from this: they assigned your former quarters to a family with a new baby. At the very least, take solace in the fact that your erstwhile quarters are being put to good use for the people living there now and it is not just a payoff for some government sycophant."

"Tell her about her belongings," Durojaiye prompted from astern.

"Ah, yes!" Ahmad squeaked. "I had almost forgotten! Before they officially evicted you, Durojaiye managed to gain access and we were able to save your possessions from the recycler. We have boxed them up and are storing them here in our place, so they will be waiting for you upon your return."

Despite the heartbreaking news about losing her

home—one that had passed between her family members for generations—Lilit could only laugh at the idea of Ahmad and Durojaiye sifting through her dirty clothes and underwear that she had left behind more than a year prior. She couldn't imagine that she had any possessions she cared that much about, and she felt guilty that they were now taking up precious room in their own limited area. When she responded, she would be sure to thank them for their thoughtfulness, but tell them to dump it all.

"Now that we have caught you up on your personal tragedies," Durojaiye said as he stepped into the foreground and gently pushed Ahmad back, "it is time to bring you up to speed on what is happening here overall. Civil unrest is growing and we are having some issues maintaining the peaceful nature of the Movement. There is a small, but growing, splinter group that is taking more radical action.

"To be fair, they were not the first to fire. The Protectors have been responding to the protests with excessive force, and there have been violent clashes between them and us. At first, it was just a few small voices in the crowd that wanted to take more... vigorous... actions, but these aggressive engagements by the Protectors have made more flock to the radicals' perspective. I am doing everything I can to hold things on message and methodology, but your return cannot come soon enough.

"Aside from those who lean towards brutality, the good news is that many more everyday people are becoming much more sympathetic to the Movement overall. Our own forces have swelled and nearly a third of the population is supporting us openly. And believe me, plenty of others are doing so clandestinely. There are even Protectors who have come to me to express that they do not agree with the actions of their brethren and what they have been ordered to do. After all, they are humans, too, and have to live here the same as—"

Lilit could not take it anymore and turned the message off. She cried into her pillow until she, at last, mercifully passed out.

Lilit was sneaking around the back wall to Isra Emerson's house, making sure there were no cameras or prying eyes to see her before she attempted to scale the solid fence. Though Isra was a member of the Terran Government Subcommittee on Terrestrial Colonies, she was one of the few who had shown sympathy to their cause, and even been quite friendly with Lilit outside of official proceedings. After the committee had rendered their decisions, Lilit wanted to hear from someone within the inner circle about why their requests were being denied, and she figured Isra was her best hope. Besides, what did she have to lose at this point?

When the sessions had wrapped up the prior week, the committee took a number of closed-door votes—or so they said. Whatever happened, Lilit could tell that Isra was not happy as they made their pronouncements. The head of the committee read out their decisions to their group, "While we are certainly understanding of the situation on Aestas, we simply cannot fund another floating city on Venus at this time. In short, the bottom line is that Aestas is just one square in the large tapestry that is the Human Expansion Program. Our limited resources must be spent elsewhere so as to maximize colonization opportunities across the entire solar system."

As terrible as this statement was to hear, Lilit was relieved to have confirmation on the Terran Government's standing and intentions on certain issues. Amongst themselves, members of the Movement had discussed rumors that the Earthers were giving credence to some loose-knit collection of religiously bent individuals who wanted to see the Human Expansion Program be put on ice and have all energies be redirected solely towards the people living on their ancestral planet. From what Lilit knew of them, these folks seemed to think that humanity belonged nowhere else but on Earth. It was comforting for her to hear that the Terran Government was still dedicated to further exploration and settlement.

Nevertheless, Lilit did not care for the answer she had just received nor the decorum in the room and called out, "And just what would these other 'opportunities' happen to be?"

Unphased, the committee head answered, "I am afraid I am not at liberty to discuss what those may or may not be at this moment."

"What does that mean?" Lilit yelled back since her microphone had been turned off.

"That means that it's classified," Isra interjected. "I'm sorry, our hands are tied just as much as yours... for the time being, anyway."

"If I may continue," the annoyed principal spokesperson interposed. "Like I said, we are empathetic to your plight, but there is nothing we can do at this instant. However, we have made several recommendations in our official report that your local government has the freedom to implement. We will leave it up to the Aestas Managing Council to decide what is the most appropriate approach to resolve your short-term housing issues."

When Lilit read the report later, she found that it contained suggestions for a number of draconian population control mechanisms. This included everything from ending immigration entirely to forced sterilization. Basically, it was a handbook on how to naturally reduce their population over several generations. Examples were given from high-density areas on Earth where they were able to demonstrate negative habitation saturation within fifty years, whether that was the intentional outcome or not. Lilit's insides roiled as she read glowing reviews about some of the worst atrocities in human history as potential solutions to their woes. It took all her self-control to keep the contents of her stomach where they were.

Amazingly, while Lilit was discussing her concerns with Xander, he took the council's final product as an overall win for Venus. "Look, we got something here, Lilit," he claimed. "The Terran Government has never before agreed to let us close our borders to immigrants, so this will bring an immediate relief. We could even encourage emigration to other colonies and, perhaps, Earth itself. Don't you see? This would tremendously speed up the depopulation process and ease our short-term pressures."

When Lilit expressed that she was not sold on these so-called benefits, but rather found Xander's proposals to be completely repugnant, he attempted again by saying, "This doesn't mean you have to give up on a second Aestas; you can still continue that fight! But this buys you, and all of us, desperately needed time to make that a reality. Please Lilit, I beg you, for the sake of the citizenry of Aestas, accept this as a victory."

Instead of an answer, Lilit chose to walk away. She decided that Xander was right about one thing: there was still critical information she was missing. It was then that she resolved that the only way she was going to get it was by forcefully yanking it straight from the horse's mouth.

Confident that she was not being watched, Lilit at last pulled herself up and over Isra's protective barrier that shielded her from the rest of the human race and jumped down to the lawn on the other side. Since she didn't hear any alarms going off or dogs barking, she walked up to the back sliding door and knocked. At first, there was no response, so she rapped her fists loudly on the door until the interior lights flipped on. A curtain moved to reveal Isra's face, followed by a look of complete shock at seeing Lilit standing there.

Sliding the glass door open, Isra simply asked, "Lilit, is that you?"

"Yep, that's me!" Lilit chipperly affirmed.

"Jesus, what are you doing here?" Isra grilled. "Never mind that for now. Get in here before someone sees you." At this, Isra stepped aside and signaled for Lilit to enter.

Upon doing so, Isra exclaimed, "I don't know how you do things on Venus, but this is highly inappropriate. For the record, I should be calling the cops on you right now."

"But you won't," Lilit declared with a definitiveness she definitely did not feel. "You never would have invited me in if that was your intention. Isra, I can see that we are very much alike, that you want to help me, help all of Aestas. That is why I could only come to you.”

Sighing, Isra then asked the obvious question, “And how do you expect me to do that?”

“Let me in on what is really going on, what you are clearly hiding,” Lilit plainly directed.

Isra chewed her upper lip for a good minute while wringing her hands. Finally, she threw her arms up in surrender and declared, “Damn it, it’s not fair. You should know; everyone should. I don’t know why we are supposed to keep this a secret, but it’s beyond amazing, Lilit; truly, absolutely and completely astounding! It’s the greatest breakthrough in space engineering since we built the elevator!”

“Tell me,” Lilit urged. Now that she had learned for sure that something was being kept from her, she knew she could not back down.

After saying nothing for several more minutes as she appeared to work through her own internal quandary, Isra said, “Okay, okay, but you didn’t hear this from me, understood?” Once Lilit agreed, Isra resumed, “Alright, HSA has developed something they are calling the ‘Torch Drive’. It is a new propulsion and energy management system that will eventually allow us to move at incredible speeds. If we can attach it to a spaceship, we could get from Earth to Venus in just three days. Mars would only take one additional day beyond that! We could be on the moons of Jupiter in just six and a half days, and reach the dwarf binary planetoid Pluto-Charon in only eighteen days."

"How is this possible?" Lilit probed.

"I don't understand the specifics," Isra admitted, "but I do recognize the possibilities. The velocities at which these vessels could travel means it would simulate 1G on board. Do you know what that means?"

"No space traveler or immigrant would ever need rehab again..." Lilit offered, realizing that, at the very least, this would eliminate the need for most of her former job duties.

"That's just the beginning," Isra started speaking rapidly as she was obviously excited about this technology. "We could go anywhere in a short amount of time, relatively speaking, that is!"

After taking a moment to giggle and snort at her own pun, Isra recovered and continued, "And, I mean, not just the entire solar system, but even beyond. It's all still a work-in-progress, but it is just a matter of time. Even though what we are looking at and have available at present is only good enough for the Sol System, in a few generations we might be able to reach our nearest neighbor Proxima Centauri in just six Earth-years! Also, with time dilation, the people aboard the shuttle would only experience three-and-a-half years. Isn't that wonderful?"

Lilit's head was spinning and she could not keep up. "I... but..." was all she managed before stammering, "Is it ready to fly now?"

"No," Isra confessed. "There are technical limitations that need to be overcome. Nevertheless, it doesn't matter: this is the future. Why put money into another floating city when soon we'll be able to populate rocky bodies with real ground everywhere in our own solar system, and then all other ones? With this amount of cosmic reach, Venus would only be valuable if we could somehow get to the surface, and that is simply an impossibility right now."

CHAPTER 28

"Come in," Xander said in his typical detached tone in response to Lilit's knock at the entrance to his expansive quarters.

Lilit did just that and gently closed the door behind her. She wanted to clear the air with Xander about what she considered their overall shared failure, but was immediately stopped short in her tracks due to the scene before her. "Xander, what are you doing?" she asked the man still surrounded by work on his desk. "We're leaving tomorrow to go up the space elevator and it doesn't look like you've even started packing yet for the return home!"

Xander looked up from the pile of materials he was poring over and appeared to close out his personal monitor with a subtle gesture only someone else with a visual implant would recognize. Giving Lilit his undivided attention, he motioned to the couch and said, "Lilit, please, take a seat."

Nervous, Lilit did as requested while Xander came around his desk and sat down on a chair across from her. He still didn't speak, so Lilit prodded,

"What is it, Xander? We've been through a lot; you know you can tell me."

With a deep exhalation, Xander began, "Lilit, the fact is, I'm not going back with you and the rest of our team members. That is, the ones who are returning and not staying here, too."

"What are you saying?" Lilit demanded. "I don't understand."

Xander did not waste time as he launched into his explanation. "You see, I've been in contact with the Managing Council and we've all agreed that I would be more useful to Aestas if I remained here as an ambassador-at-large." When Lilit tried to interrupt, Xander demanded that she let him finish speaking first. "Lilit, I'm not angry with you, but you have to know that thanks to your machinations, I have no future back on Venus. You destroyed my political career when you forced me to come here with you. However, I now see that it was for the best. Back on Aestas, there was nothing more I could do to aid the citizenry. From here on Earth, I will actually have some prospects to help with the situation, so it's better for me—for everyone—if I remain behind."

Once it was clear that Xander was done with his explanation, Lilit only had one thing to say:

"You coward."

"I beg your pardon?" Xander responded, flabber-gasted.

"You heard me, asshole," Lilit lambasted. "I didn't think you could find a new way to thoroughly disappoint me, but there you go! In many ways, I'm impressed with the level of self-deceit that you must have in order to see yourself as making some sort of noble sacrifice. 'Oh no, I'll have to stay behind on this large planet living in a mansion on the government's dime with only my hot redheaded lady-servant to console me every night! Woe is me!' Meanwhile, the rest of us who actually care about Aestas must go back to try to save our homeworld while you get to laze-away your days here in relative comfort. This is a new low, Xander. With all your highbrow talk, I didn't think you would categorically abandon Aestas."

Finally pushed beyond his limit, Xander screeched back, "Damn it, Lilit, I'm doing no such thing!"

"Lower your voice," Lilit mocked, "people might hear... that you're really a prick."

Clenching his fists, Xander spoke in as even of a cadence as he could manage, "Wake up, Lilit! Look at the writing on the wall: with the advent of the Torch Drive, Venus and Aestas are a lost cause. Who is going to want to live on the Yellow Balloon when the entire surface of a planet like Proxima Centauri B will be open to humanity! This is the end of the road for our colony! The best we can hope to do is help people live comfortably until Aestas is completely abandoned and plunges into the clouds."

Lilit was shaking with so much information coming at her at once. Xander's use of a slur to describe their own people was bad enough, but she knew that she had never told him about her meeting with Isra. Picking her first battle, she fumed, "You knew about the Torch Drive? For how long?"

Xander slumped his shoulders and admitted, "For years now. I wondered what you'd do when you found out, and this is exactly what I feared. You are going to make things much, much worse for our people. You are going to brutalize and torture them in this pointless crusade of yours. But Lilit, it doesn't have to be this way. You have all of the potential in the solar system; you could give and get so much more from life if you could just accept that this is how it is going to be, how it was always going to be."

Ignoring him, Lilit accused, "You've been spying on me, haven't you?"

Harrumphing, Xander decreed, "Of course I have! How naïve could you be? And you are doing the same to me. You think I don't know about the so-called "Intelligence Division" among the security officers of the Movement? Oh Lilit, Lilit, Lilit. You are the one who has a double-agent who is spying for Earth Central Command as your right-hand man. Or is he a triple-agent? I can't decide. Either way, it's quite a tangled web that you weave with that one!" Xander then broke into a disconcerting laugh.

Unable to take his sanctimonious diatribes anymore, Lilit simply got up, stormed out of the room, and slammed the door in her wake. Alone in her own quarters and already packed, she had nothing to do but pace and agonize over Xander's accusations. It was then that the epiphany came to her: this entire journey to Earth had been a huge waste of time. Digging through her sparse belongings, she found a small drone with a camera and turned it on to record a message to Ahmad and Durojaiye.

After catching them up to speed about what she had learned from Isra and Xander, as well as other pertinent details, she laid out what she had finally realized. "This entire time, we've been making a false assumption. We thought that we needed to change the system—the government—as the precursor to saving Aestas and Venus. This trapped us into playing by their rules and thinking there was no escape. We... I... let them dictate the terms and tried to stay in their little boxes. This was my mistake, I take full responsibility, but now I know that there is a solution.

"The reality is that we don't need them or anyone's permission to do what needs to be done. We cannot wait for them any longer with our hands out hoping that they will suddenly recognize the errors of their ways. When I get back, our first priority is going to be shifting our thinking into an approach that does not include nor need the Aestas Managing Council nor the Terran Government. We must find a way to take control of the situation, and I have some ideas for how we might go about it. Really though, the bottom line is this:

"If we want to save our world, we'll have to do it by ourselves!"

FROM LEADER TO MONARCH

Sitting in her wheelchair out in the hallway, Lilit wasn't feeling the bravado she had been preaching for the months of her journey homeward. Instead, a melancholy was coming over her now that she was actually back on Venus and feeling the pull of both gravity and responsibility. Realizing that she had months of isolation ahead of her in the Quarantine and Confinement Districts, Lilit sensed that the momentum was slipping away from her and, thus, the Movement. If anything, she would now be under the thumb of yet another bureaucrat—worse, someone in her previous position as a Coordinator, someone she used to be. Embarrassment began to bubble up at the idea of having one of her former coworkers now responsible for her well-being.

"Lilit Sarkisian, please come to the window at booth number sixteen," a familiar male voice said in perfectly clipped English. Every part of Lilit's being knew that she recognized the cadence of the voice, but it was so out of context she could not allow herself to believe it was who she thought it could be.

Rolling herself up to the glass, her heart became elated. "Durojaiye!" she shouted out to her long-lost friend behind the plexiglass partition. "What are you doing here? Are you a Coordinator now? You didn't tell me!"

Durojaiye smiled and laughed with delight. He mimed a hug through their separation barrier and Lilit returned the gesture. Finally, he spoke saying, "No, no, I have much more pressing matters to attend to most of the time, though none more imperative than seeing you with my own eyes again. The truth is, the Movement has people everywhere and has penetrated into every organization, including among the Coordinators and even the Protectors. We have infiltrated every part of society and can get into anything and go anywhere."

Lilit didn't know what to think about this revelation. On the one hand, she was delighted to see Durojaiye and excited that they already seemed to have the capabilities to sidestep the government in their quest to save Aestas. Yet on the other side, she was queasy from the sheer lawlessness and backhandedness that was required to create and maintain this clandestine network. Xander's enlightenment about how they were all spying on each other all the time and working towards their own separate agendas and goals left her quite uneasy and distrusting. If someone were willing to throw away their oath to Aestas for the Movement, then certainly they were just as capable of betraying the Movement for something or someone else.

Durojaiye saw the frown on Lilit's face and responded in kind, "Ah, you are worried about this arrangement that allows such access. Well, I have another surprise for you that may put your mind at ease. Please turn around."

Lilit did as best she could from her seat and was astonished to see that someone in a hazmat suit had snuck up on her. How she had not heard them approaching, she could not imagine, but there they were. The person kneeled so that their helmet's faceplate was in Lilit's line of sight. Inside was a bearded visage she knew quite well. "Ahmad! You're here, too!" she exclaimed with newfound enthusiasm and jubilation.

"Hello, my wayward comrade," Ahmad began. "Welcome back to the jewel of the solar system. Your presence has been sorely lacking."

Lilit giggled at Ahmad's formal greeting and suddenly she realized that she hadn't tittered like that since she had boarded the skimmer and left everyone dear to her behind. Something finally let go inside of her and, unexpectedly, she found herself completely at peace. She did not even know that she was missing the feeling until it startlingly returned.

Noticing that her tension had melted away, Ahmad declared, "I am taking you out of here. You are coming back to our place and we will rehab you there, among your people."

Shocked, Lilit probed, "What about all the rules and regulations around entry? What about the pathogens I may be carrying? You know that your former planet is filthy, right?!"

Ahmad shrugged his shoulders which had the effect of making his whole hazmat suit shift out of position. He simply noted, "We need you more, so I will be 'springing you', posthaste."

Smiling, Lilit solicited, "'We' as in you and Durojaiye, or do you perhaps mean the Movement as a whole?"

Not taken aback at all, Ahmad asserted, "Both. They need their Commander and I—we—need our friend. I have missed you so much."

The waterworks let loose and Lilit cried out, "And I've missed you guys, so, so, so desperately, too. I've needed you two more than you could possibly have known. The things I did, the horrible choices I made, the stuff I just let happen to me... I, I, I—"

Ahmad then smothered her in a hug as she sobbed into his slick coveralls. Her tears slid off her own face and down his uniform to the floor. "Shhhh, shhhh, shhhh," Ahmad offered, "It is all better now. You are here, and we are reunited again. The past is the past, and it can no longer control you. Starting today, we must only live in the present and fight for the future. Now, dry those tears, and let us go home, as a family, together."

CHAPTER 30

Rolling into Ahmad's and Durojaiye's apartment, Lilit's olfactory glands were immediately assaulted by the overwhelming pungent odor of two men living in a small space together for nearly three years. She had grown used to the luxuries on Earth like the ability to open a window, and realized that the transition back to Aestas was going to be more difficult than she originally considered. Suddenly, she felt a pang of jealousy towards Xander, and then disgust with herself for desiring anything he was a part of. Sadly, Lilit knew she could not completely divorce him from her life as he continued to send her updates from the Venusian Embassy. She was not sure why he was doing so—if it was some type of loyalty to her or retribution for himself or for manipulative reasons all his own—but whatever his motives, she would not drive him away just to allay her own revulsion.

Although Lilit had been to Ahmad's and Durojaiye's home—and, she supposed, now her home, too—countless times before, she looked around with renewed vision. Unlike Lilit's former quarters with a separate sleeping and living space, this unit was a studio with only a detached area for a bathroom. All other functions were crammed into one single room with almost no options for personal discretion.

Lilit quickly noticed that they had obviously re-decorated and brought in different furniture in preparation for her arrival. Against the wall to her left there were two beds, each raised off the ground so that a small desk with a chair and some drawers could fit underneath. These arrangements were an exact mirror image of each other. For instance, the head of the bed and the desk that were nearest to her were also closest to the door, while the other one had all of that placed the other way so that it was as far from the door as possible. With this assembly, Lilit supposed, whoever was in one of these areas would always be the maximum distance away from the other person. In between the bed/desk/dresser setups was a small loveseat. Above the couch, open shelves reached all the way to the ceiling, creating the sem-blance of a barrier amid the two sleeping spaces.

The opposite wall was dedicated to the standard combination kitchen-laundry-storage area with all of its typical accoutrements, as well as the entrance to the bathroom. In the middle of the room was now just a table that would comfortably seat four or five and could uncomfortably squish in a few more. The entryway was unfortunately framed in the center, making that wall particularly useless for anything except hangable items.

Gazing straight across at the one remaining wall, Lilit gathered that it was now going to be her "zone". It looked like her friends—or more likely, someone in the Movement with carpentry skills—had installed a ceiling to floor curtain that could be pushed aside. It was much like in the health ward to provide separation between patients but still allow anyone to easily pass through it. Noticing where she was staring, Durojaiye said, "We both thought you would appreciate some privacy and space to call your own, even if it is only big enough for a bed, a small dresser, and your chair." At that, he went over and pulled the curtain aside, revealing just that. "When you are feeling stronger," Durojaiye continued, "we can loft your bed like ours and add your own desk. There's probably enough space for more drawers, too, if you need them. For now, though, your bed must remain on the ground, for obvious reasons."

Lilit blushed self-consciously at the idea of being seen as an invalid. Based upon all of her years of helping others through this transition, she knew she should not care and admonished herself for allowing those feelings through, but that did not change her natural and subconscious reactions. Just as abruptly, she recognized that she was a stranger in her own land, a homeless drifter surviving solely on the kindness of others. She had always been her own woman and now felt completely diminished by being totally dependent upon these two men, no matter their importance to her and their place in her life.

Ahmad apparently sensed her discomfort and noted as he rolled her over to her personal outcropping, "Fear not, Lilit. This is just a temporary state of affairs and soon you will be your old self. There is an appropriate saying among the Persians that applies to your situation: īn nīz bogzarad."

"You're going to have to clarify the meaning of that for me," Lilit stated as she did not have any translation programs running at that time.

Ahmad quickly shared, "It means, roughly speaking, 'this too shall pass.'"

"I think I've heard that before..." Lilit offered.

"No," Ahmad pronounced, "you heard the bastardized western version. Until now, you have not had the pleasure of receiving the sentiment in its original form as dictated by the Sufi poets."

"You know that I have no idea what or where Persians or Sufis even are, don't you?" Lilit teased. "And by the way, where does a 'west' region begin, exactly, on a globe?"

Smiling, Ahmad said, "Of course you are unaware, but while you are here, I can teach you these and many other enriching wonders!"

To this, Durojaiye just groaned and sarcastically bemoaned, "Yay, more lessons from Ahmad's endless pool of scholarly knowledge!"

This just made Ahmad smile wider, and they all had a deep laugh together. Lilit then began to internalize that Ahamad was right, and things were going to be alright—that she was going to be fine.

After getting her unpacked and settled in as well as possible, they all sat around the central table, reminiscing and having a generally good time. Throughout the day, many of her family members and several senior members of the Movement came for a visit and to deliver news to Lilit. Some actually came to report to Ahmad or Durojaiye, which made Lilit say, "Guys, it's obvious that I am keeping you from your work. If you need to leave for a while, please do so. Don't worry about me!"

"I think not," Ahmad proclaimed. "We just got you back, so we are allowed to take some time to enjoy your sparkling personality. The Movement will survive for a day without our constant oversight."

"Besides," Durojaiye chimed in, "you think this is the only day off we have taken in the past nineteen months? Lilit, we may appear superhuman, but we are just mere mortals. We can burn out and tire just the same as anyone."

Lilit snickered and let go, just allowing the moment to wash over her. It was not to last, though. As the sun began to set, they took her upstairs to Lusaber on Level 1. Eating real Venusian cuisine seemed to bring her tastebuds back to life. Even though the embassy on Earth had its own garden, the food never tasted as fresh. There was literally something in the atmosphere that dulled the plants' flavors. Lilit was really starting to come around when she noticed Durojaiye was absently stirring the remnants of the meal on his plate. "Something on your mind, Durojaiye?" Lilit asked.

Durojaiye looked up, forced a smile, and said, "No, no, I am just distracted by something."

"You can tell me," Lilit pleaded. "You know I can help you with anything."

Appearing to be conflicted and having an internal debate to make his decision, Durojaiye finally declared, "Yes, you are right. You should know what has happened. You see, about a month ba—"

"That is enough!" Ahmad commanded at he cut

Durojaiye off. "We can talk about it tomorrow. Let her have one measly day of peace, for Allah's sake."

Squinting her eyes, Lilit sneered, "You... are hiding something... from me?!"

Ahmad shrunk in his seat, saying, "Not hiding. I just wanted you not to have to worry for a little while. Our problems will be waiting for us tomorrow. There is no need to ruin the spirit of this occasion."

Not sold, Lilit shifted her mind into Leader of the Movement mode and compartmentalized her friendships away. "Ahmad, shut up," she harshly scolded. "Durojaiye, tell me what is happening."

Looking between his two friends, Durojaiye sighed and began, "During a small protest last month, there was a skirmish with the Protectors."

"I'm aware of that," Lilit remarked. "I read the summaries that were sent my way."

"Not the complete reports, though" Durojaiye confessed.

"What do you mean?" Lilit gasped.

"I scrubbed every message that was sent to you," Durojaiye admitted. "There was nothing you could do while you were en route, so it was decided that it would be best to keep you in the dark until your return."

"How dare you!" Lilit screeched as she slammed

her hands on the table. "You aren't my guardian; you don't get to decide what I do or don't need to know."

Durojaiye threw his hands up and declared, "I agree with you, but I was outvoted. We have had to make some tough decisions to maintain cohesion within the Movement, and this was one of the many compromises I was forced to make. You charged me and Ahmad with keeping the Movement together in your absence no matter what, so this was one of the unfortunate ways we did it."

Lilit felt her anger subsiding and she placed her hands over Durojaiye's by way of an apology for her outburst. "I'm sorry," she said, "I didn't realize. But that's all over now. I'll get everyone else back in line and stop this nonsense; you guys don't need to worry about that anymore. That is my cross to bear, and mine alone."

"You are never alone," Ahmad interjected. "This is not a burden any one person can carry. Believe me, I have tried to be you these past nineteen months, and have failed miserably along the way."

"Ahmad..." Lilit whispered as she moved her hands off of Durojaiye's and put her arms around Ahmad in an awkward sideways hug. Her wheelchair continued to get in her way and she tried to stand, but found gravity had other plans. She almost tumbled to the ground before both Ahmad and Durojaiye shot up, caught her, and gently placed her back in her seat.

"Now, now," Ahmad admonished, "it has only been a few hours. You are not quite ready for that yet."

Frustrated by her lack of mobility, Lilit attempted to mentally toughen herself up. "Alright, my body may be betraying me, but my mind is just as sharp as ever. I need the whole truth, otherwise I'll never be prepared for what is to come."

"Very well," Ahmad agreed. "Durojaiye?"

At Ahmad's request, Durojaiye picked up where he left off, as if there had been no interlude. "During that... altercation... things really spiraled out-of-hand. One of the members of the Movement was killed."

"Who?!" Lilit concernedly queried.

"No one you know personally," Durojaiye acknowledged. "A more recent recruit, at that. However, as you can imagine, this lit a vitriol under the more extreme factions in the Movement, and it has spread like wildfire. I have done all I can to stop an equally violent retaliation, but there is a jihad brewing. You have to find a way to either stop it, or you must direct it, before it consumes us all."

Chapter 31

"Commander Sarkisian," the saluting young Protector greeted Lilit. "The room is all clear and you are safe to enter."

Lilit suspiciously looked the Protector over and queried, "You're Aritza, aren't you?"

"Yes, Commander," Protector Aritza confirmed.

"At ease, Protector Aritza," Lilit ordered. There didn't seem to be any change in their disposition, so Lilit continued her interrogation. "Tell me: you swore an oath, didn't you, to uphold the rule of law of Aestas, no matter what?"

"That's correct, ma'am," Aritza confirmed. There was that "ma'am" again that Lilit remembered from their first interaction so long ago, in what seemed like another lifetime. Although, on this occasion, she felt that she had prematurely aged appropriately enough since their initial encounter to have honestly earned the honorific.

Moving to Aritza's side, Lilit then inquired, "Then how is it that you can square that up with your actions today? Have you not betrayed your sacred word by joining up with a paramilitary force and over-throwing the government in what can only be described as a coup?"

Aritza began to dance uncomfortably in place before asking, "Permission to speak freely?"

"Please," Lilit said as she returned to Aritza's frontside and held out her hands.

"Commander, I have betrayed no one and changed no allegiances. My oath was to uphold the laws of Aestas and defend its people. The Managing Council, the violent Protectors, and their supporters among the citizenry were the true criminals and I helped stop their transgressions once and for all. I report to the legitimate leaders of Aestas, and that is now you. Further, as of this day, the Security and Intelligence Divisions of the Movement are no longer outside of the government. Lieutenant Yakubu has already integrated them into the Protector Force; thus, we are all one combined agency."

"So, you're saying nothing has changed?" Lilit questioned.

"Not at all," Aritza disagreed. "Things are much better already. It has been quite difficult to fulfil my responsibilities due to the corruption of my former bosses. I now have renewed hope that I can make a real difference in our society, which is what I signed up to do in the first place."

Lilit extended her hand outward and said, "Thank you, Protector Aritza."

Aritza took Lilit's hand in their own and responded, "No, thank you, Commander. Without you, none of this would have been possible."

Sighing, Lilit declared, "Unfortunately, this is just the beginning. There's a lot of work to do, but you can count on me, Aritza."

"I know that, ma'am," Aritza avowed.

Looking them over one last time, Lilit excused herself and stepped inside. She hadn't been in this space for over two years, although not much had changed. The Managing Council Chambers were as she remembered them, except there were no longer Councilors to speak of. Instead, the only other inhabitants were Ahmad and Durojaiye, who were both busy rifling through the drawers under the semi-circular raised desk. "Why, if it isn't Lieutenants Yakubu and Al Zaheri," Lilit teased, even though Aritza remained outside and could not hear her. "What type of pillaging are you two up to?"

Both looked up and smiled at Lilit's presence. "We are not thieves," Durojaiye announced, "only victorious revolutionaries inspecting our spoils of war!"

"Quite so," Ahmad agreed. "Although, most of

our findings are useless junk. But fear not, we need no additional evidence. Our case against the members of the Managing Council is already ironclad."

"And what are the whereabouts of the former Councilors?" Lilit solicited.

Durojaiye was first to speak up noting, "They have been charged with treason and placed under house arrest. Unfortunately, we need to keep them separated, so the best thing for the short-term has been to confine them to their luxury suites."

Lilit pondered for a moment before asking, "Will they get a fair trial?"

This question seemed to tickle Durojaiye as he started chortling. "Lilit, they will get whatever you say they should. You are in charge now!"

Walking around the empty chamber and running her hand across the lower desks, Lilit asked, "What do you recommend?"

Durojaiye wasted no time and simply stated "Excommunication."

Lilit was not surprised as she already knew Durojaiye's feelings, but still couldn't bring herself around to his way of thinking. She thought that everyone was redeemable, and after all her time with Xander she even understood and respected their perspective a bit. Instead, she pressed the issue further.

"Another shuttle won't be coming for a year. That is, if Earth will even be willing to send one considering the current... political situation."

The implications of this did not seem to bother Durojaiye as he added, "We should not wait. The longer they are here, the more dangerous they may become. More so, they are taking up space and resources that others could be using."

"You are not talking excommunication," Ahmad interjected. "You are talking about mass executions via defenestration."

At this accusation, Durojaiye remained completely silent, confirming that was indeed his intent. Breaking the tension, Lilit ordered, "Ahmad, set up chambers for our prisoners in the Quarantine District and, if necessary, put the overflow in the Confinement District. If anyone is still there, clear them out and get them assigned quarters elsewhere. We aren't going to have immigrants for quite some time, so I believe we can use these spaces as a jail. Work with Protector Aritza outside on getting whatever guards and other resources will be needed to watch over our... guests."

"With all due respect," Durojaiye interrupted, "I should be doing this."

"No," Lilit immediately shut him down, "I don't

want you anywhere near the detainees. Besides, I need you focused on sniffing out any remaining malcontents, counterrevolutionaries, and anyone else who might be trouble for us. Aritza can handle running the jail; I expect you to work on filling it."

Although Lilit feared Durojaiye would be upset by this, he instead smiled and bowed, saying, "How wise you have become in these past six months since your return. These are all prudent decisions. Still, you have not answered the original query on what we are going to do with these prisoners. You cannot put off making a decision for long. There will be unrest, either from the other side or from our own. I can only do so much to keep it tamped down, and not forever."

Lilit thought for a moment before making her determination. "I'll ask one of our legal experts to set up a tribunal. The tribunal will then try, judge, and sentence them. We'll make it clear from the onset that the death penalty is not off the table. To avoid any appearance of impropriety, none of us can be on this tribunal, nor any of the other senior lieutenants in the Movement. No matter what the tribunal rules, we will live by their decisions, even if they choose to execute the former Councilors."

"Let us hope it does not come to that," Ahmad fervently prayed.

Chapter 32

Lilit woke up feeling refreshed for the first time in forever. Pursuant to her initial night alone in her new sleeping quarters, she could not have been happier with the results. While living with Ahmad and Durojaiye for seven months certainly had its ups and downs, the worst part had definitely been when it was time to go to bed. There were just so many noises and disturbances all night long that Lilit could simply not stay asleep. Of course, she was also enduring the constant stress of maintaining the Movement while planning a coup of the government, so that did not help either. Now that they had been in power for over a month, she had finally started to relax.

Stretching and throwing her sheets aside, Lilit was also soothed by recognizing that she was able to once again sleep in her preferred outfit: an old t-shirt and panties. Even though she had the partition curtain back in Ahmad's and Durojaiye's efficiency apartment, she never felt like she could walk around with the immodesty she was used to. Wearing more clothing to bed just seemed wrong to her given the temperatures on Aestas, but she could not get over her bashfulness around males, despite the platonic nature of their relationships. She also felt it would make them uncomfortable if they even caught a glimpse of her sneaking away to the restroom in the middle of the night in nothing but her unmentionables, so she avoided that possibility.

Although the space she currently inhabited was tiny—only slightly larger than the curtained-off area she had been living behind just the day before—it was all her own. Her bedroom connected to a private lavatory and closet, and all of the walls were completely soundproofed. Inside this enclosure was the only place she could count on to ever truly be by herself. Putting her hand to the exterior door, she swore that she could almost feel the guards standing on the other side. Of course, it was just her imagination, so to confirm she had her A.I. pull up a view from the exterior cameras and display it in her line of sight.

To her chagrin, she found she did not recognize either of the two Protectors on duty. Durojaiye and Aritza had devised a plan to regularly randomize everything about her security detail. Who was there, who their partners were, even how long their shifts were—everything was irregular. This way, they told her, it would minimize the chance of any single bad actor having a chance at getting to her, especially as she slept. Lilit was surprised to find that Aritza was even more paranoid than Durojaiye was, which was quite an accomplishment.

Closing out the feed, Lilit entered the bathroom to relieve herself and get cleaned up and ready for the day. There was no kitchen in her microunit, but most likely someone was already making their way to the office with breakfast. She hoped that she could escape for a while to work out in the fields on Level 1, but it was getting quite difficult to find the time and ability to slip away. Although she had teased Fiona back at the Venusian Embassy on Earth when she first arrived there, now she really felt like she was packing on the kilos. Something would have to be done about this, she decided.

As she stepped outside her sleeping chamber, the guards snapped to attention. "Thank you for watching over me," Lilit commended. "Please, you can wait outside now."

"Aye, Commander!" they said in unison before exiting into Aestas's underground hallways. Alone again, Lilit looked around at all that had been accomplished in this space. A month prior, it had been the Managing Council Chambers. Since the revolution, maintenance personnel had physically separated an area to be Lilit's own personal compartment while the rest had been gutted. Gone was the raised semi-circular desk that was used to convey power over those below. Instead, there was one oval table that could seat twenty of them at a time. Lilit had chosen to have her workstation situated at the top point. At the same elevation were a number of desks and work areas, set up almost like an old rocket launch complex from the era before the space elevator.

Everything in the room faced towards a set of screens, much to Lilit's annoyance. She had not wanted them, but Ahmad had insisted it would be a better way to work together and see the same things rather than trying to do it in virtual spaces where they might be experiencing the input differently. After much haranguing, Lilit gave in and let him do what he wanted. There was one large screen in the center that was about three meters diagonal, which in turn was surrounded by many smaller monitors. Flipping them on, Lilit found that some were camera scenes from all over the colony while a large number were blank. Anyone who toiled within this revamped chamber had access to put their own views onto any monitor as well as move anything to the large center one. At the moment, it was completely empty and all the sound was muted.

Closest to the table were two desks of honor. Just as she was running her hands over them, their occupants entered after clearing their own security procedure.

"Ah, Lilit!" Ahmad flinched. "I did not expect to find you here already!"

"Well, my commute was rather short," Lilit retorted. They all had a little chuckle at that and she asked, "Were you able to sleep well without me?"

"Actually, no," Ahmad admitted. "I was quite worried about you. Durojaiye slept like a baby, though, because he has no heart."

"This is true," Durojaiye deadpanned while his mouth opened into a yawn, as well.

When they first devised the plan for this space, Durojaiye had wanted to call it the "War Room". Ahmad was the one who came up with the more benign and far less threatening "Aestas Room of Management"—or just "ARM" for short. Right as she was about to ask their opinion on something, breakfast arrived, followed by more of the lieutenants from the Movement who had become the core group for the "Transitional Leadership Assembly". They all sat around the conference table and chitchatted in a casual manner. Lilit was trying to entrench a sense of normalcy and routine into their lives. She didn't want them to be on constant edge and burn out from the exhaustion of just staying alive.

Finally getting down to business, Lilit said, "Alright everyone, I want to go over a few things before getting into today's usual business. As everyone knows, the tribunal members are almost finalized and the trial for the former members of the Managing Council will soon begin. I think we can now officially say the old Council has been disbanded, but now what? When should we cede the TLA's power and set a date for our first real free election? And what should that election cover? I mean, should we be looking at replacing Councilors within the current system, or should we be electing people to write a new Constitution?"

Everyone in the room started looking at each other before all eyes focused in on Durojaiye. "What is it?" Lilit asked him.

Durojaiye sighed and said, "It would appear that I have been nominated to bring you to your senses. Lilit, there is no reason to do any of those things right now."

"Why not?" Lilit probed, flabbergasted. "The 'T' in 'TLA' stands for 'Transitional'. We are the 'Transitional Leadership Assembly', designed to act as a temporary government until such a time that we can have the full realization of a true republic."

"She does not understand," Ahmad offered.

"Understand what?" Lilit retorted.

In response, Durojaiye stood up and walked over to the main screen. He turned it on and brought up a view from outside the chamber. The hallways were crammed with thousands of people who were chanting something, but the audio was still off.

"What are they saying?" Lilit innocently inquired.

Durojaiye slowly brought up the volume and the invocation became clearer and clearer, louder and louder. The entire chamber started echoing with it, the cacophony rivaling the sound of the bell that Durojaiye had once rung with his foot in there.

All of the people were repeating her name over and over again. "Lilit! Lilit! Lilit!"

"Wow," Lilit intoned, "I'm flattered, but that doesn't answer my questions."

To this, everyone laughed as if she had told the most hilarious joke. When they finally calmed down, Durojaiye answered, "Lilit, do you not see? Now is not the time to undertake yet another massive societal transformation. The people of Aestas have anointed you the Queen of Venus... and we are all your loyal subjects!"

Chapter 33

"It's not enough!" Lilit barked as she slammed her hands on the conference table. "One-percent here, three-percent there—this is not giving us the housing capacity we need. In the two months we've been in charge, we've barely made any headway in resolving the overcrowding problem, which, might I remind you, is the only reason we took over in the first place. We are a single-issue government and yet we are still struggling!"

"You cannot think of it in terms of individual projects," Ahmad calmly explained. "It must be looked at in aggregate. By implementing all of these solutions, we can increase human living space by at least fifteen-percent, on the low end."

"You know my policy," Lilit reprimanded.

Sighing, Ahmad parroted, "'Hope for the best, plan for the worst.'"

"Exactly," Lilit agreed. "So, I don't want to hear the upside numbers or that these are just the 'low end' of what is possible. Tell me the worst-case-scenario. Be realistic with me."

"Candidly," Durojaiye interjected, "without more extreme measures, it is more likely-than-not to peter out at a ten-point gain."

Ahmad shot Durojaiye a glare and demanded to know, "When did you become the expert statistician at this table? Last I checked, you were responsible for safety and security within Aestas."

Durojaiye turned back towards Ahmad and declared, "Overpopulation is a security issue. Lilit is right; if we do not relieve the pressure, there will be a revolt. There are expectations for this government to deliver on its promises. Waiting in the wings are the extremist factions of the Movement that want to prove that their methods are the only way."

"You mean the 'True Movement'," Aritza offered with disgust from further down the table, as far away from Durojaiye as possible—something that had not gone unnoticed by Lilit. "I wish you would let me do something about them."

"Arresting or harassing them would not resolve anything," Durojaiye espoused back. "They must be handled. Consider this: on the other end of the spectrum are the toadies of the former government who resent us completely. Should we push this so-called 'True Movement' too much, they will turn to others to realize their intentions. Ahmad, back me up here.

As someone so entrenched in human history such as yourself would know, stranger bedfellows have been made in the past."

Before Ahmad could argue one way or another, Lilit interceded. "Enough, enough, children; we don't need to fight each other here; we all want the same thing. Durojaiye, what are some of the more radical measures that those on the fringes think we should be implementing?"

"You are not going to like it," Durojaiye predicted.

"So what?" Lilit asked. "I want all ideas on the table, good or bad. Let's hear their solutions."

"Depopulation." Durojaiye stated.

"What?" Lilit questioned.

"I told you that you would not like it," Durojaiye affirmed. "Lilit, when you were on Earth, you negotiated a number of concessions from the Terran Government Subcommittee on Terrestrial Colonies."

"I suppose you could look at it that way," Lilit demurred. "And we have implemented some of that with the immigration ban. Coupling that with our own plummeting birthrate will certainly ensure in the long-term that things will get easier. But we are talking decades; we need something much more impactful far sooner."

"Right," Durojaiye agreed, "and that means getting rid of people."

"Durojaiye, we've already discussed this ad nauseum," Lilit reprimanded. "The tribunal will decide the fate of all of the alleged criminals."

"I am not talking about that," Durojaiye insisted. "I am thinking about an incentive program to leave Venus entirely."

Lilit paused, taken off-guard. She had not seriously considered a voluntary exodus before. Pacing, she ruminated on the implications before deciding, "No, I do not want to create a new Venusian diaspora and then try to get our people to return to their homeland in a couple of generations. We are a unique culture in the whole cosmos, and that deserves to be preserved and protected."

"I agree," Ahmad chimed in. "I have seen many groups scattered all over the Earth that forgot who they were and where they came from. The pressure is always to integrate into the society where you live, and that in turn leads to intermixing and the destruction of identity."

Lilit smiled to herself as Ahmad seemed to miss the irony that he himself had forsaken his roots in his quest to become a Venusian. Picking up where she left off, Lilit articulated, "Alright, then, if we are going to maintain ourselves as one people, then there is only one choice: we must have a second city."

Everyone at the table broke out into chatter amongst themselves. Rising up from the rabble were questions like, "How can we possibly do that? We don't have any natural resources! Earth wouldn't help us before; they certainly won't do so now! Would the Martians or the Belters be willing to work with us? No, they are thoroughly under the thumb of the Terran Government."

Suddenly, a voice rose up from the crowd. Durojaiye testified to all, "Ahmad has been working on a plan and he is ready to present it!"

Everyone quieted down and looked towards Ahmad. His eyes widened in shock as he said, "No, I have not verified everything yet; there are too many moving variables."

"Please, my friend," Durojaiye pleaded. "Your plan is sound and the details can be finalized. Everyone here needs to know the hope you are keeping in your back pocket. Our Queen needs to be able to deliver something to her lieges."

Lilit hated when Durojaiye invoked this royal moniker when referring to her, but she could not deny its effectiveness. Even with people who knew her well, it made them sit up straighter and listen. All the other members of their Transitional Leadership Assembly had taken up the same rhetoric and were quoted in public calling her "Queen Lilit". She even heard the chants from some of their citizens. It was out of her hands for the time being, so she had no choice but to roll with it.

"It's okay, Ahmad," she beseeched. "Even if your idea is not fully baked, I would like to hear it. I'm sure it's quite interesting."

Realizing he had been backed into a corner, Ahmad stood up, walked over to the big screen, and sent his files to be exposed for all there to see.

Ahmad brought up a representative partial map of the Sol System that was displayed at an obtuse angle so as to make the heavenly bodies contained there within easier to see. This simulation, in particular, consisted of an oversized Earth and Venus circling a miniaturized sun. As the planets continued to circumnavigate the central star, a timer at the bottom indicated that Earth and Venus got somewhat close to each other every nineteen months, more or less.

Speaking to this model, Ahmad began, "What you are seeing here should be familiar to everyone in this room. When Earth and Venus are near each other, we call this an 'inferior conjunction'. But to get from Earth to Venus, the shuttle does not leave at the exact moment when our planets are closest. Instead, the ship takes off before the conjunction happens and gets into Venus's orbit as Venus itself 'catches up', so to speak. In other words, one has to leave and head out in what we will generously call a straight line and wait for the planet in motion to reach them. We just happen to be good enough at the math that all of this happens practically simultaneously. Thus, from the traveler's perspective, it looks like an intended direct flight from one planet to the other.

"When a shuttle arrives, it only has a few weeks to offload its passengers and cargo, pack up everything going back to Earth, and take off again. Basically, the vessel makes the same trip in reverse as at that point Earth is trailing behind while Venus is a little bit ahead. It leaves Venus, goes on the predetermined track, and waits for the Earth to catch up on that end. Again, it is almost completely seamless nowadays, and you can clearly see this in the mockup I have on the screen."

With these words, Ahmad added a spaceship to the simulation with dashed strokes showing the flight paths. "Here, we only have two bodies to keep track of," Ahmad continued, "so it is rather simple, at least as far as orbital mechanics goes. Now, pay attention to what happens when I add Mercury—the planet closest to the sun—into the mix."

Upon that pronouncement, Ahmad did just that. Watching the facsimile of the solar system, Lilit saw that there were occasions when Mercury and Earth were actually next to each other while Venus was on the other side of the sun. The same would happen when Venus and Mercury were in inferior conjunction while Earth was as far away as possible, much like where Durojaiye and Aritza were currently sitting in relation to each other at the table. "Ah, Lilit, you have noticed," Ahmad observed without her saying a word. "Now watch this: coming up in this next cycle will be a syzygy."

"A what?" Lilit finally broke her silence.

"A confluence when three or more celestial bodies line up roughly in a row," Ahmad explained. "Yes, there it is! Let me pause here."

Sure enough, Earth, Venus, and Mercury were in an almost-exact column. Ahmad further expounded, "This example happens to also be when Mercury appears to be near its aphelion—the point at which it is furthest from the sun and thus closest to Venus. All celestial bodies in our solar system have an elliptical orbit around the sun, but some are more pronounced than others. We call this the 'eccentricity', and we measure it on a scale from zero to one. Zero would be a perfect circle and one... well, you wouldn't be in orbit anymore.

"Venus has an exceptionally low eccentricity of zero-point-zero-zero-seven. Basically, its orbit is in an almost a perfect circle, and certainly the closest object to being so within the entire Sol System—

whether we are talking about a planetoid, an asteroid, a comet, or anything else. For comparison, Earth is zero-point-zero-one-seven. The numerical difference sounds small, but it comes out to nearly a hundred and fifty percent difference.

"And then there is Mercury. Mercury has an eccentricity of zero-point-two-zero-six, almost thirty times more than Venus. It is rather similar to the dwarf binary planetoid Pluto-Charon, which has such an ovular trajectory that it actually crosses over Neptune's path, making it sometimes closer to the sun than the furthest out of the full main-sequence planets. Mercury would be similar if it were not so close to the sun. But what is most important to take away from that is how near it can get to us."

"Ahmad," Lilit interrupted, "this is all very... informative... but I fail to see how this is going to resolve our housing crisis."

"Please, bear with me just a bit longer," Ahmad begged. Lilit knew if it were anyone else, she would have had them sit down by now, but because it was Ahmad, she just nodded to let him continue to lead up to whatever it was he was suggesting.

"Now, let me add something to this chart," Ahmad said as he inserted the current calendar onto the screen. The date was for a point ten months in the future. "While a Mercury-Venus-Earth syzygy happens in large cycles of time, one is coming up very soon, when the next shuttle is scheduled to arrive from Earth. More so, it is not a precise alignment, but one where Mercury will be falling behind a little bit. If we wanted to go to Mercury from Venus, we must think of Venus as the center as we did with our example from Earth in the beginning. Therefore, we must leave for Mercury when it is trailing behind so that it can catch up to our vessel."

"Wait, wait, wait," Lilit jumped in again. "I think I missed something. Putting aside all my other questions about logistics and sanity, why would we want to go to Mercury?"

Unperturbed, Ahmad laid out the facts, "Mercury is nothing but a big rock. It is sixty to seventy percent metals and the rest are silicas. These are the very ingredients that Aestas is made out of. We cannot get to the surface of Venus to mine it, but we can easily do so on Mercury. There are some existing operations already there that we can take advantage of, especially to get below the surface to relative safety. But by extricating the raw materials we need from Mercury, we can bring them back with us and built a second Aestas here in orbit."

Lilit was floored by the sheer audacity of the plan,

especially coming from Ahmad. At the same time, she had to admit the possibility excited her. Here was what she was truly looking for: a project for the entire citizenry of Aestas to get behind that gave them everything they wanted while sticking it to the Terran Government by completely circumventing them. She saw that this was the scheme that would prove them all wrong and demonstrate that Venus could survive in the upcoming age of the Torch Drive.

Before Lilit could start asking questions, Durojaiye added, "This, of course, means that we will have to appropriate a shuttle that, ostensibly, belongs to the Terran Government."

"Won't they quickly notice that their ship is missing?" Lilit asked.

"That is the brilliance of Ahmad's plan," Durojaiye claimed. "If we just took the shuttle at any random time, we would have to wait months to launch at an inferior conjunction with Mercury. That would certainly give Earth plenty of time to notice their ship was missing. But because of this syzygy, all they will be able to see is that their ship has launched when it was expected to do so. We can send regular signals and check-ins from there, and they will not realize something is amiss for months!

"Even then, what could they do? Mercury will be

moving further and further away from them and by the time it reaches an inferior conjunction with Earth and it is reasonable to attempt a crossing, what actions might they reasonably take? This is not some science fiction adventure; they do not have space lasers and torpedoes! All they have are orbital platforms with defensive weaponry against meteorites. Other than that, there are just shuttles parked there for the transportation of people and goods. And, more so, those ships are not free to go off on some wild-goose chase; they all have assignments to go back and forth between the other colonies like Mars. There is no such thing as a fully-armed and ready space force. Most importantly, there are no available resources to hunt us down."

"But we'd still have to convince them to actually send a shuttle," Lilit complained. "They haven't exactly been communicative since we overthrew their hand-picked government, you know."

"Admittedly, this is a bit of a hangup in the plan and something you would have to handle," Durojaiye acknowledged. "And although I am loath to admit it, there is but one person out there who may be able to help us convince HSA and the Terran Government to make this happen."

Lilit cringed as she said, "Xander."

"Xander," Durojaiye agreed.

After the Movement had taken over, Lilit had decided to leave Xander and the rest of the Venusian Embassy staff on Earth in place. If anything, she promoted Xander to being completely in charge. Although he had given up on saving Aestas, he still professed his commitment to the citizenry and provided Lilit with important intelligence. Since the Terran Government wouldn't talk to her directly, he was their only line of communication with them.

"Alright, I'll do it," Lilit agreed. "But I understand how Xander thinks, and he'll want to know what we will offer to get this shuttle to show up. Obviously, we've forbade any more immigration, so there cannot be any people aboard except for other Venusians coming home. Those passengers alone will not be enough to defray the costs of the journey. At the very least, we'll have to pay out-of-pocket to convince them to launch, but even then, it won't be enough."

"That brings us full circle," Durojaiye asserted. "If we tell them that we are using the shuttle to depopulate Aestas by sending people back to Earth and then onward to other colonies, they will be interested as it is within the confines of what you discussed before with the Terran Government Subcommittee on Terrestrial Colonies."

"And Xander is a proponent of depopulation, as well," Lilit recalled. "We don't have to let him in on the plan, then; he'd be happy to think he'd won and would revel in us turning to him to make it a reality. This is good, Durojaiye."

"But it has to appear real," Durojaiye warned. "We need to implement an actual depopulation program here, as I outlined earlier. No one outside of this room and the select few other people we bring into this conspiracy can know the true plan until it is too late. We have to prepare as if this depopulation effort is going to happen right up until the shuttle arrives. Only once everyone disembarks and the shuttle is fully unloaded will we be able to strike. There will be backlash both for creating the depopulation program and for yanking it away. Are you prepared for such subterfuge, resistance, and blowback?"

"Should we do this, we would have no choice," Lilit conceded. "And for the record, I don't care what happens to me. This is and has always been about saving Aestas. I'll do whatever it takes and make any sacrifice to ensure that happens."

At this affirmation, Durojaiye simply gave an appreciative nod.

Chapter 35

"Now, before I fully agree to implement this plan, there are a few other things I want to go through, first, okay?" Lilit requested of the room.

Once everyone agreed, she continued. "Durojaiye, you said that they couldn't catch up to us, but what about with the Torch Drive?"

Surprisingly, it was Ahmad who answered her by saying, "Durojaiye took the intelligence you gave him and inquired with his old connections on Earth. He was able to get his hands on some current specs, thus I have been able to run a few simulations. Basically, even though they can definitely attach a Torch Drive to an object and send it careening at the speeds they claim, they have not been able to figure out a way to dissipate the heat and radiation, among other concerns. If they attached this propulsion method to a ship, all they would succeed at doing is kill everyone on board. However, I believe they would be boiled alive before they were fatally irradiated."

"Ahmad, was it absolutely necessary to be that graphic and specific?" Lilit rebuked.

"I am afraid I am to blame for this," Durojaiye tendered. "He has become accustomed to how I would want to hear the specifics about the infinite ways we may expire at the hands of an uncaring universe."

"Anyway," Lilit segued as she opted to gloss over the exchange, "if they can't use the Torch Drive for transportation, then what are they doing with it?"

"As far as I can tell," Ahmad remarked, "they are just hooking them on to rocks in the Asteroid Belt and maybe the ice-balls in the Kuiper Belt beyond Neptune so that they can be brought back into Earth's orbit to be mined for resources. It is no different than what we want to do with Mercury except that instead of going all the way out there to do the excavations, they are bringing the raw materials straight to Earth to quarry on-site. It is probably a more economical plan, though I have not run the numbers as of yet."

"In other words," Lilit summarized, "the Torch Drives are no threat to us or our operations. Further, there is no chance that any person could possibly be strapped to one anytime soon."

"Yes, exactly," Ahmad agreed.

Lilit gave a sigh of relief at taking one worry off the table, so she decided it was time to move on to the next. "Alright, so let's assume Xander is able to convince the Terran Government to release the inter-planetary shuttle and send it here. How are we going to commandeer it, then?"

At this query, Durojaiye tagged back in. "While some people on the journey to Venus were busy obsessively monitoring their rad-count and dreaming of the future," he said while staring directly at Ahmad, "I was doing reconnaissance. To the untrained eye, it may have looked like I was up to nothing, but my methodologies are quite involved and sophisticated."

"You have made your point," Ahmad shot back, "so why do you not tell us what your amazing spy-craft produced before we all fall asleep?"

Durojaiye harrumphed before continuing, "Most of the below-deck staff on the shuttle are actually indentured employees. They are people who, for one reason or another, are indebted to HSA and are paying it back with their labor. They have no love or loyalty for HSA, quite the opposite actually. Because of that, they would probably not do anything to stop a hostile boarding party, especially if we offer to help eliminate their debt."

"You mean a bribe," Lilit translated.

Shrugging, Durojaiye said, "Call it whatever you want. The important thing is that the same could be said of the few peace officers on board. HSA has not seriously considered the idea of someone trying to overtake a vessel or engage in a mutiny, and that is their critical mistake. The guards have no real allegiance to HSA or its property and would not risk their lives to protect it. They are just hired hands! Most could be... persuaded... with the same techniques."

"And those who cannot be 'persuaded', as you say?" Lilit delved.

"If you think about it this way, we are talking about removing eighty to ninety percent of the potential resistance just by making them an offer they cannot refuse. For the rest, we have more than enough of our own security forces to overwhelm and dispatch the most stubborn individuals."

Frowning, Lilit stated, "If we are seriously talking about making this pipedream into a reality, no one can die. Do I make myself clear? We lose all the moral high ground if a single person loses their life, or is even seriously injured."

At the other end of the table, Aritza suddenly broke their silence and interjected with a shout, "Queen-Commander, wait! It's one thing to talk about all of this in the hypothetical, but you can't really be considering going down this path?! Wanting to go to Mercury and find a way to get the materials and resources we need is a fine goal, but what we are talking about here is something else entirely. This is a declaration of war against the Earth!"

Durojaiye brushed aside their concerns saying, "Aritza, you, more than anyone, are capable of doing this. My liege, do you remember when you threatened to send me to the holding cells on the docking platform?" Once Lilit nodded, Durojaiye persisted, "We can use those to detain any malcontents. First, send me and the rest of the Intelligence Division up there as soon as the ship arrives and we can manage the wetware front. We will find out who will work with us, and who will be a problem. After surreptitiously tagging the potential troublemakers, Aritza and their team can sweep in and quietly remove them. Aritza, you have a lot of experience at managing prisons now, right?"

Aritza could only fold their arms over their chest and lean back in their chair, obviously realizing that Durojaiye had accounted for any of their objections.

Ending the uncomfortable quiet, Ahmad declared, "Whatever we do, we would have to do it very quickly. We have a very small window to clear the shuttle, place our people and equipment on, and get underway. The turnover is certainly tight, but it is still quite possible. Nevertheless, we can have no mistakes, no errors; everything must run perfectly, like clockwork. There is no room for any contingency. I cannot change the laws of physics, the universe, or orbital mechanics, so do not expect a last-minute miracle if we miss our chance. All I can do is harness the rules of nature and put them to use for us."

Lilit got up from her seat without a word and walked over to the large screen. She started playing with Ahmad's simulation, moving the planets back and forth, seeing when they aligned in the past and when they were predicted to do so again in the future. Finally, she turned back to the assembly and said, "Then let's do it! We have less than ten months to prepare and implement this plan, though. If I have any doubts whatsoever as we approach the go-day, then I will cancel the mission. Is that satisfactory for you, Aritza?"

Aritza was silent for a moment themselves before acquiescing. Lilit then asked, "And you, too, Durojaiye? If I choose to call it off, will you abort?"

"Of course," Durojaiye agreed.

"Good, then we have no time to waste. Let's get going to Mercury!" Lilit exclaimed with a genuine smile on her face as she excitedly thrust her fist into the air.

Chapter 36

Lilit was closely peering at Ahmad, who was standing there with his tablet in hand. In turn, Ahmad was intently watching each individual piece of equipment making its way through the docking area and onto the skimmer, looking up and down from his screen while they passed by. As every item left his sight and entered the cargo holds, she saw Ahmad check off a line on his inventory sheet. Taking every possible precaution, Ahmad had been reminding Lilit and everyone else who would listen for the past nearly ten months that nothing could be left to chance and no detail could be overlooked. Even though there was no real reason for Lilit to duplicate Ahmad's efforts, she had decided that she should be there, too.

Soon thereafter, the skimmer was fully loaded and the crew began preparations to head up to the docking platform in orbit. Durojaiye was already overhead to receive their goods. Ostensibly, though, he still had other duties he was performing. With the lull in activity, Lilit decided to broach a subject with

Ahmad that had been needling the inside of her brain.

"Ahmad..." Lilit began.

"Hmmmm?" was all he managed as he did not bother to look up from his work.

"I just want to make sure..." Lilit tried again. "What I mean is... are you really okay leaving Venus after all you did to get here?"

Ahmad paused what he was doing, put his tablet down on a counter in front of him, and turned to give Lilit his full attention. His face was completely serious as he measured his words, "There will be no Venus if we do not do this. As such, it is my sacred duty to follow you to another world so we can save this one."

During their early planning, Lilit had made the unpopular decision that she would be leading the expedition. Durojaiye, Aritza, and almost the entire Transitional Leadership Assembly had been against the idea, especially since at that point she had only recently returned and they had just taken over control of the government a few months prior. Still, Lilit would not be dissuaded because she could not ask others to take this massive risk if she was not willing to do so herself. At that, Durojaiye then indicated that he would have to go as well, principally to watch over any converts from the crew. "Besides," he had said,

"I will already be up on the shuttle before anyone else, working on turning crewmembers to our side and uncovering the troublemakers. As such, there is no need for me to return to Aestas. Aritza, you will be comfortable filling my shoes while I am gone, right?"

Whether Aritza would be or not, they agreed wholeheartedly. Lilit sensed there was still a lot of tension and distrust between the two. In private, Lilit tried to assuage Aritza's concerns and emphasized how none of them would even be in this position without Durojaiye's help and insight. For some reason, that only seemed to agitate Aritza even more. "Just promise me," they requested, "that you will always choose Aestas first, even over your... friendship... with Durojaiye... or anyone else, for that matter."

"Aritza," Lilit insisted, "all of this is about Aestas. I have made innumerable sacrifices already, and am prepared to make any and all future ones that may be necessary."

"Then swear on your crown," Aritza insisted.

Aritza's persistence that she was royalty made Lilit incredibly uncomfortable. Because of their viewpoint, there was always a wall between them that could never be surmounted. Lilit wanted Aritza to be comfortable with her on a personal level, but she constantly caught them looking at her with awe. If it would make Aritza feel better, she decided, she would do as asked. Placing her hand over her heart, Lilit stated without breaking character once, "By my royal pledge, I will always choose the interests of Aestas over those of any individual, no matter how close or important they are to me personally."

Lilit could see Aritza visibly relaxing as they said, "Thank you, my Queen-Commander."

"In exchange," Lilit interrupted, "you will also train on piloting the skimmer and the forthcoming tugboat we will be building to support the construction of the second city."

Aritza blushed at Lilit's suggestion. Although it was difficult to get many private details out of the reserved Aritza, she did learn that they daydreamed about being a space cop. It was such a silly aspiration that Lilit insisted on making it a reality. Stuttering, Aritza relented and they finally seemed to be fully in concurrence with her.

While Aritza and Durojaiye had been hesitant in backing Lilit, Ahmad had completely supported her from the beginning. But that was because he had decided that he was going as well, which Lilit tried to dissuade him from. Since he was not intimidated by her like Aritza and most of the Transitional Leadership Assembly, Ahmad had said, "I am the only person on all of Venus with any knowledge of and involvement in mining activities. Therefore, I must go and lead the expedition on the ground."

"You worked on an archaeological dig in a desert for one season!" Lilit reminded him.

Ahmad smiled broadly as he declared, "And yet, that is still thousands of hours more experience than any other person on our colony. Is this not true?"

Realizing that she had obviously fallen right into Ahmad's trap, Lilit had been forced to agree.

After this meeting, Lilit had accompanied Ahmad and Durojaiye back to their apartment. Of course, several Protectors were trailing behind, keeping a watchful eye. Much to Lilit's embarrassment, when they came across other people they usually stopped and even sometimes bowed or kneeled. "All hail Queen Lilit!" became a common cry in her presence, no matter how much she tried to discourage them. Lilt began to suspect that someone else was urging the citizenry of Aestas to react to her personage this way, but she pushed it from her mind as she had much more pressing issues to keep on top of.

Once out of sight of the public and the TLA, Lilit let loose with the only two people in all existence who still treated her like a normal human being. Even her own parents were somewhat standoffish with her, like she was some stranger who had come to their door to sell them a useless trinket. More often than not, they quickly sent her out of their home, always insisting that she must have more important things to do than waste her time with them. She knew they meant well, but it was disheartening. Lilit did not want to lose her connection to the important people in her life—or the community in general—yet it appeared that in order to be "Queen", she must be separated from them.

Not for the first time, Lilit doubted the choices she had made that had led them all to this ridiculous scheme. But that was a burden just for her to carry; no one else could ever know. She realized that she needed to project an air of confidence, otherwise the others who looked to her for hope and guidance would falter. They had a very precarious grasp on Aestas, and she could not afford to show any weakness lest it slip from between her fingers.

Suddenly, Lilit was nostalgic for the days of their mass protests. Sure, she wouldn't be able to come home for days on end and would be tired, dirty, and smelly, but at least she was out there, too, among the people and fighting the same battle. She felt so disconnected from their own cause now, like she was watching herself from the outside. That was another reason she had to lead this mission to Mercury; she needed to be on the front lines again and use her hands to actually do something. When she tried to explain all of this to Ahmad and Durojaiye, they were sympathetic, but also giddy.

"This is even more reason for all of us to go then," Ahmad noted. "After all, we were separated for such a long time while you were on Earth. I do not wish for us to be apart again."

"Neither do I," Durojaiye insisted. "I was only thinking about what would be best in regard to the long-term plans for Aestas, not my own wants and desires. I would very much like to be stuck in an even smaller space, trapped underground, for month-and-months on end, with no one but you two!"

Lilit smiled and giggled, hugged both her dearest friends, and declared, "Then it's settled. We'll never be apart again!"

As Lilit and Ahmad watched the skimmer take off, Ahmad broke her out of her memories by saying, "However, Lilit, if you are having misgivings, it is still not too late to call things off."

Lilit shook her head and professed, "No, we must do this. Nothing has changed in the past ten months that would alter my opinion and standing. We've started implementing all of the small ways we can release new housing and that effort will continue unabated while we are away. There really is nothing on Aestas that we could do that the rest of the TLA cannot handle on its own. Everything is in place. The most important thing is fulfilling our real promise: the creation of a second Aestas."

"Very well," Ahmad acquiesced. "Then, when the skimmer returns, we should have one more cargo load before we ourselves head up and start our new adventure."

"You know," Lilit segued in a slight change of subject, "Durojaiye has emphasized that the 'branding' for the new floating city is very important. Have you settled on a name like we discussed?"

"I do not know why you are putting such pressure on me!" Ahmad grumbled.

"Stop trying to deflect and answer the question," Lilit teased as she ruffled Ahmad's hair.

Sighing, Ahmad admitted, "Well, I have narrowed it down, but I do have my favorite..."

"C'mon, tell me!" Lilit demanded as she tickled Ahmad to gain his compliance.

After laughing and pushing her off several times, Ahmad gushed, "Alright, alright, I yield, please stop!" Since he did not immediately spill his guts, Lilit playfully pouted as she looked at him with exaggeratedly sad eyes. Finally, he relented and said, "It is 'Freyr'."

"Freyr?" Lilit asked. "Tell me why."

Ahmad began to explain his reasoning, "Freyr is the name of a Norse deity who is the personification of summer, just like Aestas is to the Romans. Additionally, Freyr is representative of many similar symbols like fair weather, abundant harvests, and prosperity. More so, according to legend, Freyr was willing to lay down his sword in the name of love. And yet, the sword still continued to fight, all on its own!

"It is my fervent hope that when this is all over and Freyr is flying in the skies next to Aestas that we, too, will be able to lay down our arms for love and peace. But the threat of our might will remain in the back of everyone's minds, ensuring that no one ever challenges Venus again."

Lilit was completely silent as she continued to stare at her friend. After a while, he jumped in the air and said, "Oh, you think it is awful, I am so sorry for ever mentioning it!"

In response, Lilit wrapped him in a hug and sobbed into his shoulder, "It's perfect, Ahmad! Thank you so much. We go to Mercury to free the mighty Freyr from its regolith!"

The moment ended when Lilit's A.I. interrupted to say that Durojaiye was calling. Lilit pushed the call onto Ahmad's tablet so that they could both respond. Although it felt odd in her hands, she picked up the flat computer screen and saw an upward view of Durojaiye, looking up his nostrils.

"Oh, I did not know you two were together," Durojaiye declared. "Good, then I can catch you both up at once. Are you hearing me well?"

"Yes," Ahmad confirmed. "Surprisingly well, considering your location in orbit."

"Excellent," Durojaiye said before continuing. "I wanted to let you know that two more of the junior pilots have defected to our side. With the addition of them, we now have a full-enough crew complement so that we should be safe to launch."

"But we still don't have any of the senior pilots?" Lilit prodded. Durojaiye had lived up to his word and—although it cost them a lot of money and other promises—had managed to convert the vast majority of the shuttle crew to their side. Or, more correctly, convinced them not to oppose their plans. There was no bloodshed as even those who refused to assist them peacefully surrendered and were now locked away in the holding cells on the outer space platform.

Nevertheless, Durojaiye had not completely given up on recruiting these people. He had been sharing their plight with them and Lilit knew that recordings of her speeches, interactions with the Managing Council, and protest appearances were being played around the clock, as a sort of reeducation effort. From what Durojaiye had shared with her, it was quite clear that the Earthers had no idea what was happening on Aestas. That said, she could not decide if it was because the information was being suppressed or if it was willful ignorance. Ahmad tried to assuage her with the possibility that they had no frame of reference and therefore simply did not care.

"No," Durojaiye answered in response to Lilit's query. "The younger ones are certainly more sympathetic to our predicament, especially after being informed of all we have had to endure. Unfortunately, the older and more senior pilots are staunch HSA supporters, first and foremost. Interestingly enough, they do not necessarily support the Terran Government or Earth Central Command, but they seem to believe that HSA is a buffer that is protecting them from an uncaring bureaucracy. Their views do not really differ that much compared to ours in that regard, but they seem to have some unwavering loyalty to HSA that I am having great difficulty untangling. I am not sure if it is even possible to counteract it to deprogram them, but I am willing to continue trying."

"We really only have another couple of days left," Lilit noted. "I think it's time to give it a rest and find out where they would like to stay for the next long while. Aritza has confirmed that the Confinement District is ready to receive them if they want to spend their time in gravity. There is also now a permanent Coordinator substation there, so we can offer them a rapid recovery. Emphasize to them that they are not our enemies and we do not wish them harm, but we cannot allow them free movement."

"I think that message would be better received if it came from you instead of me, their known jailer," Durojaiye articulated.

Lilit realized that he was correct. How could they

believe the person who had imprisoned them? "Alright," she agreed, "I'll record a message pertaining to this and send it up there so that you can play it for everyone who's still detained."

"Good," Durojaiye replied. "If I might add, though, you should also have Deb doll you up in some type of regalia. It will make you look more official that way, and they will take it better. These are people who very much believe in the power of hierarchy, and you can convey your superior status with your regal look and countenance alone."

Blushing, Lilit wanted to yell at Durojaiye for his misogyny, but she also knew he was in the right to say so. Few were willing to speak to her so bluntly nowadays, so she appreciated his candor. Still, not wanting to fully satisfy his distasteful suggestion, Lilit brushed it off with, "Fine, fine."

Before signing off, however, there was one last thing that was bothering her. "Durojaiye," she began, "how do we really know we can trust these people who have claimed to join our side?"

"We cannot," Durojaiye admitted. "The only thing I can assure you is that I and the agents of the Intelligence Division will all be keeping a very close eye on each and every one of them, so you need not worry about any potential betrayal."

Two months into their journey to Mercury, Lilit was alone—per usual—in her quarters inside the transport vessel. She had been given the former captain's barracks and, thus, had more space to herself than any other person aboard. They certainly had not brought along that many people, so there was technically a lot of area to spread out. At least, that was the plan for the voyage to "the swiftest planet". On the way back, they intended to fill almost every part of the ship with raw materials. During their long wait between worlds, much of their crew was involved in removing bulkheads and separation barriers so as to expand the cargo holds into the living zones. HSA was not going to be happy when they saw what they had done to their ship.

Thus far, things had been relatively quiet. There was one attempted saboteur who was revealed to be a Terran Government zealot, but Durojaiye had been able to quickly dispatch him. Currently, he was locked in his own quarters that were under constant guard. Durojaiye had wanted to send him out the airlock, but Lilit insisted on mercy. "He's not wrong, Durojaiye," she had scolded her friend. "We are thieves, we are imprisoning his innocent comrades and coworkers, we have committed treason of the highest order. Look at it from his perspective; he truly believes he was trying to save civilization from terrorists like us."

Against Durojaiye's recommendations, Lilit even went to visit their locked-up foe. She was hoping to see if he could be talked down from his grandstanding so that he could freely move about again and perhaps do some useful work instead of just being a leach, but it did not work out. He actually tried to spit in her face. However, since microgravity didn't work that way, his phlegm never left his mouth and a medic had to be called in to suction it out before he choked to death. Durojaiye shook his head and said, "It would have been more prudent to let him die by choking on his own spittle."

Putting that unfortunate experience aside, Lilit turned on her virtual monitor and looked through her messages. She had instructed her A.I. to create several filter layers to prioritize her responsibilities, but it always felt like she was missing things. The Movement, the Transitional Leadership Assembly, and the Mercury Mission were all so huge and unwieldy, and she was stretched thin as it was. She needed some clones to stay on top of it all, but knew that wouldn't really help.

While Lilit was scrolling, a large video message started downloading. From the metadata, she could see it had come from the Venusian Embassy on Earth. Everything was delayed right now because all data was being relayed through Venus, so who knew how old this dispatch really was? Still, for some reason, she felt she should wait for it to finish loading and watch it immediately. A little over an hour later, an alert went off to let her know that the communique was available. She quickly hit play and Xander appeared directly in her line of sight.

"Hello, Lilit," he began simply. "Or should I be addressing you as 'your majesty'? How about 'Queen-Commander'? Well, to me, you'll always be that damn upstart who cost me my job. Then again, you gave me this much cushier one, so how about we drop the formalities?

"Okay, you can obviously tell that I'm stalling. It's just, I don't know where to begin. Well, let me put it this way: I am completely pissed off that you commandeered a transport vessel and are taking it to Mercury! You lied to me for months and kept this all hidden from me. I could have assisted you, you know.

But really, since I am your representative on Earth, a little heads up would have been nice before I was hauled before the President of the entire Terran Government to explain what the hell was going on!

"In case you are too dense to get what I'm implying, the Earthers have realized what you are up to. I'm guessing this is much sooner than you expected it to happen, but there you go. You keep underestimating the Terran Government and Earth Central Command. You think you can pull the wool over their eyes for the sake of Aestas, but I have repeatedly warned you that it is a losing battle. Of course, you won't listen to me, so why am I wasting my breath?

"For once in your miserable existence, please believe me when I say that I'm looking out for you and what's best for the citizenry of Aestas. You, my dear, have now been made public enemy number one by Earth Central Command. They have a warrant out for your arrest and an extradition order to send you back to Earth so you can answer for your crimes. No, before you ask, I have no idea how they could possibly enforce this legal declaration, but I fear the worst. I've told you before, and you didn't take me seriously then, so I'll tell you again now: the Terran Government is willing to kill everyone. As far as they are concerned, Venus is their property and they can do with it whatever they see fit. Your little revolution is just some minor inconvenient hiccup in their grand plans.

"Despite all of our history together, despite all of our differences, I do care about what happens to you. More so, I am concerned about what happens to our people. Like it or not, you are responsible for all their lives, just as I was before you. It is a heavy responsibility, and it is one you must completely internalize and give yourself over to. You have to be willing to sacrifice yourself for the greater good. What was my sin, Lilit, that you felt you had to pluck the crown from my head? That I lived in a tiny bit of opulence to take the sting off? Well, now that is you, hiding in your own castle in the sky. It is the little bit of reward people like us give ourselves because we know in the end that we will be the bloody offering on the altar, with our throats split open.

"That is why I am asking you to do it yourself before the Terran Government does it for you. Fall on your sword, Lilit. It's not too late for you to turn that ship around and then hand yourself over to Earth Central Command. If you don't, everyone you hold dear will also be held accountable. Do you want to be responsible for what ultimately happens to them? You must realize that it cannot end well for anyone supporting you! Your only hand is to throw yourself at the mercy of the Terran Government, and beg them to let everyone else go free in peace. If you don't, I can assure you that they will make you watch while they destroy everyone and everything you hold dear. These are very vindictive people, Lilit; especially when the have been annoyed.

"I'll even sweeten the pot: if you want to take me down with you, I'll gladly accept. We'll both burn in the pits of hell, but it will be better for the rest of the poor souls on Aestas. Lilit, I may be stuck on Earth, but I still have family and friends back home. I have not forgotten them, not once. For their sakes, on my knees, I'm pleading with you: end this, end this now."

The video suddenly terminated and Xander faded from Lilit's view. She was shaking, which in turn was sending her careening around her cabin in the microgravity. Why had she watched that now when she already couldn't sleep? Completely unnerved, she knew she needed to find something to help her calm down, otherwise she would explode. She left her quarters and headed to the mess hall, hoping that there would be something, anything, there to aid in bringing her back to her right state of mind.

FROM MONARCH TO DEITY

Chapter 39

Tripping over her own two feet, Lilit started to fall forward. It was such a slow fall, though, compared to what she experienced all her life on Aestas and during her sojourn on Earth, that she was able to spin her arms rapidly enough to stop herself and remain upright. Even though they had been on Mercury for four months now, she was still having a rough time adjusting to its low gravity.

Many of the miners who Lilit's contingent had met since they arrived on the planet had grown up on Mars and had no issues adapting to life on Mercury. At first, it seemed strange to Lilit considering Mars had a radius half that of Earth and Venus, while Mercury's was just a third of that size. However, Ahmad had explained that its composition was far denser, meaning Mars and Mercury had almost the exact same gravity. As such, the immigrants from the red planet appeared to have little problem with their adjustments after their arrivals at the swift one.

Lilit, on the other hand, was struggling in a way that she had not been prepared for—both physically and mentally. Although she easily acclimatized to what was colloquially called zero-g aboard their transport shuttle, having a lesser gravity was throwing her off in ways her inner ear could not cope with. For the first time, she truly understood her former clients from when she was a Coordinator who could not manage the slight disparity in gravity when migrating from Earth to Venus. To most, including her, the negligible difference was hardly noticeable. Yet Mercury was proving too much—or rather, too little—for her and she worried that she would never be able to cope with it.

Closing her eyes, Lilit chanted her manta under her breath to herself—īn nīz bogzarad, this too shall pass—over and over again until she felt halfway normal. Even closing and opening her eyes had helped as her vision came back into better alignment. Unfortunately, one of the side effects of her now third trip through outer space had been a diminished ability of her eyes to remain focused. Ahmad was trying to find a way to modify her ocular implants to correct her deteriorating eyesight, but it was all trial and error. As skilled and knowledgeable as he was, this particular effort involved an understanding of human biology that even he lacked. Still, there was no one else to turn to, so she decided that she would pull him aside for another attempt after this meeting.

Continuing down the habitat corridor, Lilit finally approached the door to the room they had dug out to be a gathering space. The native and immigrant force on Mercury seemed to be quite amused with their Venusian guests, Lilit found. During one interaction, Gang Chiu—an important leader in the community who also acted as their primary conduit to everything else going on planet-side—explained that permanently defined space was nonsensical. They were constantly digging and moving forward, so they simply dragged their living quarters and all their scant possessions along with them, a relentless nomadic life. For Lilit, who had lived in a place that never grew or changed, the idea of incessantly relocating was unfathomable. She and the other indigenous Venusians thrived on having specifically designated rooms that could be counted on to always be there and to function as their intended purposes.

While they were culturally quite different, Lilit did find the Mercurians to be very accommodating, all things considered. Obviously, they could not ask permission ahead of time to invade their world as any messages between them could have been easily intercepted. After receiving Xander's warning, Lilit knew the cat was out of the bag anyway and decided that they should break radio silence. It took a while before they heard back, but Gang Chiu was the first to respond to their outstretched hand.

As Gang Chiu explained, there really wasn't a government, per se, on Mercury. Each group was its own private consortium that received a license from the Terran Government that granted permission to mine the planet. "Obviously, you do not have such a license," he noted, "but it is not like anyone here has any means to stop you. That said, I'm sure we can work out some mutually beneficial understanding."

Ahmad was instrumental in their parleys with Gang Chiu's crew as he was, as he declared, "quite familiar with the techniques and expectations for working within the Chinese negotiation method." Lilit had no idea what that meant as she did not realize there were differences in the way various ethnic groups from Earth approached making a deal. All she knew was that this was going to end up being some other type of bribe-by-any-other-name, though she had no idea how they were going to pay it.

Once the terms were worked out, Ahmad explained to her, "You see, Gang Chiu typically only hires other ethnic Chinese people as he finds it creates an easier and, in his words, 'better' cohesion and harmony amongst their group. That is why there are so many Martians among his employees, as Chinese explorers made up a significant portion of the early settlers on Mars, too. I know this is challenging for you to understand coming from such an amalgamation as Aestas, but on a place like Mars with nearly unlimited stretches to spread out to, most spacefaring Earth-countries created their own separate colonies. Even today, despite all of the time that has passed since the advent of a united Earth under the Terran Government and the intermixing of all locales, these populations have remained in a rather homogeneous existence and maintain most of their progenitor culture's influences."

"I think I understood about half of that," Lilit confessed, "but what does that mean for us?"

"Yes, well," Ahmad stumbled, "the thing is that there is a certain... level of morale... that Gang Chiu is concerned about amongst his crew. Basically, they are rather protective, a closed-in circle if you will. Therefore, we must do things that will allow him to save face with his people."

"And what, pray tell, does that entail?" Lilit probed to get some definitive details.

Ahmad was silent for a moment as he seemed to be looking for the right words that would make it plain to Lilit. Finally, he said, "We will sign an agreement to be subcontractors to his crew, but maintain a completely separate existence. This way, we will technically be covered under his license and he will not be guilty of any violation for helping us. However, we must work completely apart from his main contingent and go only where he says we can go. You can rest assured, Gang Chiu will direct us to mine in the opposite direction of anyone else, so our interactions will be minimal."

"That all seems fair…" Lilit tried to begin.

"I am not done," Ahmad interrupted. "Although that will be the general situation, Gang Chiu will reserve the right to pull any member of our crew, any piece of our equipment, and any other resources from our stockpiles—at any time—to work exclusively on his particular projects."

"Jesus, Ahmad!" Lilit exclaimed as she shook her head. "What else did you give away with the kitchen sink to buy Gang Chiu's cooperation?"

"Nothing directly," Ahmad admitted, "but there is definitely an overhanging threat of a future payment in order to continue to guarantee his silence, even after we leave."

"Need I remind you," Lilit reprimanded, "that our government is already overextended and there is no money to be had?"

"Not money, I fear," Ahmad noted. "It is more likely to come from tributes. I imagine that we will have to turn over a certain percentage of our mined metals. Further, when we depart, it seems likely that Gang Chiu will ask us to leave in his personal care an assortment of yet-to-be-specified pieces of the equipment that we fabricated on Aestas and brought with us. Gang Chiu has often reiterated the considerable risk he is taking not just in the here-and-now, but throughout all time, for harboring wanted criminals such as us—most especially, you, Lilit. He may also have to use what we give him to ensure the other consortiums turn a blind eye, too. Thankfully, there is a limited number of them down there, so we do not have to worry about this going on ad infinitum."

"Wow, a real win on that front," Lilit sarcastically summarized. Sighing, she asked, "And you think this is a decent and fair trade for us?"

"I would not be presenting it if I did not," Ahmad underscored.

"And have you run projections on how all of these... gifts... are going to set back our timeline?" Lilit queried.

"I have," Ahmad confirmed, "but it depends on how efficient we end up being. I really will not have an answer until we are there for about four months and I can see how things have progressed."

Now, at last, that day had arrived when Lilit and the rest of their company would find out just how badly things had gone for them.

CHAPTER 40

Opening the door and stepping into the chamber, Lilit discovered that she was the last to arrive. Such is the right of the Queen, she derisively thought to herself. Everyone stood up as she entered, so she waved them back to their seats saying, "As you were, please sit down." Once they had done so, she joined them at her place at the head of the rock that had been shaped into a table. Her chair, like everyone else's, was just a cheap, hollow plastic one that they had used a 3D printer to construct. Space was even more of a premium down on Mercury than it was on board the ship, so they only built the most basic objects, and only when they absolutely needed them.

"Alright," Lilit began, "we all know why we're here, so let's not waste any time. Ahmad, what is our status?"

Ahmad pulled his tablet up in front of him and began to recite from the figures he had displayed on screen. Lilit interrupted him and demanded, "Ahmad: summarize! What does this all mean?"

Clearing his throat, Ahmad tried again by stating,

"Ah, yes, well, at this point, we are a mere few weeks away from our next inferior conjunction with Venus and, if we want to return with what we have, we would need to launch very soon after that. However, our cargo holds are only half full, meaning we do not have nearly enough raw material to build Freyr."

"Got it," Lilit noted, her disappointment clear in her tone. "Given that, what are our options?"

"There are really only two," Ahmad assured her. "The first is that we launch with what we have, head back to Venus, drop off our load, begin construction of Freyr with what we place in orbit, and head back to Mercury at the next available opportunity."

"When would that be?" Lilit probed.

"It would be more than five months from now," Ahmad answered.

"I suppose, then," Lilit began, "that our second option would be to stay here and finish the job completely so we have a full inventory?"

"Yes," Ahmad confirmed, "but if we do not make this transfer window, it will mean we have to stay here for an additional six or seven months, depending on how far we want to push it. On the other hand, with the first option, you must also consider the time it takes to get between worlds. Depending upon how poorly things go, it may mean we only have a week to dump the cargo and turn around to head back here. That would be quite tight, and loss is possible."

Lilit pondered that statement for a moment before asking, "Loss? What do you mean by that?"

Ahmad did not hesitate as he explained, "We would have to clear the holds so rapidly that there is a good possibility we will push our inventory out with such force that some will fall into Venus's gravity well and be destroyed as it is crushed in the planet's unrelenting pressure."

"Wonderful, we'd be throwing rocks at our own planet," Lilit intoned. "Are there any environmental impacts or dangers to Aestas?"

"Environmental impacts would be minimal," Ahmad claimed. "There might be momentary disruptions from a massive updraft that could cause Aestas to shake uncontrollably for a short while. For those on Aestas, it may feel like an earthquake. However, since the rocks would be going so slow when they entered the atmosphere, there is not much they could do except implode and rain down to the surface as dust, which would result in basically zero impact from our perspective."

"I see," Lilit said as she was nodding her head, trying to convince herself that she actually did understand what could potentially happen. "Durojaiye, what is your security assessment of these options?"

Durojaiye, unlike Ahmad, did not pull out a tablet but spoke directly, "For this, it is important to take into account what has and has not happened while we have been on Mercury. Most significantly, Earth did not launch any vessel or even an observational satellite towards the planet when they had the opportunity to do so a couple of months ago. That said, they have another chance in a few months from now. Based upon what Ahmad has said, if we go with the second option, this confluence will happen before we have the next opening to leave Mercury. The longer we stay here, the more likely they are to show up in orbit. This is especially true because at some point they are going to want to send a cargo ship to pick-up what Gang Chiu and the other consortiums have been mining. We cannot forget that they have natural interests here that do not involve us."

"But would they send a security detail with their regular cargo pickup and crew rotation?" Lilit prodded, trying to anticipate how Earth Central Command would react.

"This is difficult to assess given the unprecedented situation we are in..." Durojaiye began.

"Give me your best guess," Lilit interrupted. "I trust your intuition on this."

Durojaiye appeared to consider his words for a moment before he decided, "No, they would be at a disadvantage if they confronted us here. Our numbers are such that we could, if necessary, forcibly take control of the space elevator and docking platform, and then literally refuse them entry. More so, we could easily wait out any siege and leave on our own terms. At best, they could follow behind on the way back to Aestas, but they would have no access to our skimmers and therefore could not confront us there. They must know all of this, as well, and would realize it would be a fruitless effort."

"Interesting..." Lilit considered. "Even if it is a highly unlikely scenario, we could still prepare for it, though, right? I would also rather not have to use violence to take control of the space elevator and docking platform. I'm sure you could find a more persuasive method that does not involve the potential of hurting anyone. After all, we are still guests on this world, and I'd prefer to maintain good relations with our gracious and accommodating hosts."

"Of course," Durojaiye granted. "Your wish in this regard can be granted. That said, I would like to propose a third option."

"A third?" Ahmad interceded. "What idea could you offer that I have not already thought of, analyzed, and dismissed?"

"You concentrate on the science," Durojaiye expressed. "I, on the other hand, listen to the people. This has opened up a prospect in your blind spot."

"That is fair, I suppose…" Ahmad pouted.

"Enough, Durojaiye," Lilit said to get him back on track, "don't leave us in the dark."

"Yes, my Queen," Durojaiye crooned. Lilit still felt her stomach flip every time Durojaiye called her by her royal or any other title, but it was something he had gotten in the habit of doing when they were in public. In private, everything was as it always had been, and Lilit even confronted him about it when they were alone. He had demurred and insisted that it was for the benefit of the others, but she still did not buy it. Nevertheless, aside from ordering him not to do it, she could think of no other solution, so she let it continue to stand.

Breaking Lilit from her thoughts, Durojaiye observed, "Some members of our retinue have indicated that they would like to stay behind on Mercury… permanently."

"What?!" Lilit yelped, jolted by his statement. This was news to her and she hadn't considered the possibility that any Venusian would wish to remain on this planet. She realized that it was her own bias from having such a difficult time adjusting; others were doing quite well, some apparently thriving remarkably well.

As if to confirm these thoughts, Durojaiye highlighted, "The feeling is more pronounced among the native Venusians. These people have never walked on the surface of a planet before, so this experience has fundamentally changed their worldview. Among most of them, though, the key factor has been, as they have said, 'finding a purpose'. These folks have really taken to life as miners and would like to continue this type of work for the foreseeable future. I can assure you that Gang Chiu would be glad to keep them on."

Lilit felt herself sinking, despite the low gravity. She admonished herself for not foreseeing this exact scenario since the same thing had happened to her before on Earth. Back then, too, some members of their own constituency had opted to remain behind. It was bad enough when Xander had decided to, but when her associates from the Movement chose to stay on Earth, too, it stung in a way that she had not experienced before, nor had completely gotten over. She suffered their betrayals like a piece of her heart being ripped away and thrown into the sun. Taking it quite personally, Lilit felt that leaving her meant that these people had given up on the Movement, on

Aestas, and on Venus, and were just looking out for their own future. It made her believe that she had failed them and everyone else, in some way.

"I know what you are thinking," Ahmad spoke softly to her, "but it is not your fault. Just as I did not belong on Earth, some people do not belong on Aestas. It is only natural, and we must accept whatever truth people learn about themselves."

"Besides," Durojaiye offered, "there is an opportunity in this, too. We can split up. Those who desire to stay here may do so and continue the necessary labors. Meanwhile, the rest of us will return to Venus during this window, unload, and rotate the crew. We can go home and take care of things there while everything continues as expected here. Thus, we can begin regular shuttle runs between the worlds closest to the sun."

Lilit sat back in her chair and took time to deeply ponder all that had been presented. Others in the room debated the merits of the three options before them for some time, but she was not paying attention to their conversations anymore and, therefore, did not hear what they had to say. After a thoughtful period, she spoke up and declared, "I've made my decision."

Everyone quieted down immediately, so she

resumed, "At this point, we cannot split up. If even a quarter of us left now, it would slow down production so much that those left behind would never finish in time. We have to stick together until we have enough raw goods for Freyr. The risks are relatively low and the biggest issue will be the health effects from remaining here under this low gravity for longer than we intended. That is just the sacrifice we have to make for the greater good of our people.

"However, when we reach that point six or seven months from now in which we have all the basic core materials we need for Freyr, not everyone will be coming back. Those who want to remain here will be allowed to do so, but under one condition. During these ensuing months, we will establish a permanent Venusian colony and embassy right here on Mercury. Therefore, we will not really be leaving them behind, but instead will be designating them as our emissaries. This also means that someone at this table will need to stay on to act as our ambassador—at least temporarily until a replacement can be sent, but the position could be made permanent if this volunteer desires it to be—so decide amongst yourselves who is taking up that mantle.

"The most important thing to realize is that Durojaiye is right about one thing: we are going to need to keep coming back here. That said, it is not just about Freyr; Freyr is only the beginning of our new Venusian plans and dreams. Once our second city is built and is floating above the clouds on Venus, we will need a third, a fourth, and more! That means it will be necessary to return to Mercury for additional batches of raw materials again and again and again.

"It is time to shift our thinking to the long-term; we must stop reacting and start being proactive. For that, we need a strong alliance with Mercury, maybe even one day we will join together into a confederation of the inner-inner solar system. Today will mark our new beginning, one in which we cast off the shackles of humanity's ancestral homeworld and finally start to be free!"

Happily floating in the air within the docking platform above Venus, Lilit watched with great interest as workers in space suits continued to take specifically designed components and fasten them together. Though it was hard to believe, the collection of random objects and primordial rocks were the beginning of what would one day become the future city of Freyr. However, even in their best projections, they were still years away from this being completed. Nonetheless, they had accomplished everything they had set out to do with no interference from Earth Central Command or the Terran Government. She often pinched herself to confirm it was really happening, that they were actually succeeding in giving hope to everyone on Aestas. Each time, she failed to wake up from their dream come true.

Although Lilit was having a good time just looking out the windows, her guards did not appear to be as excited. The two who had been assigned to her for this shift were noticeably uncomfortable in microgravity. While Lilit could swim through space with the grace of a fish in water—or so she was told since she had only seen such a thing in videos—the Protectors both looked like they just wanted to vomit. Lilit thought that she would have to talk to Durojaiye and Aritza about having sentinels who were specifically trained to work in near zero-g. It was looking more likely that they would need an additional division within their security apparatus to be able to address crime and safety in space.

Their integrated military, intelligence, and police services already had many specialists, and Lilit was rather concerned about subdividing them yet again. Within the confines of Aestas, there was currently a separation between general safety, overseers for prisoners and detained individuals, safeguarding people like her, and other similar allotments to make sure they had the right folks assigned to their many specific areas of concern. And that did not even begin to address how the military and intelligence branches each had their own subsectors.

In totality, Lilit was unsure how united the entire safety and security mechanism really was. To say that Durojaiye and Aritza did not see eye-to-eye would be an understatement. Truthfully, Durojaiye rarely complained about Aritza; it was usually the other way around. Somehow, though, the two continued to manage the entire defense apparatus with Lilit only infrequently having to be the deciding voice between them. She realized that it did not help that neither one truly had a formal title nor had a clear separation been established between their responsibilities. For instance, undercover agents in the public sector were provided by Durojaiye's intelligence services, but seemingly reported to the Protector hierarchy. In that same vein, Lilit had not promoted Aritza to the head of all constabulary duties; technically there were many higher ranked individuals that Aritza answered to. It was more like Aritza had become the chief liaison between the Transitional Leadership Assembly and all of the Protector detachments.

Thinking of Aritza and having officers floating in orbit around the planet, Lilit realized that the skimmer was late for the shift changeover. As part of their agreement from before she left for Mercury, Aritza was being trained to pilot the vessel. Actually, they should have been the one driving this run, which would explain why it was late; Aritza was still very trepidatious. Suddenly, the idea of having a "space police force" that Lilit had teased Aritza about before didn't seem so funny anymore, and she realized that she absolutely wanted Aritza and other Protectors up here on a more regular basis. Who knew what threats they would need to handle? The construction of Freyr was too important to leave anything to chance, so additional coverage would be beneficial. Lilit also thought that while the officers were up here that they might be able to provide additional services. Since Aritza already expressed a desire to patrol the stars, perhaps they could become the premier captain for their new tugboat, currently under construction along with Freyr? If Lilit recalled correctly, that was part of the same deal they had made.

Finally, the skimmer arrived and broke Lilit out of her reverie. To her surprise, among those who exited were Ahmad and Durojaiye. That made her wonder if Durojaiye had harassed Aritza during the trip and further slowed them down, but she put the thought aside. Waving her friends over she said, "Hey guys, what are you doing here?"

"You missed the Transitional Leadership Assembly meeting," Ahmad accused. "Everyone was quite concerned and upset. We had to hunt you down since you were not answering your calls."

Lilit then realized that she had muted her A.I. so that she could have some peace and quiet for a change. That explained why she was feeling so relaxed; she literally could not be disturbed. "Whoops, sorry about that!" was all she managed with a sly smile, believing that would be enough to forgive her unintended transgression.

"You cannot just do that," Durojaiye scolded. "You are the Queen of Venus and far too important to just disappear into the ether. What would we do if some tragedy befell you?"

"Give me a break!" Lilit snapped back in annoyance. "The Protectors you personally assigned to me were here the entire time, so I'm sure you could have checked in with them to make sure I was fine. Besides, what could possibly happen to me up here, of all places?"

Durojaiye stayed silent as Lilit thought he must have realized that she was correct. Still, the lack of response was even more disturbing, as was the look of concern and disappointment on his face, like he was admonishing one of his children for making the same mistake that he had previously corrected. "Fiiiiiiine," Lilit whined, "I won't do it again. God forbid I get to have a moment to bask in the glory of our astounding accomplishments. You know, I've been going nonstop for over five years now, but of course I can't even have a few hours to myself. That would be simply outrageous!"

Failing to illicit any sympathy in response to her rant from either of her friends who had gone through almost all the exact same situations and stressors, Lilit resigned herself to the obvious reason they were here. "I give up. What was so important that I missed at the meeting?"

Not skipping a beat, Ahmad summarized, "As you are aware, we are nearing the window when we will be at an inferior conjunction with Earth."

"Fuck! That was this one?" Lilit exclaimed.

"One in the same, and you missed it," Ahmad confirmed. "We needed your final decision."

"Damn it, I hate when you have a real reason to be pissed off at me," Lilit divulged. "I really dropped the ball, huh?"

"Perhaps you were subconsciously trying to avoid making a determination," Durojaiye diplomatically offered her by way of an excuse.

Before she could answer, Ahmad jumped in saying, "But you must do so, Lilit, and it needs to be very soon. No matter which option is adopted, there is much that will have to be done, and we need as much time as possible so that we can implement it."

Back at the ARM—a clunky acronym that Lilit was now regretting—the Transitional Leadership Assembly gathered around the conference table. Once everyone was there, Lilit began, "First up, everyone, I apologize for my absence before. This is very important and I should have been here as I promised to be. So, thank you all for being willing to drop everything and get back together again on short notice."

Everyone mumbled their forgiveness and Lilit decided to accept it all at face value. Continuing, she said, "Alright, because I cost us so much time, we will not leave here until we reach a verdict. Is everyone okay with that?"

There was more muttering of acceptance, but Lilit realized that the people in this chamber—save for Ahmad and Durojaiye—lived in reverence, if not fear, of her and would never disobey her in regard to this. Much to her own disgust, she began to feel some sympathy towards Xander. Perhaps he did not intend to be surrounded by "yes men", but it just naturally happened over time? Maybe he actually did want a diversity of viewpoints and her rejection of his offer to join the Managing Council was a mistake? Per usual, Lilit compartmentalized even her doubts so that she could lead her people in this unpredictable new age. After all, she thought, if she had tried to work with Xander from within the government that existed at that time, they would not have Freyr under construction right now. Then again, they also wouldn't have the issue she needed to resolve during this session.

Shaking it off, Lilit decided to summarize the situation herself instead of having someone else do it. "Due to our actions earlier as the Movement and then more recently as the TLA, we have created a fair number of political prisoners. These people are being held both here on Aestas in the former Quarantine and Confinement Districts, as well as in orbit on the docking platform."

"Queen-Commander, if I may," Aritza countered. "I feel you are doing yourself—and us via proxy—a great disservice by persisting in calling them 'political prisoners'. They are criminals that we have rightfully detained, tried, and punished. They are serving out just and reasonable sentences as decided by our laws, courts, and special tribunals."

"That is not true for all of them," Ahmad argued.

"For instance, the senior HSA pilots from the shuttle we commandeered to go to Mercury are all innocent bystanders that we have been holding in indefinite detention without any legal standing. Their only 'crime' was being unwilling to break their vows to HSA and the Terran Government in order to help us."

"Thus, they supported criminal enterprises, proving my point!" Aritza shot back.

"Enough you two!" Lilit barked. It was obvious that Durojaiye was having an unhealthy influence on how Ahmad treated and interacted with Aritza. "The semantics aren't that important. The only question is what will we do with them now? While a few have certainly been rehabilitated and have been able to rejoin society, the vast majority will never be able to do so. They don't want to be here as much as we don't want them, either—especially since they are a drain on our resources. Plus, being able to clear out our prisons will open up those spaces for additional housing. We are years and years away from completing, let alone populating, Freyr. We don't even have a good plan yet for how we're going to produce enough soil and fertilizer without Earth; something else we have to work on. In the meantime, these inmates are taking up valuable real estate, and the citizenry knows it. We all know it."

"And you know exactly where I stand on this," Durojaiye mentioned.

Lilit shot him a look and declared, "We will not be throwing anyone out the airlock for minor offenses just because they are inconvenient!"

"You say 'minor offenses'," Durojaiye articulated, "but what about those like our saboteur aboard the Mercury shuttle? That was premeditated attempted mass murder and regicide. And it is not like he is the only one of his ilk that we have captured over the past couple of years. Aestas is just as vulnerable as ever, and extremists have tried to take down our whole colony, desiring to perpetrate a genocide of the Venusian people. So, what will the consequences be for these vile acts? Deportation back to a place that will receive them as heroes?! That is no punishment; that is a reward!"

Finally, Lilit thought, we are getting to crux of the matter. Aloud, she asked, "Which is the larger problem: setting these people free and sending them to Earth, or the fact that we'll have to give up the shuttle we stole to do so?"

"Both are of an equal concern," Durojaiye diplomatically contended.

"Pick one," Lilit commanded.

Durojaiye was quiet as he thought for a moment

before declaring, "If I must pick between them, then I would say it is the shuttle."

"I agree," Ahmad chimed in.

Lilit was surprised to hear this from him. "Et tu, Ahmad?" she intoned.

"While I disagree with Durojaiye's and Aritza's standing on what we should do with the prisoners if they must remain here, I do wholeheartedly support their stance about the shuttle. We do not have a re-placement vehicle yet, which means those we left behind on Mercury will be stuck there. It will be like abandoning them because of ineptitude. Yes, they are building a new shuttle of their own, but like Freyr it will be a long time until it is ready."

"What's the estimated timeline?" Lilit probed.

"We do not have a lot of people there," Ahmad began, "and the few who are there do not have the proper skillsets to even build the vessel. As such, it will take them at least a year, if not two to finish con-structing the shuttle. On the other hand, if we keep our current craft instead of releasing it back to Earth, we can send them help and speed up the process. I am not saying we should not return our prisoners back to Earth in the end, just that we delay it until we have another spaceship."

"But that means," Aritza debated, "that in the

meantime we will still have to house, feed, and clothe these dregs on society while our own people suffer. How much time will you shave off with this plan of yours? A few months? That is nothing!"

"I... do not know," Ahmad admitted. "But just as you want to protect everyone here with us on Aestas, I want to make sure we do the same for our scattered brethren who have remained behind on Mercury."

"Those Mercurians are no longer our primary concern," Aritza seethed in a way Lilit had never seen from them before. "They will have to take care of themselves."

"How can you possibly say that?" Ahmad rejoined. "Are their lives any less important than the rest of the citizenry?"

Aritza bit right back, "Damn right! They abandoned us! You think I can't read between the lines? Instead of being a part of the struggle, they gave up for an easier life that doesn't involve having to make the hard decisions, like the one we have to make here, the only logical one."

"What are you saying?" Ahmad disputed. "Those on Mercury are children of Venus, just like all of us."

"Just like me, you mean," Aritza fumed, "just like my Queen-Commander Lilit, and just like most other members of this assembly. That is, everyone except the Johnny-come-latelies like you and Durojaiye."

"Whoa, Aritza!" Lilit reprimanded. "You've gone too far with this one. Ahmad is as much of a Venusian as you and me, as are Durojaiye and the rest. You apologize this instant!"

"I'm sorry, Queen-Commander," Aritza started, "but I cannot, with a true heart, do as you ask. These immigrants can never fully understand things the same way we natives do. More so, their loyalties will always be in question. Hell, Durojaiye has a wife and children back on Earth! How can we ever fully trust the Earthers' opinions when it comes to our future? They have an inherent bias towards protecting their own kind."

"Aritza, I'm warning you; you are way out of line!" Lilit chastised. "Are our enemies so few that you feel the need to attack those of us within? These are your colleagues, your comrades-in-arms, who have sacrificed just as much as you have to reach the point we are at today! What has gotten into you?"

There was fury visible in Aritza's eyes. As Lilit stared them down, Aritza's fire seemed to finally cool and then go out in a puff of smoke. "You're right," Aritza whispered. "I've let the stress of everything get to me and I've taken it out on those who do not deserve it. Ahmad, please forgive me."

Ahmad did not respond immediately as he was looking down at his hands. Finally, he raised his head and said, "I am not sure that I can. I learned something about you today, Aritza, something I never imagined was true. You carry a great prejudice, intolerance, xenophobia, and hatred within you. I expected better, especially from you."

Aritza looked like they wanted to respond, but Lilit cut them off. "You two will have to hash this out later on your own time. Now is the moment we must make a major decision on how we want Aestas to be projected outwardly towards the rest of the solar system. They think we are barbarians, and the display put on in this room today would certainly prove them right. As such, I'm going to change the paradigm for them and for us.

"It is obvious that keeping the prisoners here is causing too much discord. Therefore, they have to go. Although I can clearly see that this will be an unpopular choice both within these walls and beyond them, we must do the morally right thing and put them on that shuttle and let them go to Earth, no strings attached."

"But Lilit..." Ahmad began.

Cutting him off, Lilit announced, "I don't want to hear it; I've made up my mind. We are fighting first and foremost for our freedom. How can we possibly deny that opportunity to others? Earth, its inhabitants, and its supporters are not our enemies, despite what some people may contend. We are all just human beings trying to do what is best for ourselves and our people so that we can survive."

"I see there will be no dissuading you," Durojaiye chimed in, "but that does not mean we still cannot try to get something, anything in return for this."

"What do you have in mind?" Lilit asked.

Durojaiye answered, "We should at least negotiate with Earth Central Command to get you off their 'most wanted' list. We can offer this as a trade, of sorts, sprinkled with a shot of goodwill."

Lilit thought about it briefly before concluding, "I give you permission to negotiate, but whether we get anything for the exchange or not, that ship is launching on the expected date with all of our prisoners and anyone who wants to go with them onboard. My personal standing with the Terran Government will not be a sticking point. From now on, we are going to do the right thing and hope that the other side reciprocates. And if they don't, who cares? It changes nothing for us. We already have everything we've always wanted, and they cannot take that away from us!"

CHAPTER 43

Once the cheering had finally died down to a decibel level at which she could be heard over the clamor, Lilit smiled one last time before launching into her speech. "Thank you, thank you so much," she began. "And not just for this ovation, but for everything you have sacrificed, everything you have had to endure, and for your unyielding support over these many tumultuous years. Give yourself a well-deserved and raucous round of applause!"

As the crowd did just that, Lilit took the opportunity to look out over the tens of thousands of heads that had shown up to mark this new holiday. Once the crowd had begun to quiet down and she was able to speak again, Lilit continued, "Today, we commemorate a resolution that was made five years ago. On that day, in a small chamber on Mercury, we decided that we would stop being at the mercy of distant powers forever. In that dark hole far removed from the light of the glorious and lifegiving sun we are currently enjoying overhead, we made the conscious choice to not only overthrow our absent masters, but to cut the cord they tried to tie around our necks. They thought they could subjugate us by trying to force us to be dependent upon them, but under meters of rock we learned the truth: that we didn't need them anymore, for anything!

"That is why we have opted to mark this occasion now and forever as our very own Venusian Liberation Day!" As the crowd chanted the name of their planet, Lilit had a little chuckle to herself. She knew that the events she had summarized had not occurred exactly five years ago. Actually, it would be several more weeks until the real anniversary, but Durojaiye had insisted that this specific date would be better for observance. Since no one had a counterargument or a concern about the precise day the festivities should fall, they went with his suggestion.

Picking up where she left off, Lilit noted, "It was because of our liberation that we were able to reach this point. In a few short months, our second city Freyr will be complete and will join Aestas soaring above the clouds. Over the many years this moment took to arrive, we had to give up a lot and suffer in ways we'd never considered before. Looking out beyond all of you, I see a Level 1 that has been transformed and fundamentally changed in ways I could not have foreseen a decade ago.

"Just at the edge of this last remaining open area there used to be a restaurant called Lusaber. It was my favorite place for Venusian cuisine, one that had been here since the colony's founding. But people needed space to live, and even though it was unpopular and unfortunate, it was necessary to tear it down. In its spot, we have created new apartments, vertical farming, and grow lights and aqua gardens in every family's home so that no one would ever have to worry about food insecurity while we were losing our farmland. Still, it was not just here on Level 1, but everywhere else, too. Seventy-five percent of the Commercial District is now housing, as is twenty-five percent of the Industrial one. Every space has been used to maximum efficiency, but much was lost in order to do so. We chose to make all the hard decisions that the former Managing Council refused to.

"I want you to know how much I appreciate everything you have had to part ways with during this time of transition, no matter how small or seemingly trivial it was. Everything we have laid waste to was important in its own way; I don't want to diminish any of them by saying one was more valuable or significant than another. It does not matter if all you lost through this era was your favorite ottoman; I am humbled and grateful to you for having done so.

These gestures have made a real difference, and I will never forget that. Without you and your faith in me, the Transitional Leadership Assembly, and the dream of a better Venus, none of this would have been possible.

"But thanks to those forfeitures and for never giving in to despair when times were tough, many new hopes have arisen, as well. For instance, on our satellite colony on Mercury, our brethren were able to finish constructing a transport shuttle and we have already received many shipments using it. With this vessel and the others that will be manufactured in the future, we will be a central hub unto ourselves in the Sol System, with the ability to reach any human world on our own terms without any interference from the Terran Government.

"And I should point out that we have never been at war with Earth, though they cut us off for quite a while. Thanks to the nonstop, dedicated efforts of our people who have been trapped at our embassy on Earth—especially Ambassador Xander—I can now announce that we have reestablished diplomatic relations with the Terran Government. While I, personally, am still persona non grata, the citizenry of Aestas is once again free and safe to travel anywhere in the Sol System. The embargo and siege of our homeworld has come to an end!"

While the crowd erupted in excitement at this news, Lilit had to suppress a little frown. Though it was true that Earth Central Command would no longer restrict the movement of Venusians, the Terran Government had still refused to formally acknowledge their independence. Xander had said those in power on Earth were referring to Aestas and Venus in general as a "rogue colony" and that it was inevitable that they would rejoin the fold someday. Lilit could not see how reunification would be possible, nor did she see the need. Her speech originally included these details as she did not like to keep things from the people, but Ahmad had insisted she take it out. "After all," he highlighted, "this is a happy occasion. There is plenty of time to discuss all our other issues afterwards."

Reluctantly, Lilit had agreed to strip out the offending references, but there was something she was going to announce during this speech, and no one could stop her. The rest of the TLA had no idea she planned to make this announcement, which was the point; she knew they would try to talk her out of it. However, Lilit was quite sure this was the right place and the right time to make this pronouncement. Taking a cleansing breath, Lilit assured herself that, in the end, the rest of the TLA would forgive her for springing this on them in a very public way.

"That is not the last good news I have," Lilit shouted over the throng of humanity. "Once Freyr is deployed and populated, this intermediate time of transition will come to an end and I can fulfil the final promise of the Movement. We will have a new Constitution and a representative government will be elected, one that will be—for the first time—truly controlled by you, the people, without any restrictions. It is past time for me to step aside and hand the destiny of all of Venus over to your capable and knowledgeable hands."

At this, the multitude started chanting, "Long live the Queen! Long live the Queen!" over and over again, such that Lilit could not get a word in edgewise. She felt tears welling up in appreciation and went to wipe them away. It took a while, but she finally got the audience to quiet down again.

"No, no," she intoned. "I cannot be your Queen forever. It would be wrong for me—and any potential future progeny I may have—to do to you what the Terran Government did to all of us for our entire existence. I have no desire to maintain any hegemony over you. I will gladly stay on to help the succeeding government in any way I can, but the season is approaching for me to just be a regular person again.

"The forthcoming era has limitless potential to be anything we want it to be. I cannot see what it might hold, what challenges we might face, what joys we might discover, or even where we might go from here. No matter what, though, based on the foundation we have laid here with our own liberation, I do know that it is bright and boundless.

"Most of all, I understand this: our great struggle is at last over; we have unequivocally won!"

As Lilit was basking in the adoration of the people of Aestas, an alarm suddenly sounded through every available speaker within the colony. Pandemonium began to break out in the mass confusion, and a slew of Protectors rushed on stage to grab Lilit and sweep her away from there. "What's happening?" she screamed above the piercing assault to her eardrums. "Where are you taking me?"

None of the Protectors had an answer as to what was going on, but they said they were getting her back to the ARM where she would be safe. However, en route, the entire ground began to shake and they were forced to hit the deck. "How can we have an earthquake?" Lilit asked no one in particular. "We aren't even on the surface!"

Her questions went unanswered at that point, but after a minute or two the quaking subsided enough that she and the Protectors felt it was safe enough to continue their journey. The elevators were not functioning, so they ended up taking emergency ladders down into the bowels of Aestas. Sweating from the difficult descent, Lilit entered the ARM to find half of the Transitional Leadership Assembly had also found their way there.

Without any preamble, she raised her voice over the sirens, "Can someone turn that damn thing off and tell me what the hell is happening?"

No one said anything, but the screeching bell finally ceased. Breathing a sigh of relief while trying to get the ringing out of her own ears, Lilit asked again about what was transpiring. Ahmad got up from his workstation and put an image on the large screen. It was a blurry picture of what looked like a ball with a long tail, but any detail was difficult to make out.

"This photo," Ahmad began, "was taken just a few seconds before the alarms went off. It is difficult to make out, but this is a massive ice-asteroid. The reason it is so blurry and difficult to discern is that it came in at an inconceivable velocity, so fast that we do not have any cameras with shutter speeds fast enough to capture it. I am pretty sure no one in the whole solar system would have equipment that could do much better."

"I don't understand," Lilit interceded. "How could we not have seen something of this size coming for years in advance? Space debris tracking has always been an integral part of Aestas's security protocol and management, and we have successfully diverted asteroids like this many times in the past."

"That would be true," Ahmad answered, "for objects travelling at normal velocities. I cannot quite figure it out, but this ice-asteroid came out of nowhere and was flying at two-point-five percent the speed of light. Based on our current observational technology, it was simply impossible to see it until it was on top of us."

Flabbergasted, Lilit probed further, "That makes even less sense. How could it possibly get that fast? Where did it come from?"

"Hold on a moment," Ahmad requested before walking back to his workstation. "I was running some calculations when you came in and should have better projections now." After reviewing his tablet, all he managed to say was "Hmmmmm..."

"Care to elaborate?" Lilit scoffed.

"My apologies, Lilit," Ahmad tried, "but things have become even more illogical, somehow. According to this, the asteroid would have an origin point in the Kuiper Belt beyond Neptune, and would have left there sometime between twenty to twenty-five days ago."

"Twenty days?" Lilit asked skeptically. "Ahmad, you are far more versed in orbital mechanics than me, but I'm quite sure it would take our shuttle over a decade to get out there."

"You are not wrong," Ahmad confirmed. "It makes no sense; these figures would break all the laws of physics as I understand them... unless..."

"What is it?" Lilit attempted to pull an answer out of Ahmad as he immersed himself back in his simulations. He was completely zoned in on the task and it appeared that he could no longer hear her, so she had no choice but to wait patiently as he worked through whatever he needed to. In the meantime, she decided to check in with the others to see if they had any insights. No one had anything to offer; everyone was just as much in the dark as she was.

Abruptly, Ahmad's voice rang out, reverberating around the ARM and shocking Lilit as much as the blaring alarms had earlier. "Lilit," he shouted, "we are in grave danger! We are under attack!"

Lilit ran over and said, "Whoa, whoa, whoa, slow down, Ahmad. What are you talking about?"

Showing signs of obvious agitation, Ahmad explained, "It is the Torch Drive! As I predicted years ago, I hypothesized that they were attaching them to rocks in the Asteroid Belt and maybe the Kuiper Belt. This proves my theory was correct. It is the only way that something could move nearly five billion kilometers in such a short amount of time."

"Okay," Lilit conceded, "it makes sense that this ice-asteroid was propelled by a Torch Drive, but it doesn't mean it was done intentionally. With an emerging technology like this, there are always growing pains. Maybe some mistake happened? Perhaps they had aimed the load towards the Earth's orbit and the engine failed to initialize the breaking and insertion procedure?"

"I have considered this," Ahmad decreed, "but it does not fit. First of all, it is an astronomically small probability that it would run directly into us at all, just given how much empty space there is in general compared to the tiny size of Venus. Further, if it was aiming for Earth then it would have continued to fly off in an entirely different trajectory after it missed. We are not directly aligned with Earth right now, so it must have been aimed specifically at us. The final proof comes from the speed itself. If it had failed to cut its engines, it would still have gained velocity and come in even faster. If it had planned to stop, it would have at least flipped around so the engines were facing the other way. The fact that it reached a specific rate, stopped the output of fuel, but still never attempted to spin the side the engines faced means it must have been intentional."

"But why?" Lilit complained. "What is the purpose of throwing a rock at a place that floats in the air?"

"I am... not sure... yet," Ahmad admitted. "Nevertheless, I should note that they missed Aestas and anything critical by a wide margin. The reason we felt that 'quake'—for lack of a better word—was because of an updraft roiling through the thick Venusian atmosphere. When we were on Mercury, I discussed how a slow-moving rock passing into the stratosphere could cause such an event. Although this one was much bigger and faster than anything I had imagined possible, the principals are the same.

"Conversely, at that time, I also said that anything that went through the top layer of clouds would be crushed under intense pressures and be turned to dust. In this case, though, based upon the swiftness by which it arrived, at least part of the ice-asteroid must have slammed into the surface directly. Thus far, I fail to see what that would accomplish. Lilit, I need you to give me some time, please."

Lilit paused for a moment before agreeing and saying, "Alright, you have it, but let's pray nothing else happens while we're chasing answers."

Chapter 45

After a week of no further progress and even less sleep, Lilit realized that she could not continue at this pace, nor could the remainder of the team. She ordered them all home to rest—everyone except Durojaiye. Although Ahmad was quick to leave and return to his quarters, the rest of the TLA and other experts they had brought in took their time to wrap up their tasks and document their findings so they could easily pick up where they left off when they returned. This took far longer than Lilit would have hoped, and she impatiently waited for the gaggle of humanity to exit in order to grant her and Durojaiye some privacy.

Once she and Durojaiye were finally alone, Lilit reprimanded him, "Durojaiye, I didn't want to belittle you in front of the others, but this event has been a major lapse on your part. You are supposed to be our chief intelligence officer—our eyes and ears everywhere in the solar system—and yet you had no inkling this was coming prior to the attack. This must have been years, maybe even decades in the making! How could this have slipped past you?"

Durojaiye looked like he was considering his words carefully before declaring, "All I can offer is my apologies and condolences. You have always received from me everything I could possibly give you, but it appears that even I have limits. If there is someone you think would do a better job and be more up to the task, then you should—no, must—bring them in and relieve me of my duties."

Lilit gave a sad laugh and said, "Oh, Durojaiye, you and I both know there is no one more capable than you on this entire planet. I'm sorry, I'm just looking for answers, for somewhere to direct my anger and frustration. I shouldn't have laid the blame at your feet; you didn't deserve that. That being said, I'm not letting you off the hook entirely. I'm going to need you to step up in a way I've never asked you to do before."

"Sounds challenging," Durojaiye smiled.

Unamused, Lilit continued, "Thus far, nobody is taking responsibility for this violation of our sovereignty. Nevertheless, there must be human hands involved. You need to find out more details and get to the truth of this matter. Use every connection you have, every favor you are owed, whatever it takes."

"Whatever it takes?" Durojaiye asked for

confirmation. "Are you sure you want to unleash me in that way? My philosophy, standings, and preferred methodologies should be well known to you at this point, and you have... consistently discouraged... me from using them in the past."

Lilit thought for a moment before answering, "I do. We have no shortage of enemies. Though it is painful for me to admit, perhaps you were right all along; I have been far too lenient."

"Perhaps so..." Durojaiye agreed.

"Besides," Lilit intoned, trying to lighten the mood, "you owe me for the position you put me in."

Durojaiye looked alarmed as he said, "I am sure I do not know what you mean."

Lilit scrunched her eyes curiously at Durojaiye's seemingly worried response and tried again, "I mean, it was like they timed that ice-asteroid to plunge through the atmosphere at exactly that moment—on that day, of all days—to be as impactful as possible. After all, you were the one who insisted on creating a Venusian Liberation Day and launching it precisely on that date! Therefore, I have no choice but to blame you for all our woes and misery!"

"Oh," Durojaiye said as he visibly relaxed and started laughing. "You had me going there for a minute! Well, in that case, since I certainly did everything you have described, then I shall gladly absorb all the culpability you need me to!"

Lilit giggled and hugged Durojaiye, reaffirming their unbreakable bond. While in his arms, the overwhelming stress of their situation at last took hold and she let the dam break. Over the past week, Lilit had been trying to be strong for everyone else, but no one could offer her a similar solace. Despite the painful angle, she chose to find it in Durojaiye's shoulder.

Pulling away and rubbing her eyes, Lilit said, "I'm sorry, I've soaked your shirt."

"It is quite alright," Durojaiye assured her. "I have barely been home this week, so it is exceptionally dirty anyway."

Laughing while continuing to dry her eyes, Lilit offered, "Well, let me buy you a new one. I'm sure I can expense it back to some government department. After all, it was destroyed in service to your Queen!"

Chucking, Durojaiye countered, "No, no, that is not necessary. My shirt should easily survive a laundering and I have plenty of other ones hanging in my closet. However, before I go home to change and get some rest, why do we not sit and chat for a while, like in the old days. Lately, I have missed spending time with you just as my friend."

Delighted by the idea, Lilit agreed and they did just as Durojaiye suggested. After a while, they thought they heard something going on outside, but it was too muffled to make out. As soon as they forgot about it, the door to the ARM suddenly slid open and both Lilit and Durojaiye jumped up and away from each other in surprise.

"Am I interrupting something?" an equally perplexed Ahmad asked in the doorway. Lilit then realized that the nearly inaudible sounds they heard before must have been Ahmad negotiating his entry with the Protectors stationed outside.

"No, no, nothing," Lilit insisted. "I had just been taking out my frustrations on Durojaiye's shoulder, and then we were catching up on life."

"Ah, I see," Ahmad offered.

Since he didn't say anything else, Lilit asked, "What are you doing here, Ahmad? Didn't I send you home for the night?"

"That you did," Ahmad admitted, "but you asked me several days ago what our enemy's endgame is. I believe I have finally figured it out."

"I sent you home to sleep!" Lilit chastised. "You weren't supposed to do more work."

"I did do as you asked," Ahmad claimed. "Exhaustion quickly overtook me and I fell asleep almost the moment I walked through my door. This allowed me to immediately slip into REM, where I had an epiphany! Lilit, the answer came to me in my dreams, as clear as speaking to you now. Shocked by the revelation, I awoke to find that not much time had passed. Nevertheless, I could not rest, so I ran simulations until I could confirm the veracity of the matter. Now, I believe I know what is being done to us and to Venus—and more importantly, I understand why."

"Let's sit back down, then" Lilit proposed as she walked over to the conference table. Once all three of them were there, Lilit signaled for Ahmad to expound on his findings.

With no preamble, he launched into it. "The ice-asteroid slammed into Venus at a very specific oblique bearing. It did not exactly crash into the surface so much as it glanced off of it at an angle before imploding due to its own speed and the pressures of the atmosphere."

"So," Lilit interrupted, "did this hit affect us or the planet in some way?"

"Yes," Ahmad explained, "it changed Venus's natural rotational speed. As you know, Venus spins on its axis in retrograde, and does so very leisurely. The angle of attack was such that it would actually further slow down the revolution of the planet around its center of gravity."

"I'm confused," Lilit jumped in again. "What purpose would that serve?"

Ahmad quickly responded, "As a one-off, it is meaningless. It has barely impacted a Venusian sol by any measurable amount, nothing we cannot adjust for. However, if we keep taking hits like this, eventually Venus will start spinning in the opposite direction—the 'right' way, from Earth's perspective. Theoretically, we could even end up with a twenty-four-hour rotation, exactly the same as Earth."

Lilit concernedly asked, "How many blows like that will it take?"

Ahmad shrugged and said, "I am still trying to determine that, get a more precise number, but there are a slew of factors that I do not know. The imprecise answer I must give is simply 'a lot'. There are hundreds of thousands, if not millions, of icy bodies in the Kuiper Belt, so it is not like they would ever run out of ammunition."

"You still have not answered Lilit's core question, though," Durojaiye accused. "For what purpose would they do this?"

Ahmad considered for a moment before saying, "Terraforming. This is the first step in a long plan to transform Venus into a second Earth. They failed on

Mars, so now they have set their sights on us: the twin sister planet."

"What?" Lilit screeched in disbelief. "How could that be possible? The pressures and temperatures would easily kill anyone and destroy all equipment. That is the whole reason Project HAVOK was revived and Aestas was built in the first place! This is grade school stuff we're talking about—at least, here it is."

"Again," Ahmad stated, "it is all hypothetical, but very possible within our understanding of physics. Like I said, this would only be the beginning of many steps to lower pressures and temperatures through various other means. Consider this: even without doing anything else, just having a 'normal' rotation will fundamentally change the atmosphere in such substantial ways that Aestas will have difficulty staying aloft. It may even be impossible to keep it up in the sky, in the long run."

Lilit's heart started to race and she bellowed, "Ahmad, we can't let this happen! You are talking about the destruction of our home and the genocide of our people. How do we stop this?"

Stepping in, Durojaiye appeared to desire clarification as he asked, "Ahmad, based on your analysis, in order for our enemy to accomplish their goal, more ice-asteroids must be coming, correct?"

Ahmad affirmed this with a nod, so Durojaiye responded, "In that case, our first line of defense would be an early detection system of some kind so that we can at least have a bit of warning to deal with the incoming volleys."

"And we need it yesterday," Lilit forlornly intoned. "Moreover, it's necessary to do much more than mere detection. There must be a way to protect ourselves from this onslaught, neutralize the immediate threat, and turn the tables on them. From now on, Ahmad, this is your sole concern. Get on it!"

The day Lilit had been dreading and yet been eagerly anticipating finally arrived. Spinning around in his seat at his workstation in the ARM, Ahmad declared with glee, "We have found one! The early detection system is working!"

"Please do not be excited about that," Lilit uttered. "What's the ETA?"

"Right, one moment please," Ahmad said as he turned back around to where his tablet and keyboard lay. "Okay, given its velocity at the time of detection and the arc curve of expected increase in its speed, it looks like it is about... ten days out."

"Are you confident in that?" Lilit probed.

"No," Ahmad admitted, "these estimates are far from accurate. I only had the one prior attack to base everything off of; it is, unfortunately, simply not enough data to be assured that it will be the same. Before you ask, yes, ten days in the worst-case scenario. Probability-wise, there does not appear to be a way for it to get here sooner based on what we know about this technology."

"Ten days," Lilit frowned. "That is all we have left to stop this monstrosity. Tell me we can move it off course with our regular meteor deflection system."

"I am afraid not," Ahmad disputed. "That methodology requires making a detection at least a half-year in advance so that we could use either gravity or energy-based redirection."

"What would Earth do?" Lilit wondered aloud.

"The same thing we are," Ahmad assured her. "The procedures for dealing with space debris are well-established. If you see an incoming object heading your way, convince it to change course just enough to make sure it misses all our planets and colonies. The only thing they have that we do not are nuclear missiles on orbital platforms."

"Would it help if we had those?" Lilit delved, pondering on the various ways they might go about stealing a nuclear bomb.

"Not that the Terran Government would even let such weaponry out of their sight," Durojaiye offered as he got up from his own desk and joined Lilit at the conference table, "but even if they did, it would be no use. Blowing up a large object in space only creates many additional smaller objects that would be much more dangerous to us. Yes, we would stop it from hitting us at the angle necessary to change Venus's axial spin, but there would be a torrent of uncontrollable rubble that may slam into Aestas itself. As you know, it does not have to be much. Something the size of a baseball would decompress the entire colony so fast that we could not stop it in time. The good news is, we would probably asphyxiate before we crashed, burned, or were crushed to death."

"Thanks for that," Lilit deadpanned. "Glad to see you've maintained your always sunny disposition through these tumultuous times, Durojaiye. Alright, so we can't move it in time and we can't blow it up. Where does that leave us?"

"We can let it hit," Durojaiye proposed. "Ahmad, you said the last one barely had any effect on the planet's rotation. We can be prepared this time, batten down the hatches—so to speak—and ride out the literal storm the crash creates. There will have to be hundreds, if not thousands of strikes to change Venus's spin enough for what they hope to do, so letting one make contact could be written off as negligible impact. Since we are not ready to mount a counterattack yet, the best and most logical strategic choice would be to take the beating."

Ahmad shook his head as he declared, "Unfortunately, this ice-asteroid is not like the last one. That one was relatively small, really just large enough to work as a proof of concept. This one is much, much bigger. If it hits, our chances of surviving the updraft are fairly slim. It could be something as small as a system failure from an EMP caused by the collision or as significant as Aestas flipping completely over and plunging us all towards the surface head-first. In either case, Durojaiye's 'positive outlook' from before would also be our greatest hope."

Lilit rubbed her temples as she chastised, "All I hear are all the ways we fail. How do we win?"

"The bottom line," Ahmad noted, "is that our best bet is to get the ice-asteroid to run into something else so that it explodes and disintegrates with the impediment as far away from Venus as possible."

"Durojaiye just said that blowing it up is a bad idea," Lilit summarized.

"I am not talking about hitting it with a precision strike and breaking it apart," Ahmad countered. "What I am saying is an object of equal or more mass—maybe even less mass, depending upon its volume—can absorb the impact for us. Think of it as putting up a physical shield it can run into, but placing it further away in outer space."

"Okay, this I can work with," Lilit perked up. "What do we have that meets those requirements?"

"What about a skimmer?" Durojaiye suggested.

"Skimmers can barely reach the orbital platform," Ahmad disputed. "Each one has neither the capabilities nor the capacity to travel beyond that point. That is, even if we did have time to retrofit one or more, which we most certainly do not."

"Then what about the tugboat?" Durojaiye submitted. "It is already out in space and I know it can go as far as a shuttle. Aritza has often bragged to me about their ability to maneuver it any which way."

"It is a fine idea," Ahmad agreed, "but it is not big enough. In comparison to the incoming projectile, it is so tiny that it is outside the margin of error of expected entry points. As skilled of a pilot as Aritza has become over the past four years, they can only go where we specifically tell them to. Most likely, the rock would slip right past them without enough time for them to adjust. Even Aritza cannot react quickly enough to something moving at two-point-five percent or more the speed of light."

"Then what's left?" Lilit bemoaned. "If we want to stop it, we have to act fast. There must be something."

Everyone was silent for a long time while they considered their options. Suddenly, Ahmad shot his head up and whispered, "Freyr."

"What?" an incredulous Lilit asked, unsure if she

heard Ahmad correctly. Then she feared that had understood him perfectly and began to torture herself as her mind raced away from her, wondering what it would mean for their future.

While Lilit tried to regain control of her own runaway thoughts, Ahmad continued, "We can use the tugboat to move Freyr into the ice-asteroid's projected path. Freyr is large enough that it would cover the entire margin of error and then some. Plus, it has more than enough mass to absorb the impact completely. The projectile itself cannot change direction due to its own speed, so Freyr can act as our sword and shield."

Lilit's jaw dropped as she jumped to her feet, slammed her hands on the table, and yelled, "No! Absolutely not! There have to be other options! Someone, anyone in this room, give me something else we could use, something we could actually afford to lose!"

Instead of an answer, all the other bodies in the room palpably tried to avoid looking Lilit in the eyes. The rest of the Transitional Leadership Assembly who were there and the workers brought in to assist them seemed to have nothing to add, and Lilit cursed their uselessness under her breath. At last, Ahmad broke the tension by saying, "I am most sorry, Lilit, there just is not enough time or readily available materials to entertain any other possibility. Freyr is the only thing we have in space right now that could possibly fit the bill."

As Lilit started sobbing, Durojaiye stood up and wrapped her in a hug. In her ear, he said, "It appears we have no choice. Unfortunately, I am the bearer of more ill tidings."

"What else?" Lilit cried.

There was a moment of silence before Durojaiye stated at a volume only she could hear, "There is something much worse you must do, first, to ensure the success of this mission."

"What could be crueler than this?" Lilit blubbered.

Durojaiye sighed before revealing, "In order to get Freyr into position, someone is going to have to tow it out there and most likely have to stay there until the bitter end. We will lose both the tugboat... and the pilot."

"So, you're saying..." Lilit tried to speak through her tears that just kept coming.

Durojaiye finished her sentence, "...that you must order someone to their death."

Lilit pushed Durojaiye away with a violent shove and stared at him with the wrath of an avenging angel. In turn, he stood there placidly, only showing concern for her. After a moment, Lilit's eyes stopped watering as they extinguished the flame within. She then nodded her head in sad agreement. At that moment, though, she felt something die inside of her.

CHAPTER 47

It was only after the last person cleared out of the ARM that Lilit called Aritza in. They appeared a few minutes later and looked around in confusion at the lack of people and activity. All of the monitors were off and the lights were set low. "Queen-Commander, what's going on? Where is everybody?"

"Please, sit down," Lilit said as she indicated towards the seldom used plush chairs in a corner. Aritza did as asked, but was unable to cover up their uneasiness and concern that was clearly visible in their eyes. Once seated, though, they waited until Lilit spoke.

Lilit opened her mouth several times to start talking, but nothing came out. After a few tries, Aritza attempted to facilitate by asking, "Have I done something wrong or offended you in some way? What can I do to fix it?"

Instead of helping the situation, their questions just brought all of Lilit's feelings of guilt and failure up to the surface. She started to cry, and Aritza looked around, not knowing what to do. "How long have we known each other, Aritza?" was all she could manage between her tears.

"My Queen?" they asked in response. "It must be close to nine... no, ten or eleven years now."

"I know you don't see me this way," Lilit sniffled, "but I am human. I'm not the superbeing you've made me out to be."

Sitting up straight, Aritza declared, "I have to disagree. You are far more than a mere superior person. Look around at all that you have remade in your image! Put yourself in my shoes and imagine this all from my perspective. You'll see a world transformed under your careful gaze and mightily projected mind. To me, to most of the citizens of Aestas, you are a true God!"

Lilit dried her eyes with her handkerchief and intoned, "And as a God, I have the power of life and death within my hands."

"Yes, of course," Aritza submitted. "I've seen you invoke it many times, saving countless lives. Even when I wished to bring the sweet relief of mortality on those who betrayed us, you were the one to pull me back from the abyss. You not only protected people's physical selves, but you stopped someone like me from stepping over the edge and forever staining my soul. Without you, what would I be? You gave me the chance to discover my true self, my calling in life. I worship you for this, as do many others here on Aestas and beyond."

This was all making Lilit feel so much worse, but she forced herself to push onwards, "And if I asked you to kill for me, if I were a vengeful God?"

"I would do it in a heartbeat," Aritza pledged.

"Why?" Lilit queried.

Aritza did not hesitate, saying, "Because I have complete faith in you and your decisions. You do not make any choice lightly, and if you have made up your mind, it is with good reason. Oh, I may disagree with the decision and even the rationalizations behind it, but I will always execute your words as if they are my own thoughts and beliefs."

It was now Lilit's turn to sit up straighter in her chair as she declared, "Aritza, someone has to die..." At this, she caught them up on all the details related to the impending ice-asteroid's impact and the plan to stop it by putting Freyr in its path. "... and that means, the person who will be piloting the tugboat will have to die. But that person, whoever it may be, will be the only death we have to suffer. So, you and I, right here, right now, need to decide who that individual is going to be."

Aritza pursed their hands together and held them

to their lips as they appeared to go into deep thought. Lilit recognized that since Aritza was head of the Space Protectors, they would know who the most capable pilot would be to drag Freyr into position. She wasn't prepared for the real answer, though.

"It's me," Aritza stated plainly.

Lilit jumped up and screamed, "No! Why does it have to be you?! I've invested so much in you; seen you grow into such an amazing human being over this past decade. You absolutely cannot leave me!"

Aritza looked Lilit directly in the eyes and said, "You wouldn't have done all of this if you didn't already realize and understand that it has to be me. You knew the moment you sent everyone out of this room and made sure it was just us here making this decision. Every part of your subconscious knows I am the only choice; you are just trying to keep the truth from yourself."

As Lilit tried to disagree, Aritza cut her off saying, "Look at it clearly: no one is a more accomplished tugboat pilot than me, far and away. If this mission is to succeed, I must be at the helm."

"But it's my fault you are so talented," Lilit complained. "I pushed you into this six years ago. If I didn't do that, then you wouldn't have to die now."

"If I recall that conversation correctly," Aritza

contended, "you promised me that you would always put Aestas before your personal relationships, no matter what. Is that not so?"

Lilit could only nod, so Aritza summed it up with, "Then live by the covenant you made with me. Put aside all your feelings and send me to meet my maker. I'm ready for it; I've always been ready for it. Lest you forget, you are not the only one who is willing to sacrifice anything and everything in order to save our home. So, please, I'm begging you: make me that offering unto the heavens, a hero and martyr for all of Venus to rally behind."

"I'd rather submit myself to the endless darkness than ask you to do this," Lilit rebuked.

"Don't even say that!" Aritza shot back. "Losing me, destroying Freyr—these are just temporary setbacks. But you, my Commander, my Queen, my God... you are the embodiment of our hope. Without you, we are all lost. I believe, we all believe, that you—and only you—can see us through to the promised land on the other side."

Lilit slumped back into her chair and they were both silent for a long while. After some indeterminable amount of time, Lilit leaned forward and commanded, "Protector Aritza, I direct you to use the tugboat to bring Freyr into the path of the incoming ice-asteroid, and then stay with the second city so as to ensure that the incoming projectile is completely destroyed, and thus save Venus and Aestas. This is not your choice; you are not electing to die. I am ordering you to your death so that all others might live. Your demise will be on my conscience, and mine alone. Is that understood?"

Aritza stood up, saluted, and declared with emphasis, "Yes, ma'am!"

Lilit stood up, too, and looked Aritza over. She walked around them a few times before ending up directly in front of their face. Putting her hands on Aritza's cheeks, Lilit pulled them in close and planted a long kiss directly on their lips. "Aritza," she spoke with a sultry air through parted lips, "just for tonight, will you call me Lilit?"

"Ye-ye-ye-yes, my Quee—my... Lilit," Aritza said breathlessly.

Lilit then held out her hand until Aritza stopped gawking with awe and took it in their own hand. She then led them along, through the door, and into her private sanctuary.

Just like the large central monitor in the ARM, every single screen—whether physical or virtual—was tuned into only one thing. All eyes were watching the incoming ice-asteroid as it headed toward Freyr, which had previously been towed by the tugboat into the harbinger-of-destruction's path. Lilit had nothing more to do at this point but stand, pace, and watch the action unfold. Of course, there wasn't really anything to see. They had directed a satellite telescope to point at Freyr's location and it was returning a seemingly unchanging picture of a vaguely Aestas-like shape, albeit a deflated version. The incoming projectile was too dark and moving far too fast to really see in the human visual spectrum they were all attuned to. The only way they would know anything had happened would be when—

And then it was done. Freyr lit up and disintegrated into nothingness. It was there, and then it wasn't. There was no reverberating bang from some great explosion because there was no medium to carry sound in space to begin with. After letting the image clear, Ahmad declared from his position, "That was most assuredly a direct hit! It worked! Freyr stopped the ice-asteroid and we are all safe. I see no significant incoming tertiary debris. Everything that is coming this direction should easily burn up in the upper atmosphere, posing no threat whatsoever."

The room erupted in cheering, hooting, and hollering. People hugged, some of them even kissed. Over the years of living and working so closely together and under such trying conditions, many intimate relationships had formed—as well as fallen apart—among the members of the Transitional Leadership Assembly and their staff. Lilit was just as guilty as the rest at having engaged in a handful of affairs of varying degrees and durations that all eventually fizzled out. It seemed like the drama of life could not be contained, not even by their dire situation. However, Lilit was never able to maintain anything resembling a normal pairing; it always became painfully obvious that she was held apart from all of them. It was then that she realized how right Aritza had been about her.

After spending the night, Aritza had left Lilit's sleeping quarters shortly after dawn and went straight to the skimmer. Thus, they had been completely alone out there in the dark, emptiness of the cosmos since that point. Lilit had pretended to be asleep when they left her bedroom so that neither of them would have to deal with the pain, hurt, and re-criminations that would be mixed in with saying goodbye. By her lonesome once more, separated from all the people she loved but could never be close to, Lilit tightly held onto her own naked body as she built the resolve to become a murderer.

It was because of this that she could not join in the celebration. The relief in the room was palpable following over ten days of extremely tense waiting. Nonetheless, to Lilit, everything about it had felt wrong, even though it was all necessary. She was try-ing to find the balance between being her human self and being the God these people demanded, but she wasn't sure where the line should be. All she was cer-tain of was that she could never be normal again, not unless she did something drastic. But as a divine be-ing incarnate, was it not her prerogative to change the rules on a whim?

For now, though, Lilit was still in charge, and that would be the case for a long time to come. Instinc-tively, she realized that the plan she announced just a few months prior to finally hand the government back to the citizenry was not going to happen; that she was trapped as the Godhead of Venus. As such, she knew that she must continue going through the motions of being the leader they expected her to be. "Can someone open up an audio channel to all of Aestas, please?" she asked above the din.

"You're on live with the whole colony," someone said. Lilit was numb, so she didn't care nor notice who spoke the words.

Instead, she declared, "Attention citizens of Aestas: you are safe now! Freyr did its job, acting as our noble sword and shield against those who tried to destroy us. Obviously, we have lost a lot today, almost more than I can even bear. Yet, we cannot forget that we have gained something, too. The lesson of this day is the story of our unbreakable resilience. We have proven that no one, no matter how powerful they are, can defeat us. We will rebuild, we will grow, and we will fulfill the destiny of Venus!"

At this, Lilit signaled for the feed to be cut off, walked away from the large screen, and sat down at her seat at the head of the conference table. "Transitional Leadership Assembly, join me here," she ordered. "I want an after-action report."

Durojaiye walked over and whispered in her ear, "Are you sure you want to do this now? We can spend all of tomorrow going through the gritty details. Perhaps it would be best just to bask in our victory?"

"What victory?" Lilit fumed.

Durojaiye frowned and said, "Lilit, do not beat yourself up; you have done what was required and the mission was a success. Even you are allowed to breathe and mourn."

"Sit. Down." was Lilit's only response.

Shrugging his shoulders, Durojaiye took his place at the table as the others slowly joined them, dragging along various accoutrements with them. Lilit waited with a patience she was not feeling for everyone to find their spot.

Once they were all gathered, Lilit jumped straight into it without any tact by asking, "Tell me what, if anything, we've discovered and learned from this horrific experience."

"Quite a bit," Ahmad offered. "We can apply all of the new data we have now to the early detection system. I only have a very preliminary analysis here, but it looks like there is a noticeably distinct energy signature associated with the Torch Drive. I believe we will be able to create sensors to specifically look for these. If applied correctly, then we are talking about having something like twenty days of warning from when they light up in the Kuiper Belt, double what we had during this crisis. I mean, it would actually be a signal from six or seven hours in the past due to the speed of light, but that can be accounted for in our overall preparations and calculations."

Lilit shook her head as she pursued this line of thought further, "But will that really be enough when we have nothing left to stop these rocks with?"

Ahmad held open his hands as he declared, "It is a start. We have to try something."

"I believe I may have the solution to that," Durojaiye interjected. "I have already spoken with our Venusian Colony on Mercury and they have assured me that the plan is sound."

"What plan?" Lilit probed.

Durojaiye smiled in what seemed to Lilit such an unnatural manner given their current circumstances. "They are going to start carving out pure large chunks of the planet and delivering them to us wholesale. I have conferred with others, and it looks like we should have no problem placing them into orbit and then we can throw them at incoming ice-asteroids when they come our way. We will never need to sacrifice another totem of Venus again once these large chunks start to arrive. Lilit, do you not see: it is not over yet, not by a long shot!"

Where To From Here?

CHAPTER 49

"Successful contact and... incoming ice-asteroid has been destroyed," Ahmad announced by rote from his desk in the ARM. Lilit felt that even he sounded bored by this task of throwing pieces of Mercury at high-speed primordial meteors and obliterating the pair. For more than a year, they had been doing just that. Since they now had a fully operational defense mechanism, she could not imagine what anyone was gaining by continuing to lob rocks their way. Were they testing and probing their line and capabilities? If they were, it seemed to be mostly benefiting Venus.

At first, things were a lot more hit or miss. Several of the projectiles managed to evade their counteroffensive measures, and consequently slammed into the planet at the intended angle. Thankfully, none of those were as large as the second volley they had sent that resulted in Freyr's destruction, so the damage was minimal. The bigger they were, the easier each one became to intercept and annihilate. However, as Ahmad explained, even the failures added to their data pool. And that, in turn, made them better and better at being able to avoid getting smashed to pieces.

By this point, "Venus's Charm"—the tongue-in-cheek name Durojaiye had given their fortifying weaponry—had not missed its target in nearly six months. The solution seemed to have been perfected no matter the size of the mortar. Lilit felt the whole endeavor was uncouth. In her mind, turning these resource-rich chunks into dust was completely wasteful; they could have been put to much better use.

Sighing, Lilit ordered, "Stand down from alert status."

The lighting across the entire colony then returned to normal rather than the crimson it had been bathed in. This change signaled to the citizenry that the danger had passed and that they were free to return to their everyday lives. Lilit reflected on how quickly they had all adapted to being under constant bombardment. At that point, it had become just a minor inconvenience to stop everything they were doing, take cover, and await the potential need to evacuate. Not that they had anywhere to evacuate to, but Durojaiye had convinced her that able security theater helped keep everyone calm, which was much more important for their collective safety.

Nevertheless, since they had around twenty days of warning each time, these disruptions could actually be scheduled in. They were even able to fly Aestas itself further away, taking it to the other side of the planet from a potential impact site. This way, should they somehow miss their mark, the dangers would be minimized. The unfortunate side effect of this was the interruption of the normal light/darkness cycle, which in turn created some unusual weather inside Aestas. There were times when it became uncomfortably hot due to having to stay under the sun for long periods, and others when temperatures dipped to levels never before felt on the colony as they hid on the dark side of the planet. Before this happened, Lilit had never heard the refrigeration machinery that pushed the hot air out of Aestas turn off. The silence from the lack of whirring was deafening.

"How's our inventory looking?" Lilit customarily asked, although she already knew the answer.

"Good," Ahmad confirmed. "It was a small one, so we only had to use one of our little rocks, too. The aiming precision was spot on. I have to hand it to Durojaiye; his targeting algorithms have really made a significant impact. If we had these a year ago..."

Ahmad must have realized the faux pas he was about to commit and shut his mouth. "It's okay," Lilit

assuaged him. "Who knew one could become so pro-
ficient at this particular skillset?"

"Well, I suppose Earth Central Command," Durojaiye offered as he spun around in his chair to face
Lilit. "While Ahmad honors me by giving me credit
for procuring this code, I was merely the vessel by
which it was liberated from the Terran Government's
protected servers. Of course, I never would have
thought to look for such a thing before these incidents."

"Incidents?" Lilit questioned the word. "What an
odd way to put it. We've really become so accustomed to this life that the constant threats from
above have just become mere 'incidents' to us. How
sad."

"Or how marvelous," Durojaiye countered. "In a
couple of months, we will receive our fourth delivery
of arsenal from Mercury and our stock will be over-
flowing, based on the rate of our enemy's aggression.
If anything, we are now in a better position than we
were a year-and-a-half ago on Venusian Liberation
Day when all this began. I know we skipped over hon-
oring it this past year, but we should think about
bringing that holiday back again."

"I don't believe that's a very good day for festivities anymore," Lilit sulked. "You'll have to come up

with a different one, a better one."

"How about the anniversary of when we overthrew the Managing Council?" Durojaiye proposed. "I think that would have been a few weeks ago."

Frowning, Lilit queried, "Don't we have any historical events to commemorate that are not wrapped up in violence and tragedy?"

"How about the day Ahmad and I stepped foot— or rather wheel—on Aestas?" Durojaiye joked with a smile.

"Oh, I like this idea," Ahmad chimed in. "We could call it: Ahmadojaiye Day!"

"What is wrong with Durojmad Day?" Durojaiye countered.

Lilit giggled and scolded them, "Don't make me laugh, you two! Can't you tell that I want to be miserable and depressed?"

"Too bad," Ahmad declared. "Come on, let us go topside. We have all been locked in this chamber for far too long, staring at these same walls. We need to bask in the sun on this beautiful day."

"As any true Venusian would want to do," Durojaiye agreed.

Lilit hesitated, but quickly changed her mind and acquiesced. After all, wasn't she the most Venusian of them all? Didn't she need the sun to fuel her?

After walking around what remained of the accessible area of Level 1, Lilit, Ahmad, and Durojaiye—as well as Lilit's slew of Protector guards—returned to the ARM. Although being outside had certainly refreshed her somewhat, it did not quite quench her thirst for freedom from the restraints of responsibility. Lilit would have liked to have been able to mingle with the regular people milling about, too, but her gaggle of visible security officers made that all but impossible; besides already being the most famous person in all Aestas. Additionally, there was the unspoken threat of plainclothes agents intermixed with the crowd, ready to pounce if necessary.

To Lilit, of course, all these efforts seemed over-indulgent. She admitted that there certainly were dangers to her well-being in the past, but it seemed like Durojaiye had been able to purge pretty much every naysayer that might be a potential threat to her. He was certainly not as convinced as she was in this regard, so the impregnable wall of humanity remained between her and the rest of society.

Per usual during any public appearance, there were cheers and chants of "Long live the Queen!" Since they had just blown another ice-asteroid to smithereens, patriotism was running high, leading to plenty of clapping and shouts of appreciation. Their band came upon some children who were kicking around a soccer ball and they stopped what they were doing to cautiously stare at the Queen with curiosity. Lilit realized that in the over eight years since their coup against the Managing Council, thousands of babies had been born who knew of no other life than living under her rule.

Once back at the ARM, Lilit had everyone available gather around the conference table. She started the impromptu session by noting, "Today, I saw some children who have never known anything except my hegemony. How can they truly be free if I continue to hold on to my power and never grant them the democracy they deserve?"

"Those children would not be alive today if not for you," Ahmad countered. "And I mean that in a lot of ways. Prior to the Liberation Day attack, the birthrate on Aestas had skyrocketed. That is, compared to its abysmally low level from before the ousting of the Managing Council. The hope you have instilled in the citizenry has literally translated into the existence of more babies, despite having not re-solved our overpopulation issue completely. Yes, there has certainly been a drop-off in the past year, but overall, we are at least treading water."

"Moreover," Durojaiye chimed in, "now is not the time to end your reign. You need to see us through the current situation. Once this has passed, too, then you can talk about taking the next steps."

"Did you just paraphrase and use my mantra against me?" Lilit laughed. "Well, I guess I deserve that. Alright, fine, I give; we'll get through this osten-sible issue of rocks falling from the heavens first, but we need a way to bring it to an end. The problem is, though, that in the past year and a half, no one has come forward and admitted culpability. More so, no demands or ultimatums have been made of us."

"I mean," Ahmad offered, "it must be HSA, Earth Central Command, and/or the Terran Government, or some mix of all three. No one else has all the re-sources, knowhow, and motive to pull this off and to keep it up for so long."

"Of course, I agree," Lilit stated, "but that doesn't resolve the main problem: who do we talk to so that we can bring this to an equitable conclusion? Setting up this ploy must have been years, if not decades, in the making. I don't need Isra Emerson to tell me that they have obviously been redirecting the resources that should have been going towards building a second city on Venus into this effort."

"And, it is as Ahmad has highlighted many times," Durojaiye brought up. "With their failed attempts at terraforming Mars due to its diminutive size and lack of magnetic field, they have set their sights on Venus, a closer Earth-analogue planet. Despite this decision, they were equally aware that the people of Aestas would never have agreed to readily give up their home, but that does not matter to them. If we are talking about the Terran Government or any of their subsidiaries, you must realize that from their perspective, they own Venus and can do whatever they want with it. Very few on Earth will stand up for us, so they have no fear of retribution or mass protests in their own backyard. If anything, they have used the rise of the Movement to paint us as usurpers that they must contain."

"So, this is why no petitions have been made?" Lilit probed. "They are just waiting until they connect with the perfect shot and destroy our world, then they'll swoop in? I don't buy it. Why not ask us to lay out terms to surrender to them?"

"Perhaps they are not ready yet," Durojaiye

hypothesized. "They might still need something else, some other tool that is not quite complete. These ice-asteroids may be massive attacks to us, but they could just be little warnings or potshots to them. They refuse to answer our calls because they are not at the point where they feel the need to talk to us."

"What more could they possibly need?" Lilit harangued. "You're saying what they've done so far is still not enough?"

"Durojaiye is right," Ahmad expounded. "There is much more that they will require before they are ready for a terraforming effort. For instance, they will need a giant shade in orbit to block out the sun. This, in turn, will help cool down the planet. They must be constructing it somewhere, probably on a platform around Mars or Ceres. If Aritza were still with us, I am sure they would say that we should stop playing defense and start going on offense."

Wincing at Aritza's name, Lilit asked, "Are you saying that we should commence a blind hunt for this sunshade and blow it up? How would we even go about doing either of those things?"

Ahmad shrugged and said, "In mythology, Venus and Mars were forbidden lovers, and together they produced the beautiful Harmonia."

Lilit laughed and said, "Oh, you of all people,

would like to have an affair with Mars, huh?"

Blushing, Ahmad said, "You were the one who talked about a confederation with Mercury. Although we have nothing official yet, perhaps it is time to explore an alliance of like-minded colonies and seal it with a mutual protection pact. After all, 'Cine Cerere... friget Venus.'"

"What does that mean?" Lilit wondered aloud.

Ahmad clarified, "I was paraphrasing a very old Earth saying. It means, 'without Ceres... Venus would freeze.'"

Throwing cold water on this line of thought, Durojaiye noted, "No one will want to be in an alliance with a nation that is already under attack. Yes, they may sympathize, they may even send arms and intelligence, but they will not stick out their own necks for us. A student of history such as yourself should be well-aware of this fact."

In recognition of this simple truth, Ahmad hung his head in resignation.

"I disagree," Lilit perked up. "I believe that all avenues of peace and cooperation are worth pursuing. Maybe they won't bear fruit during our current conflict, but this is just temporary, right? Any connections we make now may prove useful in the future. Ahmad, I cannot afford to lose you at home, so put

together a team of people to investigate all these possibilities. I see no reason not to explore every
potential avenue available to us."

"In that case," Durojaiye said, "then there is perhaps one additional path that should be pursued."

"What are you thinking?" Lilit asked with suspicion as she narrowed her eyes.

Durojaiye laid out his concern, "In order for our
enemies to have been so successful at remaining elu-
sive, they must have had someone on the inside
helping them, someone invisible to us all."

Lilit did not have to think too long to come up
with a name that fit that description, "Xander."

"It is not yet possible to confirm that at this
point," Durojaiye admitted, "but he has always been
so chummy with the Terrans. This was true even before you two left for Earth."

Lilit ruminated on this idea a bit more before declaring, "While I'm sure that Xander has provided
intelligence to the Terran Government, he would only
do so to ease the pain of the transition he envisions
is coming and to protect lives. Xander is a lot of
things, but he would do just about anything to avoid
any violence befalling us. Preserving life is his number one goal. No, Durojaiye, if this ghost of yours is
real, it must be someone else."

After another eight months of disintegrating ice-asteroids at a safe distance from Venus, Lilit barely even paid attention to when the alert system was engaged. Ahmad was getting to the point where he wanted to hand the entire solution over to an A.I., but Lilit was still concerned that it might attack a friendly object or vessel. After all, they were still receiving shipments from Mercury and doing construction of their own in orbit. Besides, she did not want to do anything that might scare off Mars or Ceres from approaching them like the potential of a robot striking them unprovoked.

Their ambassador had arrived on Mars after departing from Aestas during an opportunistic transfer window. The inferior conjunction came when Mars was relatively close to the sun in its highly elliptical orbit and Earth was almost completely on the other side of their shared central star. That meant that Earth Central Command would not have been able to intercept or interfere with their mission. Ahmad, Durojaiye, and the rest of the Transitional Leadership

Assembly were convinced that it was worth the risk to have a representative on Mars as the face-to-face engagement would create a human connection that could not be ignored.

Ceres, though, was another story entirely. It was significantly further away and the chances to travel there were so infrequent that it just did not seem worth it. Even the Terran Government was quite sparing with their missions there due to the difficulty of navigating within the Asteroid Belt. Ahmad gleefully told everyone, though, that the Belt did not look like it does in the movies with tons of giant rocks close to each other that required a crack pilot to circumnavigate. "Actually," he said during one meeting, "the average distance between a couple of asteroids is nearly a million kilometers. Earth and Luna are two and a half times closer than that!"

The true problem, he noted, was making it to the right target and being able to gain orbital insertion without just flying by entirely. "We call Ceres a dwarf planetoid," Ahmad had continued, "but it is on the smaller side of even that designation. If you compare it to other heavenly bodies, even the four Galilean moons around Jupiter are fifty to a hundred-and-fifty times Ceres's mass. I honestly would not trust myself to get the math right and arrive there safely."

Due to this, their ambassador to Mars was pulling double-duty as a de facto one to Ceres, although there was no chance of her ever visiting there. Still, since the communication time was generally more favorable between those worlds—although there were occasions when Venus would technically be closer to Ceres than Mars was—it made sense to have her be their main gateway and contact point.

Despite having a person in place, not much had transpired with either Mars or Ceres. Neither one was owning up to building a sunshade that would eventually need to be placed in orbit above Venus, and the intelligence officers that Durojaiye had sent along had not come up with anything yet, either. However, there was some positive momentum as Mars had expressed a particular interest in direct trade. Opening a new market and giving their idle shuttles something to do when they were not aligned with Earth certainly piqued everyone's interest. "It's not much," Lilit told the rest of the TLA one day, "but it is progress. Let's hold on tightly to that fact."

Nevertheless, both Mars and Ceres were quite concerned about potential retaliation from Earth. Talking to Venus and allowing a representative into their midst was one thing, but openly supporting Aestas was apparently too risky. "That said," Ahmad had declared during another get together, "they still would like to do business with us. It is just that they would want all their goods to pass through Mercury—and for us to provide the shuttles in the first place—so as not to alert the Terran Government."

"Oh," Durojaiye chimed in, "you mean they want to set up a smuggling route? Well, this sounds like a job for me, then!"

Lilit laughed and asked, "When and how did Mercury become the center of the Sol System?"

The swiftest planet had turned out to be critically important to them, and not just because of the arsenal it provided as a shield against the ice-asteroid bombardments. Once they were satisfied with their overall stockpile level of retaliatory rocks, they could finally allocate far fewer resources from Mercury towards defensive measures and could finally use the raw materials for their original intended purposes.

Uninterested in the specifics of the latest incoming projectile, Lilit queried, "Ahmad, did we get an update on New Freyr from Mercury?"

Seemingly perplexed by the non sequitur, Ahmad replied, "Eh? Stand by, I was not looking at that right now. I am sure I have an update around here somewhere or the other."

Sighing, Lilit responded, "Oh, never mind, then,

if you're busy. I was just looking for something to do while we waited."

After their fourth Mercury supply run, they had sent a construction crew back on the returning shuttle to join those already living at their colony there. Lilit had decided that Freyr's essence would live again through a newly built second city, but that it would be safer and easier to construct it in orbit around Mercury rather than transport the materials to Venus to accomplish the same goal close to home. There was some pushback since Venus already had all the infrastructure and not everyone was keen on moving to Mercury for several years to make this happen, but Lilit surmised that they couldn't risk an errant piece of debris destroying all their hard work once again. The death of another Freyr would devastate the citizenry, and her.

When the time came, they would tow New Freyr back to Venus, just as Aestas had originally come from Earth. Lilit felt there was something poetic about that, with cities being built elsewhere and then conveyed to them as already finished works of beauty. Though she missed being able to take the skimmer up to the orbital platform and watch it come together, the risk mitigation—as Durojaiye had put it—was worth it. Nothing had changed for them; if they were to survive as an independent world, they needed more living and working space.

As the lights changed from crimson to their regular white settings, Lilit huffed, "Finally! Now we can move on and do some real work today!"

Her cheer was short lived, though, as suddenly the lights switched back to the darkest red and a loud alarm started blaring.

"Ahmad," Lilit shouted over the screeching siren, "what the hell is going on? Did you miss the ice-asteroid or something?"

"What?" Ahmad shouted back, "Hold on!"

The irritating bell was silenced at last and the lights returned to normal. "Was it a false alarm?" Durojaiye asked.

Ahmad did not respond at all as he was intently combing through something on his tablet. After not getting an answer for a while, Lilit felt her patience wearing thin and said, "Come on Ahmad, what's the deal already?"

Lilit desperately wanted to just slip away to her sleeping quarters and get some shut-eye. Even though they were now able to easily obliterate any threat from the Kuiper Belt and the attacks did not require her direct attention, she had decided that that it was her duty to be sitting there for each and every engagement. Over the past few weeks, the rate had certainly picked up, but it wasn't beyond anything they could handle. Unfortunately, though, the interception points were coming at inopportune times, meaning Lilit had not had a full night's rest in quite some time. She was feeling it in her bones.

Lilit was drumming her fingers on the conference table when Ahmad started bowing up and down while chanting, "Oh no, oh no, oh no, it is real, it is all real."

Concerned, Lilit got up and put her hand on his shoulder. When he didn't respond, she started shaking him and said, "What is it, Ahmad? Talk to me!"

Ahmad seemed to snap out of it and looked her directly in the eyes as he inquired, "Lilit?"

"Yes, Ahmad," she assured him, "it's me. Are you okay?"

Ahmad frowned, pushed Lilit's hands away from his shoulders, and went over to the large screen. There, he put up a partial representation of the Sol System, displaying only the Kuiper Belt, Venus, and the sun, all in disproportionate sizes for illustrative purposes. "Look here," he said as he pointed to a region of the Kuiper Belt that looked pretty much like any other one. Suddenly, a huge portion of the digitally representative rocks were outlined in red.

Lilit stared aghast. "How many?" she rasped.

Ahmad shook his head saying, "Hundreds, thousands, maybe even more. So many of them lit up at once and they are so close together, relatively speaking, that we cannot accurately differentiate one from another. Even in the best-case scenario, we do not have enough arsenal to take out more than a quarter of them. Please do not make me tell you what happens in the worst outcome. It does not matter anyway; we are completely helpless!"

"No!" Lilit cried, "It's never over! Tell me what terrible things we need to sacrifice this time to save Venus and keep Aestas afloat. Who needs to die? Who do I have to kill? What piece of my heart and soul must be ripped away?"

Ahmad returned to his desk, leaving Lilit alone at the screen. From there, he declared, "Lilit, there is no feasible way around this, except one. We need to stop the ice-asteroids en route, and very soon. Frankly, if we do not find a way to force them to engage their reverse thrusters in the next nine days or so, there will be no way to stop them in time before they crash into us."

"Good, good," Lilit wildly floundered. "Yes, this is what I'm talking about. All we need to do is hack them and get them to pump their breaks, right?"

"Lilit..." Ahmad began, "we have been trying to do that for years and are no closer to gaining access. The A.I. required to guide these ice-asteroids is amazingly precise and protected in ways no one here has ever seen before. They are practically fully autonomous and very few methods appear to exist to even interface with them. We simply, honestly, cannot make a miracle breakthrough that has eluded us this entire time with just the few measly days that remain before us."

Lilit pulled at her hair as she probed, "Where does that leave us? What are our choices?"

"I see only two," Ahmad professed. "The first is that we accept our fate and die with dignity."

"Including all those children out there who didn't ask for any of this?" Lilit shot back. "You want me to make a decision to tell hundreds of thousands of people to simply roll over and die?"

"We do not really have anywhere to evacuate to," Ahmad argued. "The shuttle is between worlds right now, so all the skimmer could do is take a few hundred people up to the orbital platform where they would have a much longer and more painful demise by starvation or worse. The compassionate thing to do would be to allow them to perish with Aestas, quickly and quietly."

"And the other option?" Lilit solicited.

"Swallow our pride and beg for mercy from the Terran Government. They most likely have a way to either stop or redirect the Torch Drives."

"If we do that," Lilit complained, "then these past twelve years will have been for nothing!"

"But we will be alive," Ahmad offered.

Lilit turned towards the screen and addressed the red-highlighted rocks, "Die as a Venusian or live on as a failure under the thumb of the Terrans—are these really our only two possible futures?"

The digital asteroids' lack of a reply, as well as the absence of one from anyone else in the room, was proof enough that these divergent paths were their only potential avenues. Lilit began to rack her brain, looking for something they missed, some magic rabbit she could pull out of her hat. She had defied the odds for so long that losing was not even a possibility she considered anymore. There must be some type of white knight who could swoop in, she thought, some way to make what they claimed was impossible to become their reality once again.

And then, in her mind, the puzzle pieces suddenly started fitting together. At first, it was just a vague impression, like a word she was trying to recall, or the blurry recollection of a deceased loved one's face. More than a dozen years of doubts, oddities, recriminations, surprises, and more began to paint a picture, one she had not consciously considered before. She wondered if she knew all along, deep down inside, and had just been fooling herself, but then she realized that it was more than that, something much more devious. Her entire existence for ages now had been planned and coerced with the premeditated intent to get to this exact inflection point. All of it was simply about this one small moment in history and the decision she would be forced to make.

She felt so dirty, so used, so abused.

"Get out!" Lilit abruptly shouted, "Everyone clear out of here! Except you two: Ahmad and Durojaiye; you stay." When the rest of her cortege did not start moving fast enough, Lilit reprimanded, "Come on, come on, let's go, out, now, chop, chop!" This she ordered while making the same motions with her hands.

Eventually, after several more minutes and directives, they all finished filing out, leaving just Ahmad and Durojaiye at their workstations and Lilit standing alone with her hand on the large screen. Leaning her forehead into the monitor, she quietly said to the physical display, "I always hated you."

CHAPTER 53

After being silent for a long while, Lilit backed away from the large observation screen and whispered, "I get it now; I finally understand..."

At this declaration, she moved around all the other desks and slunk down in her seat at the head of the conference table. Ahmad turned around on his chair, left his station, walked over, and sat down next to her. "What do you mean?" he asked his one and only righteous symbol, leader, monarch, and deity.

Instead of answering him, she turned towards Durojaiye who still sat at his own desk with his back to her. "Durojaiye," she sneered, "now I know what your assignment was."

Durojaiye did not move or respond in any way. As Ahmad stared confusingly at her, Lilit said to Durojaiye's back, "Your job was to come here and raise our hopes so that we would think we stood a fighting chance. That way, when the time came for the Terran Government, Earth Central Command, and HSA to implement their real plan, we would have already exhausted ourselves by believing that we could somehow have won. And when that happened, we would realize that we were completely outmatched and outplayed, and despair in the revelation that we never stood a chance in the first place. It was all one long con game to make sure we wasted our energy, dreams, and resources on pointless side projects before the real invasion began, so we would know just how utterly defeated we were and would no longer fight back. God, Xander even tried to warn me…"

"Lilit!" a shocked Ahmad chided. "What are you saying? This is our dearest and most trustworthy Durojaiye you are talking about!"

"Wake up, Ahmad!" Lilit yelled back, at last acknowledging him. "He's been manipulating us from the very start."

"I cannot believe that!" Ahmad shouted in return.

Lilit expounded, "Then let me lay it all out plainly for you. Do you think it was mere happenstance that you and Durojaiye met and paired off? He already told us that he had been evaluating everyone and everything going on aboard the shuttle from Earth. He waited, watched, observed, and planned for the ideal moment to spring his trap. He glommed on to someone who had all the resources and skillset necessary to succeed on Venus, but had none of the confidence, a person who reeked of imposter syndrome. In you, he found the perfect patsy to be his own cover.

"And then he discovered me. Oh, no, I don't think he was looking for me in particular, I'm not that ego-centric. Yet right from the beginning he saw that I checked many of the boxes he was looking for in a savior-figure. There I was: a native who happened to also be descended from the founders. More importantly, I was young, pretty—but not so beautiful that I was unapproachable, more the 'attainable' type—energetic, connected, well-spoken, charismatic, authentic, and many other beneficial qualities. I never told anyone this, but I went to see Chigozie while I was on Earth. That's right, and she practically spilled the beans then and there! I was just too busy, exhausted, messed-up, and goddamn oblivious during that timeframe to realize what she was alluding to. I thought she was concerned that I was having an affair with her husband, but even she knew from just one look and a few brief words that not only had Durojaiye recruited me, but why.

"Whatever I lacked, he worked with me on, grooming me into his iconic vision. I never wanted to speak to groups of people or large crowds; that was all under his tutelage and urging. I never desired to be involved in politics at all; he found an issue that bothered me and kept digging and digging until he got me to turn it into a noble cause. All I craved was for my clients to have the space to live comfortable, enjoyable, and productive lives, and not be packed in like sardines. Yet, from that simple wish, this is where we ended up. At no point did I decide for myself that I wanted to be a revolutionary!"

"But you were the one who started the Movement," Ahmad observed.

"Was I? Who even brought up the idea of a popular resistance in the first place? Who was the person who recruited the initial two people to join us? Who organized all those early meetings and rallies? Who created a network and merged together many disparate voices under one roof? Who drafted a division for espionage and a military wing? Who initiated a coup against the Managing Council? Who pushed you to come up with the Mercury plan? Who was it that even said that they could be a community organizer, but only to fulfill someone else's objective? It was Durojaiye! It was all Durojaiye!"

"I... I... I...," was all Ahmad was able to say before Lilit interceded.

"Oh, Durojaiye," she mocked to the man who still refused to show his face, "you were good, almost flawless. But there were times you messed up, weren't there? You pretty much always maneuvered us into thinking these were our own personal ideas and that we were doing them of our own volition, but even you are human and slipped up on occasion. When you volunteered for me to go to Earth, that was a huge mistake. You said then that you feared what Xander might do if you hadn't acted, and I took that to mean you were afraid of what he might do to me. But no, the truth was that your plan might be ruined if he did anything to me! Thus, you risked it all and, luckily for you, it ended up paying off.

"But the biggest mistake you made was when the first ice-asteroid hit. I always thought it was just poor luck it slammed into the planet while I was giving a major speech about our victory and liberation, but it was you who pushed for that exact date and time. And when I called you out on it, you took the blame to disarm me! I bet that you thought it was a bad idea, too, to align it like that—too suspicious—but that you were ordered to go through with it by your real bosses. Then you even followed it up by magically coming up with Venus's Charm immediately after Freyr was destroyed! Fuck, I've been so, so stupid. For over twelve years, I ignored all the warning signs and let you do this to me and my home."

"If everything you have said is true," Ahmad weakly interrupted one last time to argue a losing battle, "what does it mean about our friend?"

Lilit howled, "Our friend? Our friend?! Oh, poor, poor, gullible, adorable Ahmad, you still don't get it. Come on now, isn't it as clear as the sky above our heads? Durojaiye was never our friend; it was all a sophisticated, cynical ruse."

"Durojaiye, please speak up, please defend yourself," Ahmad pleaded to his unresponsive companion. "Tell her it is not true... Durojaiye... please..."

Durojaiye finally spun around in his chair and plainly stated, "These are not mutually exclusive things. I have my assignment, and we have our friendships. Our relationships are real. I care very much for you, Lilit, and you, Ahmad. You are some of the most important people to me in the whole solar system. If needed, I would lay down my life for either of you. I would have died here today, if that had been your wish and final decision."

"But you betrayed us," Lilit cried.

This appeared to at last break Durojaiye's impervious wall of placidity as he screamed back, "I did no such thing! What did I tell you on the first day we met? What did I remind you of at every opportunity? That I was a spy, that I had a duty and obligation to Earth Central Command, that I was working on my assignment at every moment since I left my home, and that I could not go back to my cherished and most precious family until it was completed. I have never, not ever, lied to you."

"No, Durojaiye, I suppose you never have," Lilit seethed. "You just never told the truth."

They were all silent after that, except for Ahmad who was whimpering as he attempted to hold back the tears that kept flowing as the reality of Lilit's words and Durojaiye's confession sunk in. After collecting himself, he granted a look of pure disgust towards Durojaiye before turning to Lilit and asking, "What do we do now?"

Lilit also had salty rain running down her own cheeks. She wiped them away with her sleeves and requested, "Durojaiye, contact your handlers. Tell them that your operation was a complete success and that we are prepared to negotiate the terms of our surrender, including the complete evacuation and abandonment of Aestas. Just please, stop the incoming volley before it's too late so that we can save all these innocent people's lives."

Durojaiye took one last long, penetrating look at Lilit and then Ahmad before nodding and stating directly, "Yes, I will do that. Please excuse me." At those words, he stood up and walked out of the room, as well as their lives, forever.

Lessons of the Past

When he heard the knock at his open office door, Captain Edward Hersch looked up from his tablet and saw Marco Chung standing there. The young deckhand had been an eleventh-hour replacement for the originally assigned crewmember who was found comatose in a hospital after being severely beaten. Last Edward had heard, it was not looking good, but he would not know their fate until they returned to Earth after this mission to Proxima Centauri B. Already he couldn't even remember what their name was.

"Ah, Marco," Edward said, "good to see you. What can I do for you?"

The morose-looking youth who seldom smiled continued standing in the doorway as he stated, "I finished that book about the history of Aestas and Venus that you wanted me to read."

"Oh, that quickly?" Edward rhetorically asked. "Well, don't just keep standing there, come inside and take a seat."

Marco hesitated for a moment and then flopped onto one of the chairs in front of Edward's desk. From what little information Edward had been able to glean from the fledgling crewmember, it appeared that Marco never had anyone in his entire short life who really provided him any type of support system. Edward saw some potential in Marco and had decided to take him under his wing as a mentee and an apprentice, of sorts. Afterall, HSA always needed the next generation of interstellar pilots to take Torch Ships out to their existing two extrasolar colonies and to continue the search for the next potential one—as well as perhaps finally find some sign of extraterrestrial life out there. It was quite vexing that they had not found any yet, but he remained hopeful that the discovery was just around the corner.

"So, what'd you think?" Edward inquired.

"I don't get why you wanted me to read this," Marco pouted. "I thought you'd need me to bone up on ship operations or something technical like that. I mean, if you wanted me to learn some history, why not just have me review a key-point summary from the local Archive. This was so... I don't know... it felt like a drama."

Edward furrowed his brow at this response before querying in a non sequitur, "Marco, how old are you now?"

"I think I just turned nineteen—back on Earth,

that is," Marco explained.

"Yeah, time dilation can be a bitch to keep track of," Edward granted. "Don't worry about it so much."

"Yes, sir," Marco formally conceded.

"At ease, soldier!" Edward jokingly ordered. "And that, right there, is one of the reasons why I wanted you to read this book. History isn't just about memorizing the bullet points; it is about experiencing the emotions of joy and sorrow through the eyes of those who were forced to weather it. More so, there are lessons we can learn from what they had to endure. Lilit Sarkisian, Ahmad Al Zaheri, Durojaiye Yakubu, and their compatriots were just a few of the people who went through the loss of Aestas, the destruction of Venus, and the dissolution of their families. However, it's through their accounts that we can take what would be just disconnected facts and turn the whole situation into a compelling narrative that comes alive and speaks to our very being. Using that, we can find relevancy in our modern lives."

"I suppose it's just easier for me to understand the facts and figures more than the people," Marco contended. "And I'm confused about where it ended. It seemed like there would be a lot more to say about what happened to Venus, so I looked it up myself."

"Oh? And what did you pick up from your dive

through the Archives?" Edward inquired.

"Well," Marco began, "although the impending massive volley that prompted the Venusians' capitulation was cancelled and the ice asteroids were halted in their tracks, it was only a temporary reprieve. Per the terms of the surrender agreement, Earth Central Command was eventually allowed to restart launching the Torch Drive-propelled projectiles towards Venus in order to complete their plans. Of course, the pace was tempered and highly scheduled to allow an orderly and safe evacuation of Aestas to proceed.

"The rocks then began hit the planet unabated at an oblique angle so that the compound effect slowly changed the direction and rotation of the planet. As predicted, this caused catastrophic changes in the atmosphere and Aestas had difficulty staying aloft. The installation of a sunshade in orbit further degraded the situation until the last remaining residents had no choice but to land the colony on the surface. Unfortunately, HSA was not able to cool off the ground temperature as quickly as they hoped, and Aestas's internal thermal regulation systems could not keep up. Due to this, the final few people within Aestas had to be evacuated, as well. To this day, the shell that was the colony is still there, slowly decaying.

"Originally, the Terran Government believed that once Aestas was forced to land that they could just bury the whole structure to protect it from the elements, sort of making it into an underground hamlet like on Mars. But they hadn't counted on their actions causing the world's existing vulcanism to shift into overdrive. Basically, the surface filled with lava, making it worthless for their original terraforming plans. As a result, Venus was completely uninhabitable for a spell, at least as far as floating in the sky or being on the ground were concerned. Even nowadays, the conditions remain far too extreme down there to be viable for use outdoors in any way.

"Since that time—and so as to get something out of all the time and resources that were directed towards these efforts and not let the whole thing go to waste—some raised towers were constructed with cities sitting atop the pylons, kind of like that ancient twentieth century cartoon *The Jetsons*."

"You've seen *The Jetsons*?!" an astonished Edward interrupted.

"There was a reference to it in one of the articles I was reading," Marco plainly offered, "so I watched a couple of episodes to familiarize myself. It wasn't really my taste, but after viewing it, I figured it was right up your alley."

Edward didn't know whether to be impressed or insulted, but he chose the high road in the hopes that Marco was showing signs of progress. Deciding not to take the bait in either direction, he simply requested, "Go on..."

"Well, anyway," Marco continued, "due to building those *Jetson*-like structures, we are still able to take advantage of the cooler temperatures and lower pressures higher up in the sky without having to find a way to float. However, in the end, the surface of Venus was abandoned as a potential terraforming opportunity. This, though, was mostly because of other factors.

"While all of that was happening on Venus, a technology was developed to transform asteroids into livable habitats. As I'm sure you are well aware, this was accomplished by hollowing out the rocks and setting them into a rapid spin so that it created 1G-like forces on the inside using centrifugal force. The colonies built inside these asteroids became the preferred destination to emigrate to in the Sol System. Meanwhile, as Torch Drive technology progressed and Plan B—I mean, Proxima Centauri B—was settled, any remaining desire to try to build a second Earth on Venus fell by the wayside. While technically Venus has more people living on it now than during the era of Aestas, it is basically considered a disappointing, if not failing, colony."

Edward stayed silent at the end of Marco's soliloquy, pressing his hands together and bringing them up to his mouth in quiet contemplation. After pondering for a moment, Edward finally said, "Marco, that is all technically correct, but your summary is about as dry and impersonal as it could get. In all your research, did you learn anything about what happened with Lilit, Ahmad, and Durojaiye?"

Taken aback, Marco claimed, "I... didn't think to look up anything about them."

"And therein lies the problem," Edward chided as Marco's expression became more and more distraught. "Marco, don't look so upset, I'm not saying this to be mean to you. Listen to me: I have confidence in you and believe that you could have a bright future in this industry, if you want to. Nevertheless, if this is going to be your path in life, you have to make an effort on the people-front. This job isn't just about taking passengers and cargo from Point A to Point B, but about managing the wildly different ways individuals see the universe and react to it. With practice and thoughtfulness, I could see you one day sitting in this chair and advising some young protégée of your own about their prospects."

Marco was quiet for a moment as he took in what Edward had said. Finally, he looked up and uttered, "Thank you, Captain, and I'm sorry, you're right. You've been very kind to me, and I guess I'm just not used to that. I promise you: I'll try harder, I'll get better, and I'll make you proud!"

"That's all I ask," Edward declared. "I want you to see the inadequacies and failings along with the amazing feats we humans can achieve. And that includes our bosses at HSA and the Terran Government! Look, what they did to Venus was a mistake that caused unnecessary heartache and suffering all in the name of progress. Some may consider it blasphemy for me to say this, but HSA is not perfect and neither is the Human Expansion Program. You must be able to look at even what we do on a daily basis with a critical eye."

Marco did not respond, but appeared to be internally processing this new information. Edward then realized that this meeting had been going on for quite a while and he was neglecting his own duties. To move things along, he asked, "Something else on your mind?"

"Since you asked," Marco said without hesitation, "you've piqued my curiosity. Do you know... what I mean to say is... what happened afterwards to everyone, with Lilit, Ahmad, and Durojaiye?"

Edward chuckled and decided he could spare the time. "Easier for me to tell you than for you to research it and find out yourself?" Marco tried to object, but Edward cut him off. "I'm kidding, Marco, relax. Let's see here. Well, Durojaiye is easy. His spy mission was complete and he went back to Earth to rejoin his family. He stayed there for the rest of his life and rarely ever left his village again. Now there was a guy I thought you'd understand; he was so straightforward and no-nonsense, but believed in doing things right, or at least doing what he thought was right. Then again, he had a much better sense of humor."

Marco did not react at all to being playfully jabbed, so Edward sighed and continued, "Lilit and Ahmad stayed on Venus for a while and tried to aid in evacuating the colonists as things got worse and fell apart. They were largely responsible for the exodus from Venus that helped populate Mercury, before the hollowed-out asteroids you highlighted before became en vogue, that is. At some point, even they couldn't take it anymore and moved to the so-called 'Venusian Colony' on Mercury, too, where they eventually got married and had some kids."

"Wait, what?" Marco finally reacted with genuine

surprise. "I thought that Ahmad was asexual?"

"You're not wrong," Edward explained, "but sometimes, when you go through a traumatic experience with someone, there is no one else in the whole galaxy who can possibly understand you anymore. People can find solace in one another, use each other for comfort, even if they don't share a romantic love. It's a form of avoidance coping. I'm not saying it was a good idea or a psychologically sound thing to do, but that is just what happened."

"Wow," was all that Marco could muster at this revelation. Edward could tell that Marco's wheels were rapidly spinning inside his mind as he was still trying to piece together how Lilit and Ahmad's relationship could possibly work. Smirking to himself, Edward felt glad that he had finally discovered a way to challenge Marco's preconceptions. Having successfully pushed Marco into thinking outside his own impressions of the universe for the first time, Edward made a mental note to find similar ways to challenge him in the future. By Edward's estimation, Marco would need all the help he could offer if he was ever going to make any headway in life.

After letting Marco twist foreign concepts in his head for a few moments more, Edward intoned, "Well, because that happened, descendants of theirs are still around to this day. Who knows, maybe even you or I can count them among our ancestors? Did your parents ever tell you anything about your own personal history?"

Marco frowned and noted, "My parents both died before I could get to know them. I have no memories of them whatsoever."

"I'm sorry," Edward flinched. "I wasn't aware."

"It's okay," Marco brushed off his concerns. "I don't like to talk about it, but I don't really think about it either. I guess, it doesn't really make a difference to me nowadays."

"Hmmmm..." Edward offered. "In that case, when we get back to Earth, you should take a DNA test. We could learn a lot about your familial past and find out exactly where you came from."

"I'll take that under advisement," Marco acquiesced without making any real commitment.

Realizing this was going nowhere, Edward cleared his throat and concluded his story by saying, "Anyway, back to what we were talking about before: due to Lilit's and Ahmad's prior experience, they were able to build a very successful mining business on Mercury; so much so that they eventually bought out the rest of the competition and created the monopoly consortium that still exists there today. Their knowledge and expertise were crucial in the efforts to settle the Asteroid Belt and they and their progeny consulted and participated in many of the earliest efforts to carve out the inside of rocks to become new homes for the human diaspora. In the end, though, they never moved into one and instead always returned to Mercury."

"Why'd they do that?" Marco probed.

"Unfortunately, it's not really recorded anywhere, at least nowhere I've ever been able to find," Edward admitted. "But I like to believe that they stayed there so they could keep an eye on the Venus they remembered. Every once in a while, they would be able to go out on the surface of Mercury and watch that oversized yellow dot as it made its way across the horizon."

The very first thing I wrote for this story was that epilogue you just read—or at least, an earlier version of it. I had just finished a draft of **COMPENDIUM OF HUMANITY'S END** and had sent it off to my editor, so I suddenly found myself with time on my hands. Although I technically did not put together a comprehensive outline for this narrative until later, I already knew many of the key points, most especially who the core characters were and where they were going to end up.

Marco Chung was fresh in my mind, so I realized how much the events portrayed in this book would have influenced him and his outlook. If you go back and read his tale, you may notice several direct and indirect references to the proceedings in this novel. Taken together, it is all part of an overarching theme that weaves through many of my former and future books: that all events in history are interconnected, and that the past can inform even the seemingly far-flung, distant, and unrelated future.

I pride myself on being able to write linearly,

starting at the beginning and maintaining my momentum until I reach the end. However, this story did not give me permission to do that and demanded that I treat it quite differently. During the juncture in time when I wrote the epilogue, I had not even decided that the book would be told through only Lilit's perspective. After Captain Edward Hersch's account came to fruition, I slowly began to realize that having several different viewpoints scattered throughout this book could be problematic. Still, I was not quite ready to accept the revelation that Aestas was Lilit's story to tell, and hers alone.

The next step came when I wrote what is now entitled **A FUTURE INTERLUDE**. I'll spare you all the various iterations before I settled on a final layout and naming convention for the book, but that section did not begin life as Lilit's chronicle. For a couple of years prior to formally composing this book, I had been workshopping the kernel of the key ideas around Aestas. In the build-up to what eventually became **ALWAYS DIVIDED, NEVER UNITED** (the book Ahmad recommend Lilit read, but she didn't have the time), I wrote an essay for Medium entitled **FORGET MARS, LET'S COLONIZE VENUS**. There is a short, two paragraph introduction where a nameless person is on their journey from Earth to Venus, and specifically names Aestas as their final destination. This was also the origin of the derogatory nickname for our erstwhile colony: "The Yellow Balloon".

Almost a year to the day later, I entered the *New Worlds Challenge* at Vocal where I was instructed to "write the first chapter of an exciting new science fiction story." For that, I presented **AESTAS: THE YELLOW BALLOON {VOCAL NEW WORLDS CHALLENGE}**, which expounded on those original couple of paragraphs while also eliminating much of the purely technical examinations. The unnamed character turned into Ahmad Al Zaheri, while at the same time the piece also introduced Durojaiye Yakubu. Ahmad has remained relatively the same since that introductory point, but Durojaiye transformed from merely an enigmatic figure into... well, you know what now.

That brief proto-prologue was depicted entirely from Ahmad's perspective. My intention originally had been to maintain that while adapting it for this book, but then Lilit Sarkisian happened. At first, Aestas was going to be about many different people who all had their own agendas and endgames. There were extremists from Venus, Earth, Mars, and other colonies; politicians looking to make deals and compromises; and average people who were just getting caught in the middle of all these machinations.

In other words, things would bounce around from Ahmad to Lilit to Xander to Isra to Gang Chiu to plenty of others—a messy conglomeration designed to move the action along its path.

Once I started to develop Lilit's background, character profile, and individual arc, though, it became obvious that all that rigamarole was unnecessary and needlessly complicated. Lilit could unilaterally experience the various factions pulling her one way or another, even be a part of many of them. Venus was always going to be destroyed by some group who wanted to terraform it due to population growth and general expansionist pressures. No matter what, there would be a running question of what makes a unique people and culture, when do they become indigenous, who has the power to decide whether those persons have a right to self-determination, and should they have the freedom to choose their own fate in the context of the needs of a greater humanity?

Nevertheless, to explore these concepts and plot points, only Lilit was needed as the central personality and driving force. Therefore, all other characters and extraneous storylines fell by the wayside so as to focus on Lilit's experiences and perspective, aside from the epilogue, of course. A few things would, by logical inevitability, remain beyond her purview, but that only added intrigue to her tale. Omniscience can be a crutch; real people have no idea what is going on in anyone else's head, not even those closest to them. This one resolution to concentrate on Lilit brought the entire framework into focus, something it—quite frankly—lacked until that stitch in time.

As such, the next thing I did to shape this book was to adapt what once was Ahmad's introduction into Lilit's interlude. Again, this happened before I had a complete outline. Something was spilling out of me; Lilit was commanding her story be known. Who was I to deny the future Queen? Interestingly, it would not be until months later that I would know why Lilit was up in the middle of the night and needed to calm her nerves. Just to be clear, although the Interlude was written first, it was intended to be exactly where it lies in the book; it was not pulled from a later section and placed there as you might believe by its timestamp. Its purpose was to lay the groundwork for the key scientific principles of how this universe functions, as well as give a preview of the characters and all that was to come. Nonetheless, it does still fit in perfectly with where the plot would be at that instant in the timeline. If you did not do so during your original readthrough, I recommend rereading the Interlude after Chapter 38.

With a draft of that written, I had a prologue and an epilogue of sorts, so what would be the next rational step? Of course: it was the ending! Though not precisely the same as the final product, all the key elements were there—Lilit's epiphany, Ahmad's denial, Durojaiye's justifications, and Venus's surrender. The conclusion, for me, was the necessary convergence of concepts into what would be the definitive story; that I needed to transport and document all that transpired as the relationships between these three people evolved from strangers to chosen family to tragic figures caught up in what their deep friendships and strongly held beliefs had wrought. From there, I finally felt prepared to outline the key points of that journey.

To do that, I also wanted to make sure that I not only had a good grasp on the scientific principles presented, but that I worked within the confines of orbital mechanics, physics, and other such endeavors. For internalizing the convoluted workings of transfers between planets in particular, I cannot express enough gratitude to the **Solar System Scope** website. This 3D, interactive model of the Sol System allowed me to much more easily visualize and understand the whys, whens, and hows related to the frequency of inferior conjunctions, far better than just reading all of the relevant facts and doing calculations in Excel. I highly advocate that you play with their online tool yourself to better comprehend the rotation of planets around the sun and enjoy the occasional syzygy!

All that said, if I made a technical error of some kind or other with any of the science, the fault is entirely mine and not with the wonderful experts that have lent their knowledge to me. And before anyone points it out, yes, I am thoroughly aware that one does not use a degree symbol with the Kelvin temperature scale. However, I decided that humans would ignore the directives of *The Thirteenth General Conference on Weights and Measures (1967)* and would gravitate towards the familiar instead of the formal. Always trust that people will embrace the proletariat and spurn the bourgeoisie.

Beyond that, there were plenty of fascinating—at least, to me—discussions that had to be cut either for flow, because they no longer fit, or due to just being too long or complex. For instance, I touched on the sunshade that would need to be put above Venus's view of our central star, but did not get into details behind that requirement. Even if the Terran Government and HSA were successful at getting Venus to change its axial spin to be somewhat Earth-like, as well as deliver a plethora of water to the planet, it would still not be enough to cool off the surface fast enough, and certainly not have it be a permanent fixture. With just those and other potential terraforming efforts, Venus would still only have its temperatures reduced down to something like 65°C to 80°C. For a hellish world like this to be considered on the outskirts of "habitable", the temperature would have to be lowered to around 45°C, and even that is quite high for most humans to handle year-round. One "reasonable" way to accomplish this that has been proposed would be to block out the sun for large stretches, meaning the sunshade would then need to be a continual, if not permanent contrivance.

Something else in that same vein that I would have liked to discuss is that those temperature figures are "on average". Just as on Earth, if you are on the equator, it would be a lot hotter, while it would be cooler towards the poles. I would have liked to explore HSA's plans on where and how they thought they were actually going to settle on the surface, but it was not meant to be. The details would be superfluous and would only have distracted from the main narrative with their textbook-style interruptions. I've read plenty of hard science fiction books that have done this—and have certainly composed such unfortunate prose myself on occasion—so I did not want to make the same mistake again.

These are among the lessons I have and continue to learn as I grow as an independent author. And much of that education has come from my team of fellow freelancers, including editor Jessica Schmidt and cover artist Xee Shan. Thank you for all you have done to help my visions come to life! And while you are very important to me, no one holds a giant hot ball of plasma to my bestedest partner Caroline. I love you[3], and look forward to traveling the stars with just you!

At last, dear reader, that brings us to you. First off, you have my eternal gratitude for spending your precious time and hard-earned money to read this novel. If you enjoyed what you have consumed here, I would greatly appreciate your help in spreading the word by leaving a review, posting messages on social media, or just telling friends and family about it. As an independent artist, word-of-mouth is my primary growth mechanism, which means I cannot do it without you. Deprived of that, I would have no defense if an ice-asteroid came crashing down from the sky.

J.P. Prag | Last Modified: September 22, 2023

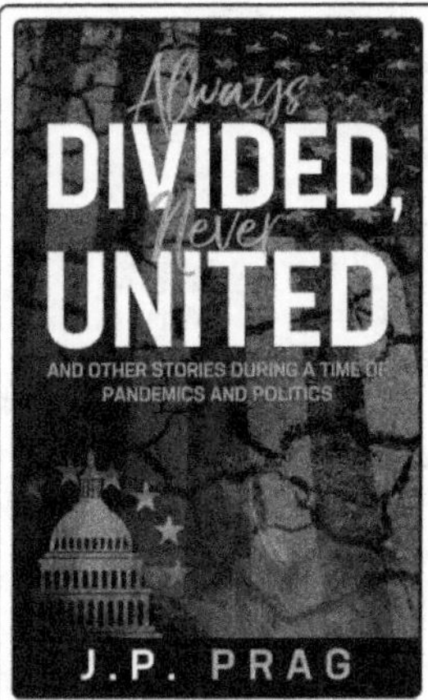

ALWAYS DIVIDED, NEVER UNITED
AND OTHER STORIES DURING
A TIME OF PANDEMICS & POLITICS

Have the troubles of our age ripped us
apart more than any point in history?
Or has it forever been this way?

https://amazon.com/dp/B09YDM25MB

NEW & IMPROVED - BOOK 2

NEW & IMPROVED

THE UNITED STATES OF AMERICA

Is there a way to save America and
ensure justice and freedom for all?
There is...if you are willing to rethink
and rebuild the entire Constitution!

https://amazon.com/dp/B08FCPB5JN

NEW & IMPROVED - BOOK 1

IN DEFENSE OF...
EXONERATING PROFESSIONAL
WRESTLING'S MOST HATED

Parts of wrestling history have been
presented with overtly critical
comments and outright lies. It is past
time to bring truth to the wrestling fan!

https://amazon.com/dp/B08F3Y7L6K

STARBUILDERS

Stars moving, children mutating, a world rapidly changing. As Nothaar Akii seeks the truth, he stumbles upon a dying universe he never knew existed.

COMING SOON...

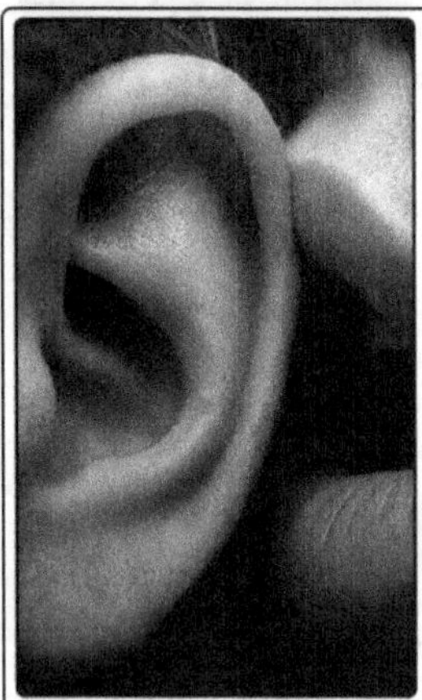

LOST RUMORS

Discovering several days of his life are missing, Riley Furman tries to piece together what has transpired, shattering who and what he believes he is.

COMING SOON...

GENERATION
- WORKING TITLE -

On an interstellar generational ship, the all-women population is tightly controlled. That is, until a baby boy is somehow born.

COMING SOON...

UNTITLED 1
- WORKING TITLE -

How does this strange boy who says they should not have even met yet know these things about her, things she has never uttered aloud?

COMING SOON...

DICTATOR AND DAUGHTER, DECONSTRUCTED

Sage Katz just got the shock of her life: the surprise return of her former dictator father! Worst of all, he now wants to repair their relationship.

COMING SOON...

HERRENVOLK

Following a century of being cut off from the world after establishing their secret society, Hitler's "perfect people" are rediscovered.

COMING SOON...

For the record, J.P. Prag is a Pisces.

Even though it doesn't mean anything, what is notable is that ten of the eighteen stars in Pisces (that are nowhere near each other) are known to host planets. One of the planets called "GU Pisces b" takes around 80,000 Earth years to circle its sun. It is also worth highlighting that some of the stars in the constellation are not singular balls of plasma at all, but are entire galaxies! Further scientific examination has revealed many other faint galaxies, nebulae, and other stellar objects within the Pisces general area. A couple of those galaxies are on a collision course, so look out for that over the next several hundred million years or so.

When not observing stellar objects at the Ladd Observatory, J.P. Prag can be found several blocks away at his home and office in Providence, Rhode Island, U.S.A. with his partner Caroline and their many tall ferns and philodendrons, lazy lying down cacti, outside pet squirrels (including Squirrel the Raccoon), and a stuffed sloth named Peeve and his new buddy Skvishy. That's where he wrote this and his other published works that you should add to your reading list right now!

For more irreverent details (and perhaps some pertinent ones, too?) and contact information, please visit **WWW.JPPRAG.COM**.

Version History

Number	Date	Note
0.00	2023-03-22	Draft Started
0.10	2023-04-26	Shell Outline Transfer Complete
1.00	2023-06-09	Alpha Draft
1.50	2023-06-30	Alpha Draft – Edited
2.00	2023-08-02	Beta Draft
2.50	2023-09-13	Beta Draft – Edited
3.00	2024-01-17	Final Release Form

Copyrights and Disclaimers

First Edition April 2024

Printed everywhere on the planet Earth from the nearest regional production and distribution center.

Edited by Jessica Schmidt
HTTPS://WWW.FIVERR.COM/CURIOUSWOMAN271

Cover art by Xee Shan
HTTPS://WWW.FIVERR.COM/XEE_DESIGNS1

ISBN 979-8-9874980-5-7 // eBook
ISBN 979-8-9874980-6-4 // Hardcover
ISBN 979-8-9874980-7-1 // Paperback

Basil Junction Publishing
7 Knowles Street
Providence, RI 02906

WWW.JPPRAG.COM

This mildly modified reprocessed image of Venus has been provided courtesy of NASA (Public Domain)